A Day in Eternity

Kathryn Gabriel Loving

SOUL
JOURN
BOOKS

ISBN 978-0-9839838-2-8

For Andrew, with love.
May the blessings be.

Oh! Brave New World, what proof have we
That all the things that tarnish thee
Will definitely never be
Continued in the Next?

—John Gillespie Magee, Jr.

CONTENTS

1. Slipping 1

2. The Higher We Soar 3

3. East of Eden 15

4. Dancing the Skies 29

5. Memory is a Deceitful Institution 39

6. What Else but Love? 51

7. A Secret to My Soul 61

8. Brave New World 77

9. Letters from America 91

10. Through Adversity to the Stars 101

11. The Harvard 115

12. If You Have Not Chaos 121

13. Take Me to that Far Hill 129

14. There Flies a Nobler Heart 149

15. Icarus Reborn 157

16. The Opening of Doors 163

17. I Find Them Laughing Beside Me 185

18. Falling Star 195

19. The Surly Bonds 199

20. Neither Here nor There 201

21. The Gypsy's Prediction 211

22. Zagazig 233

23. The Forces of Flight 241

24. On Laughter-Silvered Wings 263

25. Healing the Dream 265

26. Notes and Acknowledgments 269

27. Further Reading 271

1

SLIPPING

ANSON ROE'S BODY slammed against something solid and came to rest inside a heap of twisted metal and debris. After moments of falling and rising through gradient phases of consciousness, he felt nothing but an aching nicotine craving that wouldn't leave him alone. He started to reach for a tin of Player's in his breast pocket then remembered he'd smoked all the cigarettes he'd brought from England. *Bloody hell*, he thought. *Now I'll have to go back to rolling my own.*

Gradually he became aware of swollen eyes, screaming ears, and labored breathing. He realized that the plane he was flying was no longer airborne, the cockpit that cocooned his body no longer existed. Instinct urged him to pull himself from the wreckage before it caught fire. By sheer willpower he moved ever so slightly, triggering an explosion of pain in his cranium and sending bolts of lightning down his spine to his extremities. In rapid succession, an iridescent light cascaded through his optic nerves and bubbles of pleasure hummed throughout his nervous system, squelching the pain and placing his awareness—elsewhere.

The floodlight in Anson's mind dimmed, and there appeared before him his old dorm room where he'd attended agricultural aviation school in America. He'd spent half of 1978 in this cramped cell, with its avocado cinder-block walls and orange-striped curtains. A stack of flight manuals lay open haphazardly on his former desk. Orchestral music blared from the small television set on his make-shift coffee table, heralding an Air Force film he'd watched every night when the station signed off the air.

1

He allowed his imagination to glide with the T-38 Talon supersonic jet as it rolled, looped, and rocketed through voluminous clouds against a cobalt sky. "Oh! I have slipped the surly bonds of earth on laughter-silvered wings," echoed a baritone voice as if from heaven. "Sunward I've climbed ... and done a hundred things you have not dreamed of." These words had always uplifted Anson, but he considered the final line a bit too sentimental. "Put out my hand, and touched the face of God."

I may have to rethink my position on that, he realized as the room faded. Dropping into the abyss, he had another thought. *Where is Vivianne?*

2

THE HIGHER WE SOAR

ANSON ROUSED TO familiar environs on his feet and physically intact yet unaccountably dizzy. He took a moment to allow his mind to catch up with what he was now seeing—neither crash site nor dorm room, but the little Oklahoma airfield where he'd sprayed crops in 1980. In front of him stood Panhandle Ag Air's hangar as testified to in bright-red letters across the length of the steel building. The company's pair of buttery-yellow Volkswagen Beetles, each accented by large, black polka dots, huddled in front of the hangar. He gazed on the nearby runway that cut diagonally across the square-mile airfield, a perpetual welcome mat for aerial workers and the occasional visitor. He pivoted on his heels, visualizing a pilot's view of the short-grass rangeland of the High Plains imposed upon by acres of crops flourishing in the radiant heat of the morning sun. He relaxed, for he'd always felt at home here.

Anson's smile flattened. *Something's not right.* He had no memory of driving to the airfield that morning. He couldn't shake the sensation that he was on the wrong continent, in the wrong hemisphere, as if he'd been literally plucked from one place and reinserted into another. A scene flashed before his eyes—not the usual field of cornstalks, but cotton tended by farmers wearing muslin turbans rather than tractor-logo caps. The vision left him just as abruptly as it came, nearly throwing him to the ground in its wake.

The dream of crashing the aeroplane must have put me off my stride, he told himself as he regained his senses. Wondering if he was still dreaming, he fluttered his eyelids more than once. *No, no change.* He shook his head to dispel the alarming images, while his mind slipped into place as easily as pulling on a pair of old shoes.

Still, something about the absence of people at the airfield impressed upon him. Overhead the sky was void of air traffic. The nearby highway, usually overrun by eighteen-wheelers day and night, looked empty. As far as he could tell he was alone—no sight or sound of another living soul for miles around. He stumbled to the hangar and tried the doors. They were locked. If the VW Beetles were present, he reasoned, then the Pawnee and Thrush were probably in the hangar, everyone gone for the day. Longing for home himself, he reached into the pocket of his cargo pants for the key to the company Beetle assigned to him and found nothing. He searched his other pockets with the same result. He rushed to his Beetle and discovered he'd left the door unlocked, but there was no key in the ignition. He searched the floor under and around the driver's seat—all the other seats had been pulled long ago to make room for equipment. He leaned to rummage through the glove box and found only a map and tire gauge. The car was a coffin in the heat and smelled of chemicals. He stepped out and rushed to jiggle the door handle of its mate, but of course it was locked.

That's bloody inconvenient, he thought. *How am I to get home?*

He removed his cap and scratched his head. *If only I had a cigarette.* He wondered if Vivianne had returned from the *Daily Record* yet. Sometimes she picked up a pack for him on her way home from work. He could use a cup of good ol' American joe to clear his mind—Waster's Choice, she called it. A shot of Jim or Jack would do nicely too.

The landscape suddenly swirled around him in a brief fit of vertigo. Heatstroke would explain his lapses, he thought once he stabilized. *Best get out of the sun.* He stormed around to the north side of the hangar to stand in a narrow band of shade and have a think.

Straightaway he started obsessing over Vivianne. They'd quarreled recently. The timing and context escaped him now, but he knew how these arguments went. She'd grumble about him spending too much time at the airfield. He'd explain that his boss squeezed him for every penny he paid him, that he kept him working from dawn to nearly midnight hosing out the hangar or overhauling an engine. He'd contend that she needed to learn that his career came first, that he'd borrowed, begged, and all but swindled tuition money from everyone he knew for commercial flight school in Georgia. Not only that, he'd wasted more than a year struggling with Immigrations for over-staying his visa, and he didn't know how long he could maintain a crop-dusting career at his age. Now that he was finally flying, he needed to concentrate on that. Most of the time she understood, but in his opinion she sometimes lost her perspective—like all women.

Yet in his mind Vivianne was not everywoman. By world standards, he didn't think she would win beauty pageants, but he liked the way her olive skin gave luminosity to her coppery-brown eyes and her untamed black hair lent an air of Bohemianism to her otherwise quiet demeanor. She was an ideas person in search of a few windmills to tilt at, much like himself. He'd never imagined he'd find a woman like her in the proverbial No Man's Land of the Oklahoma Panhandle.

"Flat land is so surreal," she'd told him once. "In New Mexico, there's always a mountain in view, something to chart against. Here, I don't know where I am half the time. It's not fair that you get to soar among the eagles while I'm stuck on the ground."

"You'll cultivate an eye for the subtle beauty of this place," he'd responded.

"A survival mechanism, I suspect," she'd retorted. "I bet even we could appreciate beauty in hell."

The Panhandle, with its scarcity of water and trees, incessant wind, and harsh climate, was deemed inhospitable by most, but it was definitely not hell to Anson's eye, for it had its moments. He had arrived in March and watched as Spring dipped a brush in pots of black-eyed Susans, purple prairie clovers, scarlet sage, or Texas bluebonnets, and painted broadly across the earth tones of the plains and freshly tilled farmland one color at a time. Even the dandelions conferred a brilliant yellow river against the bruised purple of an approaching storm. He longed for verdant England, but the Panhandle was the only place where he could land an aerial-spraying job in all of America. He felt he needed to capitalize on this opportunity to accumulate flight hours, or he would never be able to work in England. "Make hay while the sun shines," Anson's employer always said. His job here was just a stopgap, a sojourn in what he hoped would be a long, global career. He could think of worse places to be.

———

In the early weeks of Anson's tenure at Panhandle Ag Air, he'd reveled in the excitement of flying by day and the solitude small-town life on the High Plains afforded him during his free time. As summer came on, a longing for stimulating companionship of the feminine variety created a foothold in his psyche. Not that women weren't available, they were, but he didn't fancy the typical farm girl physique and sensibility. Vivianne appeared suddenly as if his imagination had created her.

He was taxiing his Pawnee to the hanger after a particularly grueling day of spraying when he spotted her leaning against his Beetle. He quickly surveyed the possibilities, the camera bag hanging off one shoulder, the poured-into blue jeans, and the camel-colored, western-style boots stacked on three-inch heels that failed to disguise her petite stature. She waved self-consciously to him as he stepped onto the wing. *Ah, unsure to boot ... perfect!* He had underestimated her from the beginning.

When he hopped to the ground, her smile broadened in amusement. *Bloody hell!* He looked down at his body. Crop-dusting ruined clothes, so it didn't matter what one wore on the job. This morning he'd donned his pink khakis and work shirt, both stained by a stowaway red rag in the hot wash. His face turned the same peppermint tint as his clothes.

"Anson Roe?" She thrust a hand toward him.

"The same." He politely waved off her hand as he rubbed his own with the culprit rag. "Sorry. Grease, sweat, insecticide. Not a good combination."

"I'm Vivianne Keene ... from the *Daily Record* in Guymon? Nice hat." She pointed to the baby blue baseball cap on his head. He'd sewn a Union Jack patch to the front and had written "A V ROE" in black Magic Marker across the bill. He hoped the flag said, "Yes, if you haven't guessed by the accent, I'm English. " Everyone asked anyway.

"Thank you, ma'am," he said. He suspected he was grinning like a fool.

"I was told you might be willing to hire out."

"For what?" he teased.

Her thick black hair billowed in the wind, and a single dimple showed in one cheek when she smiled. "A lift, actually. I need an aerial shot of the wheat mountains stacked outside the grain elevators."

"Sorry, love. I'm knackered."

"Anyone else available?"

"Afraid I'm it."

"I'm on deadline." She looked disappointed.

"Ah, well, on second thought there's a bloke sometimes lets me use his private plane on Sundays. I'll take you up tomorrow in exchange for copies of the photos."

"Deal."

"Come early before it gets too hot."

"How about seven?"

"Six would be better."

"You got it," she said.

He admired the fit of her jeans over ample hips as she walked away. When he saw her climb into a barn-red Volkswagen Bus he became smitten. "And you can buy me breakfast afterward," he called out, which elicited a wave of acknowledgment from her before she drove away.

Anson arrived at a quarter to six to prep the Piper Cherokee, only to find Vivianne already waiting in her van. "You're early," he said.

"What? No pink?" she replied.

"Ha ha." He began to perform a quick check of the green-trimmed, white plane. She followed him as he walked all the way around it, sliding his hand along its seams and rivets with a pat here and a tap there as if it were aerial foreplay. He helped her climb into the cockpit and strap into the seat, relishing the nearness to a warm-bodied female and eager to show off his flying prowess. He couldn't get over the shimmer of those copper-speckled eyes. He climbed into the left-hand seat next to her, worked through his preflight warm up, and started the engine. Once the prop began humming, he taxied toward the runway. Before long, they were airborne.

The grain elevator complex, virtual skyscrapers compared to all the one- and two-story buildings in the region, stood just minutes away from the airfield by car and instantly rose into view. "What do you want me to do?"

"Circle," she shouted, looping an index finger in the air.

"I'll need to get high enough to avoid the power lines and antennas."

She nodded. "It's a zoom lens." He enjoyed the way she demonstrated it by twisting the lens to enlarge and contract the metal cylinder within it in a manner that was unintentionally suggestive. She selected camera settings, put the viewfinder to her eye, and began snapping and re-cocking in rapid succession. He flew around the concrete silo towers, which he'd heard could potentially store three billion bushels of grain before railroad cars took it to even larger elevators to await market. Despite the vast storage capacity, a mountain range of wheat sat on the ground next to the tracks. Vivianne burned through a roll of film in no time, while he flew a number of passes at varying heights and distances.

"You're part of the problem," she later told Anson over a plate of scrambled eggs in the Texhoma Café.

"How do you figure?" He was methodically striping a thick slice of Texas toast with a honey squeeze bottle, first one direction, then the other.

"There is no cause without an effect."

"You learned that at university, did you?"

She waved off his comment with a chuckle and continued. "All those chemicals and fertilizers you spray on the ground, in addition to all the water being pumped up from the aquifer ... it all helps to produce a record bumper crop. Meanwhile, President Carter imposes a wheat embargo on Russia for invading Afghanistan, and now the entire system is backed up. The farmers have no choice but to dump the wheat on the ground, which then rots in the rain. The economy suffers. The farmers don't care because they'll be reimbursed no matter what, while taxpayers foot the bill."

"You've obviously thought this through," he said, still focused on the work of art his toast and honey had become. "Everybody must eat. The world's food supply would diminish by half without fungicides and insecticides. They have aerial application down to a science now. Universities study the chemical droplet patterns and adjust the spray nozzles accordingly. We're professionally trained to be careful." He pointed a clean butter knife at her. "You would do well to look into the industry if you call yourself a reporter." He spread his honey grid out to the edges of his toast with the same knife then waved it in the air again. "Become more informed before you make a judgment. You'll call me a hero at the end of the day."

He looked up to see her staring at him. "What?"

"Why do you spread the honey out like that?" she asked. "I mean, what's the point?"

"I like every bit of my toast to have a consistent amount of honey on it with no wasteful spillage. We spread the chemicals on the fields in much the same way." He noticed Vivianne looking at her own toast, perhaps considering how she had unconsciously slathered it with butter and raspberry jam. He had to admit he enjoyed making people squirm.

"You know who you remind me of?"

He shrugged, trying not to look too curious.

"The sea captain in the *Ghost and Mrs. Muir.*"

"Rex Harrison?"

"Hardly. More like Edward Mulhare, television version."

"How so?"

"Oh, not the hat obviously, or the pink trousers, but the close beard and mustache. Impatient, frank, logical—well, logical at least in terms of your own universe, I'm willing to bet. And charming, very charming."

"My hair's a bit more ginger than his, but I'll go along with your assessment if you women are attracted to that look."

"Can't speak for all of us. I suppose it's the careful British accent that reminds me of a character living in the nineteenth century. And I'd say your beard is more of a rust color with bits of wheat in it like a tweed."

He took note of her scrutinizing his looks so closely. "Mulhare's Irish. Contrary to what you Americans think, we don't all sound alike."

"Well, he didn't sound Irish in the show. To me your accent sounds, I don't know, pompous?"

"So I've pulled it off?" Anson smiled with mischief.

Vivianne flicked her head to one side in a qualified agreement.

"You'll hear many accents when you come to England." This approach of inviting American women to his country usually worked for Anson as a means to an end. They all loved the idea of a little jaunt to Great Britain, whether it manifested or not. He wouldn't mind if anyone took him up on his offer, for if he could have his way, he would bring all Americans he met to England and vice versa.

Vivianne arched her eyebrows. "What makes you think I'd go to England with you?"

"I wasn't offering to take you," he said, backtracking. "You strike me as the type of woman who wants to see the world, that's all."

"You're saying I'm worldly?"

"Potentially."

"Oh, I've got potential," she said in a forced Brooklyn accent.

He ignored her taunting. "The way I have it figured, ninety-nine percent of the world's population is quite happy to lead a small, routine life with head down, nose to the grindstone. Only one percent stands apart from the fray. And then there's a special corner of that one percent, the rare breed of person who rises above it all and even helps improve humanity along the way."

"Obviously you count yourself in that special corner of the one percent."

He nodded. "I'll have to monitor your progress, but you might be included in that group as well."

"Sounds like delusions of grandeur to me." She wasn't buying it, but she looked amused, if not a little intrigued.

Anson shrugged. "The higher we soar the smaller we look to those who cannot fly."

"Quoting Nietzsche now," she teased. "You've just proved my point."

"Nietzsche stole from me, actually."

"Riiight." She laughed and took a sip of her iced tea. "Why the hat?" She nodded to his headwear bearing the Union Jack.

He grabbed the brim and pointed to the patch. "Oh, this is just to toy with the locals, match their zealous patriotism with a little of my own."

"Interesting. Proud of your heritage, are you? Tell me about your home. I'm curious about what you've been doing for the last, what, thirty years?"

He grinned. "Curious, eh?"

She raised her shoulders. "Just being a reporter."

"Okay, I'm what you Yanks might call a military brat. I was born in a little thatched-roof cottage in a village in Essex. Went to school in Asia where my father had served in the Royal Air Force since World War II. Spent my teens and twenties in Norfolk. And yes, I've just turned thirty-one."

"And the accent?"

"The King's English, you mean? Comes from elocution exercises in grammar school. Mother was a stickler for proper enunciation, which I'm afraid does come off as sounding a bit posh to you Americans."

"You're an elitist, then."

"You'd have to make up your own mind on that. What about yourself? How did a woman like you end up here?"

"I graduated from the university a few weeks ago. Needed to find my first job in journalism, but the local papers wanted more experience than I had. I drew concentric circles in hundred-mile radii around Albuquerque on a map and sighted on Guymon, just three rings away. Wouldn't you know, Guymon has a newspaper."

"Population 10,000? Hardly a real job, now is it?"

Vivianne pouted flirtatiously. "The *Daily Record* is the largest paper in the region and owned by a multimedia corporation."

"So, you called for an interview sight unseen?"

"No, I decided to check it out first. Arrived early one evening when the building was closed and the street deserted."

"That's one thing about being here. Bugger-all to do."

"I'm with you on that," she said. "Anyway, I peered at the web press through the store-front windows, and instantly my heart pulled at me."

"Nothing like a printing press to make a girl feel at home, I imagine."

She placed a hand over her heart. "The smell of ink and newsprint, the promise of a byline for a job well done—there isn't anything like it. On a hunch I presented my degree in journalism with a minor in ecology to the editors the next day, and they invented a job as the soil and oil reporter just for me right on the spot."

"Clever girl. You are in a special corner of the one percent." Anson sat back.

"Oh, typing up a tedious list of oil prices or sounding the alarm on the latest insect scare is not the adventure I'd hoped for, but I can tough it out for a year or two and then move on to Denver or any place greener than Oklahoma."

"It's a stopgap, just as Texhoma is for me. I'd guess you're in your mid-twenties. What took you so long to complete your education?"

"A marital hiatus that lasted approximately three years."

"I daresay. What happened?"

"I wanted to do something exciting like join the Peace Corps. He'd been a medic in Vietnam and wanted to settle into mainstream life. We were at cross purposes."

"Fair enough."

"How did you become a crop-duster, of all things?" she asked, interrupting his next question.

Having finished his toast, he lit a cigarette and sat back to tell how he'd traveled to Kenya and the Sudan to develop a business. When that didn't pan out, he'd gone into motorcar racing but realized there wasn't a lot of money in it without frequent wins. It was when he became a farm manager in Norfolk that he'd discovered crop-dusting. He'd enrolled in flight school in England and then attended agricultural aviation school in Georgia. He decided to skip the bit about looking for a suitable candidate to marry him to settle his visa woes, now that she seemed genuinely interested.

She started gathering and pulling her thick curls off her neck with one hand and fanning her glistening face with the other. "It's already hot this morning," she said.

"You haven't adapted yet, have you?" He stroked his beard and smiled to himself in the suspicion that his secret powers were working. Then he noticed his own damp palms and rubbed them on the legs of his trousers. *If it weren't for those eyes of hers, I'd be fine.*

3

East of Eden

ANSON LEANED AGAINST the hangar wall feeling grateful for the thin strip of shade the building provided as the sun climbed overhead. He looked at his vintage Timex aviator's watch, thinking it was Sunday and wondering if Boss would show up after church to check on his airplanes. He could catch a ride with him and avoid the ten-mile hike home. *Hmm.* He tapped the watch face when he noticed the second hand wasn't moving. He twisted the rewind knob, but the mechanism wouldn't budge. *Must have broken the crystal during one of my blackouts.* "Bloody watch," he said aloud.

Annoyed, he removed his cap and mopped his head with a handkerchief from his back pocket. He forced himself to take his mind off Vivianne for a moment and put it on his finances, but then he realized he'd left his diary at home. No matter—he'd gone over it so many times, he felt it was embossed on his mind. With his regular monthly wages minus expenses, he was still about £17,000 in debt by his calculations. Not where he wanted to be in this, the fourth year of his five-year plan, having had the bad luck of fighting with the U.S. government over his visa for the past year. He'd hoped to be flying in England by now or perhaps somewhere exotic and on his way to becoming solvent. Once he earned a comfortable living, he planned to work on an automobile invention he had in mind and then move into philanthropy. He'd met Vivianne at least a year too early according to his plan. *Life's not always predictable*, he'd often thought. *I must take my consolations when and where they come.*

He'd taken full advantage of the presence of Vivianne. He re-called how quickly they'd warmed up to one another, each being the only interesting person the other knew in the Panhandle. He regretted not having the funds to take her places, but there was so little to do in Texhoma that it didn't matter that he was broke. Easily remedied with a bit of imagination, they'd drive to a deso-late farm road and watch one of the region's spectacular light-ning storms while listening to a staticky country radio station. Sometimes they'd lay crossways in the tire ruts of a dirt road, drink beer, and sing along with tunes blasting from an eight-track player. "Sky Pilot," by Eric Burdon and the Animals, par-ticularly inspired Vivianne's contemplation of their rock 'n roll koan: Is it truly impossible to fly high enough to reach the sky?

Occasionally, they'd scrounge together a few dollars to spend in the TO Lounge next to the motel where he lived. The county was dry, and so the lounge served only diluted beer or sold soft drinks to go along with shots from the bottle of hard liquor the patron stored there for "personal use." Vivianne came out of her shell after a couple of beers despite the low-alcohol content, and then she would practice her Spanish and dance *Rancheras* with the Mexican migrant workers who frequented the place. She loved to dance and Anson enjoyed watching her. After a few rounds the routine became disconcerting to him, especially when she would be spotted later by a truckload of workers in town and one would yell out, "*¡Aiii, viva Vivianita ... bailar La Bamba!*" He doubted his mother would approve, and he wanted her to like Vivianne.

"Vivianne, I want you to know I'm planning an extended tour of Europe for you beginning with an introduction to my moth-er," Anson announced to her one evening in the TO Lounge only two weeks into their romance. He'd mulled it over and began to realize that she could be the woman for him, and he thought he might as well get on with it.

"Oh?" Vivianne was bent over the table and sighting on the cue ball with her pool stick. She stood and gave him a quizzical look. "I wasn't expecting that."

He raised his eyebrows. "I'm aware," he said and continued in a businesslike manner. "Thereafter we shall undertake a thorough study of the European way, and perhaps the North and East African ways, comparing our findings to the American culture. At that point we will likely need to raise funds for our next excursion, which I think should begin with South America, then the continent of India, and possibly Sri Lanka. This should take no more than five years. There should follow continuous work and travel."

"You must be joking."

"I assure you I'm quite serious. Don't you want to travel?" He knew from their discussions that her ambitions were not as well defined as his, but at least she wanted the same kinds of adventures that he did. She wanted to become a writer and photographer, which would be enhanced by living in other countries.

"I hardly know you."

"What do you want to know?"

"I know nothing of your friends and family, your history, your character."

"Hence the trip to England." He crossed his arms against his chest. "You know, I'm only a deviant."

"Hardly reassuring."

"That depends on your perspective."

"Anything you'd like to know about me before embarking on such grand adventures?"

"I'm not so curious to know more about you," he said. "You're clearly a most unusual woman in that I feel so comfortable in your company. What else could I want to know? I desire the presence of a sane, intelligent, brave, and intimate feminine person in my life. I never credited this country with the means to produce such a specimen. Even good, old home hasn't done much of that. Women like you are a rare commodity. I wonder why they're not better appreciated."

Vivianne stared at him with her eyebrows arched and jaw slightly slackened. *Just the reaction I was aiming for*, he thought. He liked keeping her guessing.

"Is your ego sufficiently inflated? I hope so. It will be in good hands."

She sauntered to him and looked him in the eye. "You're so strange, English." She threw her arms around him and stood on tiptoe to kiss his lips.

He stiffened his neck and pulled away. "Not here."

"Why not?"

He glanced toward the bartender serving some ranch hands. "Makes a man look weak."

Looking offended, she took a step backward and put her hands on her hips. "I sometimes think you were born a century too late."

A week later Anson showed Vivianne the house he intended to share with her. She had been renting a room from an elderly woman in Guymon and complained about her lack of privacy and inability to bring home male companions without everyone in the small, mostly Christian town knowing her business and raising eyebrows. Not that she had any male companions until she met Anson, but it annoyed her to know she couldn't be herself there. Apart from enjoying her company, her contribution to rent and provisions would help him whittle down his debt. He knew living together so soon would be unwise under normal circumstances, but he didn't have that kind of time. He'd be returning home to England at the end of the season and then traveling on to Africa or someplace profitable.

"This is where you want to live!" Vivianne exclaimed as she turned her VW Bus into the long, oval drive in front of an abandoned farmhouse virtually encased in steer-sized tumbleweeds. Vintage tractors and other farm implements were left to rust in the center of the drive.

"Ideal, isn't it?"

"It's in the middle of nowhere, and frankly it's a dump."

Anson could see she was disappointed. "That's the best part. The nearest neighbor is a half-mile away. No one snooping around wondering when we're going to visit their church."

"What about water, utilities?"

"See that windmill?"

"The one missing its blades?"

"Doesn't need them. A motorized pump pulls water up from a well and into that cattle tank, and another motor pumps it into the house. So water's free."

"I see two tanks over there."

"The farm owner's nephew runs a herd on the land, which uses the tank on the opposite side of that rope fence."

"What's filtering the water in the people tank?" She sounded aghast.

"Nothing, but we won't actually drink the water from that tank. I'll cover the people tank with plywood, and we'll haul in drinking water in glass jugs from a spigot inside the shed and boil it as needed. Any stray bugs we inadvertently drink will fortify our digestive systems against dysentery when we travel to under-developed countries. There's more. See that thing that looks like a giant iron grasshopper?"

"You mean the pumpjack?" she asked with an indignant tone. "Being an oil reporter has taught me a few things."

"Maybe you don't know it's pumping natural gas, piped into the house for free."

"What's the rent?"

"Hundred a month plus some painting and repairs," Anson answered.

"Seems overpriced."

"Don't be rude."

"Sorry."

"May I continue?"

"Please, carry on."

"I had difficulty tracking down Hale, the owner—sort of a soft-spoken, short, roly-poly chap. Talks a lot about global government conspiracies. Lives in Kansas City with his mail-order bride. True story. She couldn't live here anymore. Everyone in town says the place has been empty for years because he refuses to sell or rent it to anyone. I think he let it out to me to thumb his nose at them. A kindred Bohemian, I suppose. Come on, let's explore."

Anson unlocked the front door to the farmhouse and held it open for Vivianne to walk into the stifling living room. He could see she was trying to keep her expression neutral as she stepped those high-heeled boots into what probably looked like a disaster area to her. "Even the ghosts have left," she said.

"Oh, come now. You have no vision. We can clean this up in no time."

"No AC?"

"Boss said he'd sell me a swamp cooler. By the way, what's a swamp cooler?"

"Operates through water evaporation," she offered. "Only works in dry climates."

They nosed their way through the two bedrooms. The closet-sized bathroom featured a cast-iron tub sitting on stacks of two-by-four blocks of wood, an oddity which they presumed was meant to accommodate the plumbing. The result provided the bather an inadvertent view through the window. Fine-grained sand sifted from behind the bluebonnet wallpaper every time they took a step on the warped floorboards. "I bet that dirt's from the Dust Bowl days," Vivianne speculated. "Could be history right here." Later they would peel off the faded wallpaper only to discover several more layers of roses or peonies or daisies, each layer of which had been nailed into place every square inch or so. When they eventually shredded off the final layer, five decades of dirt avalanched to the floor and exposed the loosely-spaced wall boards that formed the bathroom. This effect allowed peeping from surrounding rooms into the bathroom, a feature Vivianne never learned to appreciate.

Anson next showed off the dining area, his favorite room in the house. The triple set of windows stretched nearly floor to ceiling and would offer a view of sunsets over the run-down outbuildings and the prairie once the tumbleweeds were pulled away and burned. He hoped she'd see her furniture set up nicely in there, for he had none. "Imagine the rustic photos you'll create."

"The sun stained the glass panes yellow," Vivianne complained. "They'll never scrub clean, and the screens are in shreds. Can't open the windows without the bugs coming in." He was pleased to see her pause and admire the view. She craned her neck to scan the sky. "Looks like a thunderstorm coming our way."

Anson followed her gaze. A thundercloud roiled on the horizon with a finger pointing toward Texhoma. "I think the place is brilliant."

She smiled. "It suits you."

They walked through the out-dated kitchen and into the conservatory. Vivianne gasped at the columns of empty strawberry baskets, plastic margarine tubs, milk bottles, gallon-sized jars, and egg cartons stacked to the ceiling. "People who grew up during the Great Depression saved everything," Vivianne commented, shaking her head in amazement. "I suppose Farmer Hale's mail-order bride decided she could live without these in the big city."

From the conservatory they descended the stairs to the basement full of boxes and odds and ends. "There could be priceless antiques down here," Anson said. He started going through the heap of old toys and tools with the enthusiasm of hunting for hidden treasure.

Suddenly, a slow *tick ... tick ... tick* sounded from a stack of boxes in the corner. "That's a rattlesnake, sweetheart," Anson said. He could hardly contain his exuberance.

"I grew up in the desert, and I can tell you rattlers do not shake their tales so slowly. Must have bumped a wind-up toy."

They listened with anticipation for a moment and heard nothing. As soon as Anson took a step toward the origin of the noise, the rattle shook with so much conviction there was no mistaking its identity—or their imminent danger. They skipped steps as they flew up to the ground floor, through the front door, and into the VW Bus. Anson slammed the sliding side door for extra measure.

"I've never been that close to a rattlesnake before." She cringed in exaggerated fashion.

"Well, I've never even seen one. We've got to catch it."

"Why?"

"Can't live here knowing it's in the basement. I need to get a good look at the bugger."

Vivianne sighed and shook her head. "Mad dogs and Englishmen."

At dusk the two were back in the basement, Anson with a looped wire attached to a broomstick, and Vivianne standing on a trunk holding a flashlight and trembling so badly she could barely keep the light steady. After moving several boxes, he found the snake coiled against the wall. "Now, Boss says all I have to do is persuade the snake to stick its neck through the loop, and then I just pull the wire tight."

"Won't be that simple."

He made several attempts, but the snake could not be persuaded. Vivianne bolted up the stairs more than once, taking the flashlight with her and leaving Anson in total darkness.

"That tears it!" Infuriated, he lunged for the snake and grabbed it behind the head. "Find me something to put it in," he bellowed. "Hurry!" Vivianne handed him the small metal trash can near his feet. He thrust the snake inside it and quickly covered it with the metal top of a TV tray lying within reach. "I'll need something more secure."

Vivianne scrounged up a gallon-sized pickle jar. "But how are we going to transfer the snake from the trash can to the jar?" she asked.

Anson realized they'd forgotten to bring some kind of carrier, so focused was he on capturing the thing. "I'll think about that later. Let's get it back to my motel room and proceed from there."

"Like this, you pressing the tray on top of the can with your bare hands? What if you trip and fall? I can't have a loose reptile with fangs in my Bus, let alone the room!"

"Always so negative, woman! There's no electricity in the house yet. Where else can I get it into the light?"

Giving Vivianne no other choice but to acquiesce, he climbed the stairs with his dangerous load, handling it as if it were nitroglycerin. Vivianne ran ahead to negotiate the doors. Outside, lightning streaked across the night sky with an immediate thunderclap, and instantly water flooded the ground. Once Anson settled inside the Bus, she closed the side door and slipped into the driver's seat. She slowly stepped on the clutch and eased the stick into gear. The VW lurched forward when she stepped on the accelerator. "Easy," Anson whispered. The dirt road to the farmhouse, being so far out of Texhoma, had not been graded for a while, and the effect was like driving on a washboard, especially now that water rushed over it. The snake hissed and rattled with every little bump. Each ferocious sound it emitted raised Anson's heart rate, and he began sweating. He concentrated on keeping the tray clamped down on the can with fighter-pilot focus.

In the motel room, Anson placed the tray-covered trash can next to the pickle jar on the floor, and they stepped back to study the containers from a safe distance. "Now, how does one decant a snake from that dust bin to that jar?" he asked, pointing to each receptacle. "Can't just pop the tray off and stick my hand in there. Snake won't fall for that twice."

"First we must puncture holes in the lid, or it will suffocate."

"Yes, yes, I have a hammer in the Beetle."

"The best way to get the snake into the jar is to treat it like a pineapple upside-down cake," she explained when he returned.

"A what?" With one knee on the carpet, he began hammering holes in the lid.

"Cover the can with something like a plastic garbage bag. Turn it upside down, remove the can, and then pour the snake into the jar."

"Without getting bitten."

"Hopefully, it will be too confused to strike."

After scrounging a pillow case in the motel laundry room, Anson performed the task in the bathroom sink basin. "Success!"

he exclaimed. He screwed the lid onto the jar and sat it on the nightstand between the two beds. They flopped on the mattresses and examined their trophy.

"A diamondback, maybe," she offered. "Or a prairie rattler. A juvenile, I'd say. Not very long or fat. You probably couldn't have caught an adult."

He was only half listening, so enthralled was he with the snake's reactions. Every time he tapped the side of the jar, the snake reciprocated. The fangs smacking against glass scared them both despite the protective barrier, but only Anson savored the adrenalin rush.

"I daresay I need a drink." An hour and a few drafts later, the two returned from the motel lounge. They'd left the room dark to relax the snake, but when Anson turned on the nightstand lamp, Vivianne chuckled and pointed to the reptile. "Wonder why I didn't notice it earlier." Anson had placed the jar on top of John Steinbeck's novel he'd been reading, *East of Eden*. She fetched her camera and snapped a couple of shots.

"You're a rum 'un," Anson said.

"*I'm* odd?" She replaced her camera in its bag and then faced him with hands on hips. "That snake is not sleeping here tonight. Either it goes or I go home."

"No way it's escaping that jar, and you're not driving back to Guymon after drinking."

"What if we awaken in the middle of the night and knock the jar to the floor or a tornado hits the motel?"

"You're being ridiculous."

"Yeah? I say you're being careless. It sleeps in the car. Yours, not mine."

Anson sighed. "You win."

"For once."

She held the door for him as he carried the jar outside. Without watching the ground, he stepped off the curb with one foot and stubbed the other over the parking barrier. As he fell to the ground, the glass container slipped through his hands and rolled across the parking lot with the snake tumbling inside. It finally came to rest near the rear wheel of a semi-truck without shattering. The snake came back to life, rattling and spitting as Anson placed it on the floor of his Beetle.

He carried the snake around for three days, taking it indoors with him wherever he went. As part of their business day, Anson and his boss Dan typically visited the farmers in the cafés. The farmers rarely visited their own fields. Instead they'd sit around the tables drinking stale coffee and say something like, "Heard Charlie's sprayed for root weed. Y'all reckon I got root weed?" Dan would answer, "I'll check if you want me to." Now all attention was on the rattlesnake, inspiring personal stories of terror and legend. "Rattler struck me while I was on my hands and knees weeding my garden," one man said, showing Anson a truncated index finger. "Had to chop it off at the knuckle." The snake elevated Anson to a new level of respect, if not hero worship. He soaked up the attention.

On the third day Dan, a short, muscular man with a crew cut, took Anson aside. "You've got to get rid of that snake."

"I'll take it out to some barren spot and let it go. Vivianne says something about it being an integral part of the predator-prey cycle and an important citizen of the biotic community. Needs to eat, anyway."

"That's a load of crap," Dan said. "They're good for nothing. You've got to kill it."

Anson nodded in resignation. That afternoon he drove outside of town and stopped by the side of a dirt road. He emerged from the Beetle toting the economy-sized pickle jar and held it to the sun to admire his treasure one last time. Tired from its ordeal, the snake did not rattle or strike the glass but instead felt the air with its tongue. Anson's eyes dampened. Admittedly carting his trophy around like this might have been considered inhumane by some, but he'd done no real harm to the creature. He nestled the jar in a shallow ditch next to the car and loosened its lid. He fetched the shovel he had wedged crosswise within the car and opened the passenger door where the seat had been removed. Standing on the running board, he leaned over the door as his shield and toppled the jar with the blade tip of the shovel. The lid bounced clear of the jar, and the snake vanished between sage and rabbitbrush.

Later he found Dan in the Sale Barn Café. "It is done." That's all he would say on the subject, and Dan, being a veteran Marine, nodded once and allowed him his privacy.

One evening, not long after releasing the rattlesnake, Anson had accidentally hit a harmless bull snake with his VW in front of the house. It was that half-hour after sunset when it was still too early for headlights to illuminate much of anything. He jumped out and ran around to the back of the car to see the mangled snake heaped by the side of the drive. When he returned with a shovel and pail to remove and bury it, another snake had stretched it out as straight as a yardstick and laid alongside it.

4

Dancing the Skies

"I CAN SEE why this place is called 'no man's land,'" Anson mentioned to Vivianne one evening.

"No place for a woman either," she replied. She'd come home that day reporting that her life had been threatened over her coverage of a scandal at a grain co-op. "But we've misunderstood what is meant by that term." She raised an index finger and proceeded to explain that when Texas sought to enter the Union as a slave state in the mid-nineteenth century, it forfeited the rectangular strip of land that protruded from Oklahoma proper under the Missouri Compromise that prohibited slave ownership above a certain latitude. The region belonged to no single body of government until the Oklahoma Territory annexed it forty years later. "Hence it was called 'no man's land.'"

"That's quite nice," Anson replied. He appreciated the idea of the Panhandle being an in-between place of liberty and sovereignty, though he knew from experience that such freedom had its price.

Living on the ramshackle Oklahoma farm was the quintessential American experience to Anson. He knew that Vivianne appreciated the logic in living on the farm for its negligible rent and remoteness. Even so, the dust, the heat, the mice, the insects, and the necessity to boil drinking water had all been a nuisance to her. She wasn't attracted to farm life, in and of itself, wasn't interested in gardening or baking pies or joining local quilting clubs. No, she was too occupied with her newspaper job for all that. Something about the inconveniences made her thrive anyway.

Vivianne lectured him frequently about their little farm being a microcosm of the Panhandle's ecological macrocosm. They experienced to a smaller extent whatever epic event came to the High Plains, without the comfort of proper air conditioning, window screens, or modern appliances. First there was the heat wave that eventually claimed 1,700 souls across the United States. Next came the grasshoppers—he'd had no idea there were so many different kinds of grasshoppers. They ate everything: cereal boxes, clothing, stationary, even his postage stamps! He'd pull on a pair of trousers only to find a leg occupied by a spiky orthoptera. Once the grasshopper scourge dissipated, green bugs hung in clumps from plant stalks and converged on street corners in crawling chartreuse carpets. Anson celebrated the pestilence as the potential boon to the crop-dusting industry that it was.

Vivianne hoped for a tornado for its photographic value, but none came their way. Electrical storms occasionally killed the generator, which in turn killed the water-pump operation. They had to re-prime the pump manually, a process that required her to stand outside the pump house to ensure that water was siphoning properly from the exposed water tank. Standing next to a pool of water during an approaching electrical storm made her nervous, but it had to be done. Besides, he loved the way the atmospheric ions made her skin glow.

Vivianne's curiosity about flying had grown into an infatuation, which made him wonder if she was more attracted to his pilot's license than to him. He suspected she was more drawn to the romance of aviation, and to the perspective of the world airplanes afforded the flier, than she was to the actual mechanics and physics of flight. She repeatedly petitioned him to take her to the air again so that she could see the region from the sky.

Anson finally agreed to take her flying as long as she was willing to pay for the aviation fuel. On the eventful day he insisted on cooking her a proper breakfast, with thick, fatty bacon and piles of baked beans all laced by plenty of garlic and oil. If she complained about how long he was taking to cook, he moved that much slower. They finally got airborne about mid-morning when rising heat thermals made for a bumpy ride. He began their sky cruise by circling over their own farm as well as other farms whose owners they knew. She spotted some migrant workers swimming in a windmill tank, and he banked the Pawnee several times for her to get some shots. He flew her wherever she wanted to go, but with so little geographical relief there wasn't that much to see. Soon they both began losing interest.

"Put down the camera, sweetheart," he said after she'd shot a roll of black and white film she would later process in the newspaper's photo lab. "It's time for your first lesson." He'd already spent the previous week explaining the theory of flight, and now it was time to put it all into practice.

"Great!" She handed the camera to him, which he cradled in his lap. She placed her hands on the control wheel in front of her, while he let go of its companion wheel.

"Now remember to turn the wheel sideways to control the ailerons on the wings, which control the rolling and banking. Push the wheel forward or backward to control the pitch. Your foot pedals control the rudder, which controls the yaw." She turned the wheel a bit too enthusiastically, and the wings immediately wobbled from side to side as she struggled to keep the plane horizontal. "Don't steer it like a car," he snapped. "Watch your wing tips and make small corrections." As she checked the wings through the windows on either side, the plane started to dip. "Whoa! Pull up!" he yelled. She pulled the yoke quickly toward her, and the plane pitched upward. "Now you've over-corrected," he said. "Watch the altimeter and rate of climb so that you're not diving up and down like a dolphin in water." When she stabilized the plane to the best of her ability, he cautioned her to keep watching for air traffic, not only in front of her but also below and above at all angles.

"I think I've got the idea," she said. "You take control for a while."

He'd been waiting for this moment. "Let's go crop-dusting." Before she could react he swooped down to a hundred feet above a desolate farm road. His flight path segued from crops of milo to deep, rugged gullies, making sudden steep climbs and sharp turns along the way. He followed up with a few wingovers, lazy eights, chandelles, and the like.

By now she was wide-eyed and sheet white and desperately trying to open the window next to her. "Get me on the ground!" she demanded. Before he could land at the Texhoma airfield, she was sick in her lap. He taxied to a stop and hopped to the ground. She climbed out onto the wing and sat to peel off her trousers. Stripped down to her bikini underwear and T-shirt, her face splotched with the redness of tomatoes. Since he was holding her camera, he noticed she had one shot left on the roll. He photographed her from behind, forever etching her shame in emulsion.

––––––

"You misspelled tertiary again." Anson pulled smoke from his cigarette deeply into his lungs and slowly exhaled. "That makes three." He had a week's worth of her newspapers stacked in front of him and was working his way through Saturday's edition spread across the table. Living together for about two months now, they'd settled into a lazy Sunday morning routine during which he'd proof Vivianne's articles for typos, grammar, syntax, and story flow over breakfast, several cups of instant coffee, and half a dozen cigarettes.

"As in tertiary oil exploration?" she asked with resignation. "How did I spell it?"

Anson knew she hated this ritual, but he loved to watch her wriggle, ostensibly to make her a better writer. "With an -ery rather than -ary. Same as always."

"That's what editors are for."

"Yes, but you don't have a proper editor, do you? Was he gone again this week?" Vivianne had told him that the managing editor frequently disappeared with the household-hints columnist for hours at a time. A tiny staff of unschooled writers and an absentee editor made it imperative that she do her own editing, section layouts, and darkroom work. She reveled in it, but with daily deadlines always looming she made many mistakes. The job was further compounded by the fact that she didn't know the first thing about agriculture, which she worked to her advantage. Everything was new to her, and she turned every curiosity into a story, every piece of farm equipment into the subject of abstract photography. Anson loved watching and participating in the serial documentary she'd made of her job, and he was willing to bet the readers were beginning to look at their mundane lives in a fresh light.

The two sat at the antique wooden table and chairs Vivianne had managed to stuff into her VW Bus when she moved to Oklahoma. In just one trip, she'd brought area rugs, lamps, linens, kitchenware, and a small, backless couch that served as a bed. They also made use of the scant furniture Farmer Hale had left behind. Anson contributed nothing to the household, being the itinerant pilot in temporary quarters.

Anson unfolded Sunday's paper and turned to Vivianne's section on agriculture and energy. "Ho, is this your photo?" He looked up to see her beaming at him.

"You see my credit below it, don't you?" The photograph in question was an aerial of a small aircraft flying above a miniature farmhouse surrounded by a dozen manicured rows of plant life. A thin, white cloud trailed behind each wing.

"'Crop-dusters are angels of mercy to farmers,'" he read. "That's quite a cutline. How did you get this shot of the Cessna AGtruck?"

"Someone at the paper actually asked if I was standing on a building or a really tall ladder." She chuckled and shook her head. "Do you know of a building high enough around here where I can take that shot? See how small the fuel tanker looks?"

"So you shot it from another aircraft, obviously." He wanted her to answer the question without further commentary.

"I approached an ag-spraying company at the Guymon airport last week and persuaded one of the pilots to take me up."

"You're good at that. Why didn't you ask me?"

"It will be a long time before I get into an airplane with you again." She pulled a face. "I needed to climb back on the horse, so to speak, and I wanted to experience what it was like to spray the fields myself. I knew Dan would never approve of my sharing your one-seater."

"Are you saying you flew in an ag plane?"

"A Grumman Ag Cat," she taunted.

"An Ag Cat? You dog!" Anson's voice grew louder with excitement. The Grumman was a biplane with a radial engine—a chariot of the gods in his opinion. It was heavier but more powerful than his Cessna AGtruck. *Did she notice the power? Bloody woman.* "A one-seater?"

She nodded. "It was wide enough for both of us and had two seat belts, for training I suppose. I was asked not to give them credit for fear someone from the FAA or their insurance company would see the photo in the newspaper."

"Whatever possessed you to do this?"

"You challenged me to learn more about the crop dusting industry."

Anson stared at her a moment. "I'm ... I'm absolutely stunned."

"That's what I was going for." She sighed. "You have to understand ... my heart leaps every time I watch you fly. It's like a delicate aerial ballet, a syncopated choreography, the way you approach the field at high speed, pull up steeply at the end of a swath, pirouette at the apex, then nosedive over the field again. It looks so gentle and artistic ... from the ground."

Anson was tickled by the way his skill affected Vivianne. "You were hoping for some insight into my psyche," he teased.

She shrugged. "Maybe just a little."

"Go on, then. Tell me more."

Vivianne explained that she was at the field by five in the morning before the air started to warm up. There was a stiff breeze but not enough to squelch a day's work of spraying. The plan was to shadow the co-worker's airplane so that she could photograph it as it sprayed chemical on the ground, meanwhile experiencing crop-dusting vicariously from her own plane. Once her crash helmet, camera, and seat belt were in place, the pilot gave a thumbs-up to the pilot of the Ag Cat, and the two planes took off simultaneously.

"Well ... what did you think?" Anson could hardly stand the suspense.

"The ballet had all the delicacy of handling a jackhammer as it's pounding a concrete sidewalk."

"That's right." He grinned.

"The Ag Cat is so heavy and clumsy that the vibration jerked my mind all over the sky. There was no power steering, just a joystick to counterbalance the brute physicality of working the rudder pedals with the feet. The pilot had all of his limbs going at the same time. Not for the fainthearted, I see now."

Anson nodded in agreement. "Dan always tells me: 'Don't show up at the field in your aircraft.'"

"What else would you show up in, a tractor?"

"Feels like that sometimes. If the pilot 'shows up' at the field, it means his flying is stiff and jerky. You want to fly by the seat of your pants. It's a whole-body skill requiring eye-hand-feet coordination and enormous strength."

"In other words the pilot must become one with the aircraft, as if he were soaring over the field without the machine."

"Exactly. Not only that, we constantly have to be thinking about invisible wires, oil pipe stands, power lines, and houses all previously mapped out in our heads before ever going up. We carry as much as 200 gallons of liquid chemicals, and so we have to push every last horsepower out of the aircraft to climb out of a ground effect on a hot day, and then … oi! Where did that power line come from? We throttle a bit more at the last minute just above stalling speed, then we abruptly do an about-face and get the nose down to start another row. No time for celebrating or sightseeing."

"It's a wonder you don't kill yourself."

"Some do. Most of us are not barnstormers anymore. There's been efforts to build stronger aircraft to reduce injury on impact. Never mind all that. Please continue."

"Anyway, our two planes flew side by side but staggered. As the lead plane dipped to spray the crops, we were right there shadowing it about ten feet above the ground."

"So you were spraying insecticide. You'd be a bit higher if you were fertilizing the crop."

She nodded. "The ascent at the end of the row was sharper than I'd anticipated. Then we rolled into a steep bank and dived straight toward the earth with nothing between my face and the ground except the windshield. The plane leveled out just in time over the next swath. Did you know I've always hated roller coasters? I can barely tolerate a Ferris wheel."

"So what did you do?"

"I concentrated on taking pictures to offset the airsickness. My experience with you has taught me not to shift focus beyond what is in my lens. I also knew that if I stopped to inform my mind what I was doing, fear would grip my senses and my stomach would protest. Eventually the rows of plants converged to look like a jagged-toothed monster with long, green limbs. I was forced to abort, and I motioned to the pilot to land."

"Did you lose it?"

"No, I didn't, but I also didn't regain my senses for two days. I felt like I was drifting at least a foot above the ground."

"I didn't notice."

"You've been busy, and I wanted to surprise you." She thought a moment and then added with a hint of shyness: "I don't completely accept or condone what you do for a living, but I must tell you I have respect for you as a pilot."

"You're such a romantic." He beamed at her, enjoying the moment and feeling genuine affection for her. *If this isn't love*, he told himself, *it bloody well should be.*

This heat is most certainly getting to me, Anson thought as he held his head in an effort to stave off the endless memories flashing through his mind. To him the conversation with Vivianne about her joy riding in the Ag Cat had occurred just the previous Sunday. At the same time, he had the distinct feeling that it had happened months ago, that they'd traveled to England together since then. Where they stayed and for how long, he couldn't for the life of him remember.

He lowered to the ground in the shade of the Oklahoma hanger and laid flat on his back. It wasn't long before he closed his eyes and started dreaming of spraying crops from the air again. This time he saw the ground coming up on him, and he lost consciousness.

5

MEMORY IS A DECEITFUL INSTITUTION

ANSON STIRRED ON his gravelly bed with a start. Through blurry eyes he gazed at the milky-blue sky overhead where a lone turkey buzzard sailed idly upward on a thermal. *Hope that bird's not circling for me*, he thought, wondering how long he'd been asleep this time. It seemed like hours to him, though the shade provided by the hangar wasn't much wider than it was before his nap.

The heat didn't help his dizziness. "At least it's a dry heat," he said out loud, mocking the local attitude in an exaggerated Oklahoma drawl. His head throbbed, and his tongue swelled with thirst. He knew he should try the hose behind the hangar despite the water being hot and rubber tasting. *Why am I being so lazy?* He rolled to his side and willed himself to stand on his feet. *Oi ... too quick.* He sank to the ground on his knees then fell forward, catching himself with his hands so that he was on all fours. "Hate to say it, but I think I'm going to need some help here," he said aloud in resignation.

The drone of an aircraft engine suddenly rumbled in the distance. At first he thought the racket to be another figment of his imagination, but soon a relic flying machine appeared on the horizon and angled to align with the runway from the northeast. *Ah, someone to the rescue.* He squinted, wishing for his aviator sunglasses likely nicked by Vivianne who rightly thought they enhanced her looks. The plane took on more form as it flew closer, a low-winged, center-propped, mustard-colored tail dragger that resembled Boss's precious Thrush, yet the wheels were retractable rather than fixed. He blinked and looked again, not trusting the mirage that was deftly dropping its front wheels and then the rear wheel onto the runway without bouncing. *Well done, you,* Anson thought. Now he could see a red, white, and blue roundel decorating the fuselage, which was flanked by a thick, black buzz number 43 and serial number 2866. Feeling hopeful, he scrambled to his feet and limped toward the taxi lane.

The aircraft headed straight for Anson and coughed to a stop in a burst of smoke. Two hands forced back the bay-window canopy, and a slender man at least six feet in height unfolded from the cockpit. He pulled the leather pilot's cap off his head and shook out a respectable complement of gray-speckled black hair for a man of about sixty. He removed his Irvin jacket and dropped it in the back seat of the plane, revealing a fighter pilot's battle dress with Canadian insignia on the left shoulder. The uniform was completed by a white silk scarf knotted around his neck and knee-high leather boots with the fleece-lined tops turned down, which looked ungodly sweltering to Anson. Grabbing a cloth-covered canteen from the cockpit, the pilot hopped to the ground directly in front of Anson. His pencil-thin mustache framed a grin as he extended his right hand.

"Pilot Officer John Magee," he said with a crisp English accent. "You must be Avroe."

"Avroe?"

The pilot officer tapped his own forehead, nodding toward Anson's hat.

Anson rolled his eyes upward to his baseball cap and remembered he'd inscribed AV ROE across the bill. "Anson Vincent Roe's the name."

"Alliott Verdon Roe's aviation company, called Avro, was an early aircraft manufacturer and made many of the first military planes."

"Hmm, interesting coincidence," he said, wondering if his father'd had Avro in mind when he named him. He pointed to the plane with boyish glee. "I say, is that a Harvard Trainer? Had one of those hanging from my ceiling when I was a boy."

"Yup, the 'pilot maker,' Mark IIB, one of the first built in Canada in 1940 to train pilots on the advent of the war. The Yank prototype was called the Texan, but the Harvards were Anglicized and fitted with guns and racks to hold practice bombs. Did some instrument training in this very one at the flying school in Uplands, Ontario."

"You're a long way from Canada."

"Oh, she can go about 800 miles on a tank. I fueled up somewhere in Illinois, but I underestimated how much gravy I had left after circumnavigating a storm. On my way to an air show."

"You're spot on the Oklahoma-Texas border here." Anson pointed a thumb over his shoulder. "Air force base in Amarillo is just a hop and a skip that way if that's where you're headed."

Magee grinned and shook his head. "So close."

"I assume you were in the Canadian Royal Air Force," Anson said. "Yet you don't sound Canadian."

"And you don't sound American. Actually, I am American but was raised in England. Long story. Yourself?"

Anson laughed. "I'd like to hear that story. I'm from East Anglia, here flying for the local aerial spraying company." He paused, still lightheaded and confused about his state of mind. He remembered his fierce thirst. "Is there water in that canteen you're holding?"

"A swig or two. Be my guest. Was hoping to refill all fluids."

"Everything's locked down. I've been waiting for someone to show up." Anson tipped the canteen to his parched lips and swallowed more than a few gulps. "Cheers," he said as he handed the canteen back to Magee. He wobbled on his feet.

"Steady on. You're looking a bit rough, old man."

"I admit, I'm shattered."

"We should break into the hangar, Avroe, and get you out of the sun," the older pilot said in a conspiratorial tone. "I have a spanner in the bus."

"Oi, if you knew the boss, you wouldn't even joke about that. He's an ex-Marine pilot and meticulous about his possessions."

"Wouldn't want you to clap out, would he?" Magee didn't wait for an answer. In an instant he was standing on the wing again and leaning into the cockpit. "Here, have a vitamin C." He tossed an orange to Anson.

Anson peeled the skin with desperate fingers and devoured the orange in no time, relishing the sweet juice as it squished in his dry mouth and ran down his throat. "Lovely, thank you, ta."

Dan's hangar was little more than a rectangular steel building and large enough to hold two agricultural airplanes. There was a pedestrian entrance on the short side, and on the long side a sliding door wider than the wing span of the planes. Magee approached the people door and lifted the heavy wrench to clobber the knob. He hesitated. "Something tells me your boss would be cunning enough to hide a key." He slipped his fingertips under the metal door jamb in a few places and soon discovered a key wedged beneath it. He unlocked and opened the door. "There you go."

"Clever man. Well done." Anson laughed self-consciously. "Embarrassed I didn't know about the key."

"I'm an old lag when it comes to aerodromes."

Anson headed right for the work sink, found his coffee mug and barely rinsed it out under the tap before filling it. He swigged down the water and refilled it again for an encore. Remembering his guest, he offered it to Magee. "Sorry, we've no clean cups."

"Brought my own." Magee filled his canteen and took a drink. He wiped his mouth with his white scarf.

"Right. That canteen looks brand new," Anson said. He was amazed by the detailed level of authenticity the man had managed to achieve with his costume. "Is it aluminum?"

"Enamel coated." Magee turned his attention to the two aerial sprayers, each equipped with tubing and nozzle systems attached to the trailing edges of their wings. "Which one is your hedgehopper?"

His visitor's WWII jargon brought a smile to Anson's face. He crossed to the Piper Pawnee and lovingly stroked its nose. "This is my kite." He knew a few slang words of his own, thanks to his father. "It has a six-cylinder engine, 260 horsepower, and a payload of 1,200 pounds."

"And the other?"

Anson looked wistful. "The Thrush Aero Ag Commander is Boss's pride and joy. Holds it out there like a carrot. Afraid I'll prang it. What did you fly once you were trained?"

"The Spit, of course."

"The Supermarine Spitfire? Ho, brilliant!"

"I was only nineteen at the time. Enlisted at eighteen."

"How did an American-born, English-raised teenager enlist in the Canadian Air Force? More importantly, why?"

"I was born in Shanghai, actually."

"Small coincidence. I lived in Singapore when I was a lad, but now I'm confused."

"Simple. My mother was English, my father an American missionary stationed in China. Spent my formative years at a proper British school. Then in the summer of 1939 my parents sent me to the States on the Queen Mary so that I might appreciate my American heritage. I was to return to England in September to finish my final term, but England declared war on

Germany that very month. The U.S. State Department wouldn't allow its citizens to sail to Europe, and in the meantime the ship was pressed into military service. What's more, my passport was mysteriously canceled. I became stranded in this country."

"I have a similar situation."

Magee paused for a moment. "Is that so? Well, my parents made use of my own miserable situation and installed me at a college preparatory school in Connecticut. I was to enter Yale on scholarship in the autumn of 1940. But over the summer Germany brought the war to Britain's shores, and I became more desperate than ever to help defend her."

"The Battle of Britain."

"That's when hordes of Messerschmitts flew over England like rows of militarized hornets and bombed our strategic centers mercilessly. Our Hurricanes and Spitfires swatted back the Luftwaffe in three months' time, although Germany continued its lightning war on London and other major cities for another eight months. All along the Royal Air Force was grabbing able young men by the hundreds and throwing them in the air with only a few hours of training."

"You among them?" Anson asked.

The fighter pilot shook his head. "It was not meant to be. I missed the initial wave of recruitment because I could not travel without a passport. However, I discovered that Canada was accepting Americans in their air force, and I saw that as my ticket back to England. I enlisted in Ontario in September during the peak of the air battle in 1940. Alas, the RCAF did such an excellent job recruiting that the whole system backed up, and they were being more thorough in their training by then. It would take me a good nine months to get back to England and another few months of training before I was allowed to engage the enemy.

By the time I got to England the battle in her skies was long over, and we were flying sorties over France."

Magee lifted a leather boot upon the chair and rested his forearm on his knee. To Anson, he looked like a living portrait of an ace fighter pilot straight out of the pages of *Life* magazine, dripping in style and confidence. "Funny thing … I was a pacifist at first, but I became enamored by the idea of flying long before I took to the air. The throb of an aeroplane engine was music in my ears. It had all the power of Beethoven, the grandeur of Wagner, the eagerness and intensity of Strauss." Magee's hand became a gliding machine as he spoke. "You see, the aeroplane was not a weapon of war to us but a flash of silver slanting the skies, the hum of a deep-voiced motor, a feeling of dizziness, the speed and ecstasy. Before I began my actual flight training in that Harvard, as well as half a dozen other types, I knew I had found my place in the sun. Flying was in my blood!"

Anson sat with mouth gaped open, barely believing who he was seeing and what he was hearing. "Yes, yes, I feel the same way," he stuttered. "Only I don't engage in dog fights as you did. Weeds, fungus, insects … these are the enemies."

"Your flying is no less aerobatic and harrowing. Some of the same maneuvers, I suspect."

Anson nodded, feeling he found a comrade in this serendipitous encounter. "Woman I'm involved with says that watching me spray a field is like watching a ballet. At least, I thought she was mine. No longer sure." Anson studied the ground, trying to remember.

"Ah … ." Magee smiled. "None of them belong to us, my friend. That's why God invented aeroplanes. And isn't it wonderful to be born with gifts you enjoy using?"

"Indeed. You can watch your life from the mezzanine, or you can participate in the performance, discover your talents, and relish every moment. But it involves risk."

"Have you been known to shrink from risk?"

"No." He began thinking about the seemingly random selection of genius when another dizzy spell came upon him. In one moment he was leaning against the Pawnee, and in the next he was abruptly plunging into warm salt water, venting air bubbles and swallowing liquid as he sank. He began flailing with his arms and legs wildly in panic, but recognizing that his lack of control was just a prelude to drowning, he stilled himself by sheer willpower, shot upward, and began to tread water with more control. As his head bobbed above the undulating boat wake, and as salt water stung his eyes and nostrils, he saw his father standing on the bow of their Star Class sailboat with his hands on his hips in a familiar posture that said: "Serves you right for telling me what to do."

In a flash Anson was back in the hangar, staggering from shock and more than a little surprised he was dry. Slowly he began to realize he'd been held in bondage momentarily by an old memory of when he was a boy of ten. The incident had occurred just off the coast of Singapore where he crewed for his father at the Royal Yacht Club. He recalled having a talent for manipulating water and air currents for speed and distance as it suited him, synchronized with his own motor currents and what he could only describe as a cellular memory for sailing and navigation. He'd been so sure of his skills, he often shouted orders to his father while on board, which didn't sit well with the old man, the result being an unexpected dip in the Straight of Singapore. Soon he would take his B Class Helmsman Certificate and begin skippering yachts of varying classes, crewed only by adults in competitions against other adults and winning cups. The racing club members would come to call him "Little Nelson." But the day his father threw him overboard had forever altered their relationship, and he'd vowed to leave home as soon as possible.

————

"Are you all right, Avroe?" The pilot was calmly eyeing him. "Your mind went elsewhere for a moment."

"A little swim down memory lane." Anson's senses had returned, but his mind was still murky from the experience. "I'll be shipshape in a moment." He cringed when he recalled his father saying everything must be "shipshape and Bristol fashion." He'd always interpreted that to mean that one's attitude must be tidied and docked against any rising tide of emotion.

"Memory is a deceitful institution," Magee said.

"Indeed," Anson agreed. "And dangerous."

"Not always. With lingering hands it transfers the most squalid, the most ordinary, moment into something at once tender and lovely, as a rose once blooming, now blown beyond the realm of earthly colors. You're right—it's dangerous too the way it makes one cry out for the past, believing in it still, when in reality the past is but a memory, the future but a dream."

"The present, I suppose, is all that matters."

Magee nodded and smiled. "'We are a part of all that we have met,' as Alfred, Lord Tennyson, wrote, but I think he may have been wrong. Yes, the present—the tangible, changing, moving, breathing but above all tangible present—is all that matters, is all that is of significance."

"You're a philosopher, are you?"

"I have a lot of time at my disposal." He clapped both hands together. "Right. What you say we get something to eat?"

Anson couldn't remember whether he'd eaten or not. "The town is two miles that way. Long walk in the heat."

"Saw some vehicles from the air."

"No keys for the Beetles. We're stuck here."

"I know I saw a car 'round back," Magee insisted.

"What?" Anson peered out the window over the work sink. He blinked to make sure what he was seeing was really there. The Delta 88, which he'd bought for Vivianne to drive while her VW Bus was at the shop being rebuilt, was indeed parked outside.

———

"Where's the Bus?" Anson had just come home for his afternoon tea to find Vivianne asleep on her day bed in front of the chilled air blasting from the swamp cooler.

Vivianne's eyes fluttered open, and she stretched and yawned. "On the highway shoulder halfway to Guymon," she said. "Caught on fire while I was driving home from the paper."

"Destroyed? No, first, are you all right?"

"I'm fine but the engine area is burned pretty badly. Thankfully the fire was put out before it could spread beyond the firewall. I think the fuel injector you installed to fix the vapor lock came loose and doused the engine. It just burst into flames."

"Did you use the fire extinguisher?"

She shook her head, still looking jolted by the episode. "Some of the migrant workers from the lounge stopped and barred me from getting it out of the back of the Bus. I couldn't remember the Spanish word for it. A farmer stopped, and I screamed at him to fetch the extinguisher. He sprayed foam on the engine, and the ordeal was over in seconds. He was kind enough to drive me home."

"I can't believe you're here sleeping, not trying to do something about it," he said.

"What can I do, out here in the middle of nowhere? Don't know anyone except you. You were busy flying."

Anger instantly opened the capillaries in his face. "I only had a few minutes to grab a bite to eat before going back to the fields. Now I have to stop everything to tow the Bus somewhere to have it fixed. What are you going to do without a car? You have to get to work somehow."

Vivianne shrugged, fighting back tears. *"Extintor de incendios,"* she said.

"What?"

"That's how you say fire extinguisher in Spanish."

———

Anson began recalling that Vivianne's insurance company gave her $1,500 to repair the burned out VW, which was more than it was worth. The claims adjuster, feeling particularly generous after celebrating her birthday with perhaps too many margaritas, told Vivianne over the phone that she could keep the vehicle rather than forfeiting it to the company to sell for scrap. Anson had the Bus rebuilt for $600. He now vaguely remembered spending much of the remainder on flights to England. Not expecting to return to Oklahoma, they'd given the Delta away to a friend the day they left the country.

Anson was prepared to accept these new details as his memory now presented them, yet here he was in an American airfield, and there sat the Delta behind the hangar, aglitter in the sun in all its glory. He reached into his pocket and pulled out a fob containing the keys to the Delta as well as his work Beetle. He stared at them a moment, for they had not been in his pocket when he previously checked there. This updated version of reality made his head throb even more, and it was too much for his mind to absorb. His knees buckled, and the room began to spin.

As he felt his consciousness slowly slip away again, he observed a different reality. Now he was surrounded by plane wreckage. He could hear men shouting instructions to each other in a foreign language, and he could see a flurry of shocked, worried faces looking down on him. This reality flickered like a film strip in a slow projector.

In the next moment, he was back in the hangar with the WWII fighter pilot holding him upright by his armpits and shouting, "Avroe! Avroe!"

6

What Else but Love?

AS ANSON REGAINED consciousness, he felt himself being lowered into his swivel chair by the fighter pilot. Magee handed him his mug of water. "Drink slowly."

Anson sipped the water and put his head between his knees for a moment. "I'm ... I'm sorry," he said once he started to recover. "Thought I was losing my grip. Too much sun, I think."

"What you need is a good nosh. Would you like me to drive to town for a couple of burgers?"

Anson didn't want to ask the man to do that for him, but he questioned the wisdom of his going anywhere public where he'd run into people he knew. That would be more than his unstable mind could handle. "Best we go to my house. Vivianne doesn't do much grocery shopping or cooking, but I'm sure I could turn out something."

Magee secured the Harvard and Anson carefully seated himself behind the steering wheel of the Delta, leery of succumbing to another fainting spell. He pulled down the visor and found his aviator glasses clipped to its underside. After donning them, he put the key in the ignition and turned it. A light tap on the accelerator inspired a roar from the motor as if it had been driven every day. Magee entered on the passenger side, and Anson steered the Delta out of the hangar parking area, down a dirt road, and onto the highway. The steering wheel gave him something solid to grip and he relaxed. "We're in business."

"Indeed. What do you call this motor vehicle?"

"A 1972 Delta 88 Royale. She has a four-barrel Rocket V8 engine."

"I daresay it feels like a boat. Does it go fast?"

Anson glanced in the rear-view mirror at the empty highway behind them and, seeing no one in front of them, floored the accelerator. The sedan shot forward, and before long he had the speedometer needle quivering at the one hundred miles-per-hour mark. Magee was grinning like a teenager, and it became obvious that trying to impress a Spitfire fighter pilot was futile.

Anson's awareness transported to a memory of speeding along a dirt road between two ripening cornfields. Vivianne screamed in terror next to him as she gripped the door's armrest for dear life. The giant cornstalks blinded him to any approaching cross traffic when he sailed through the intersections. He gritted his teeth with glee and immersed himself in the present experience.

Magee's voice abruptly brought his attention back to his current passenger. "I used to scare women that way too in my convertible Packard, which I affectionately called Mephistopheles," he said. "They'd as soon pound you with their fists as fall into your arms for protection."

Anson laughed and nodded. "Too right! We have that in common." He was beginning to think Magee was a mind reader.

"Suspect we have more in common than you know." Then, quite from nowhere, Magee broke into syncopated verse:

"We 'marched' at noon, with laughter
In Chevrolets, and Fords,
With power-caps for bullets,
And swagger sticks for swords."

Anson looked askance at his passenger. "I beg your pardon?"

"Oh, just a little something I scribbled out when I was a lad in Officer's Training Corps. Here's another:

"They marched at dawn, in silence,
And fell before sunrise;
With rotten flesh for faces,
—And cavities for eyes … ."

"What do you call it?"

"Bottom-rung poetry, I'd say."

"So, you're a pilot, a philosopher, *and* a poet? What an odd combination." Anson turned left onto the first farm road that veered north just before entering the limits of Texhoma.

"Fancied myself a poet. Started writing to impress a girl who composed poetry herself. She was the daughter of the headmaster at my school in England."

"Did it work?" Anson turned right and headed east. "The poetry, I mean."

"Impressed the father."

"But not the daughter."

He sighed. "I always suspected she found me too immature even after I joined up. I thought the uniform and mustache made me look older, more dapper. Knowing her, she saw right through the facade. In the end the poetry became a means for expressing my adolescent angst and preoccupations."

"Preoccupations with what?"

Magee shrugged and looked at Anson. "Death, mostly."

Anson pondered the man's answer. The young John Magee may have been preoccupied with the unavoidable fears of a war-torn world, but he clearly survived. The man didn't appear to be depressed, Anson thought. Quite the contrary. He seemed rather jolly.

"This is me," Anson announced as he turned onto the road in front of the farmhouse he shared with Vivianne.

"What's that?" Magee pointed to a tall, four-legged creature leaning against the mailbox post near the road.

"Why, that is a doe." He wrinkled his brow with feigned disbelief that the fighter pilot didn't recognize the animal.

Magee chuckled. "Looks alive."

"Stuffed by a professional taxidermist, I think. Vivianne and a mate visiting from her hometown found it on the plains, loaded it up in her Bus, and set it up here as a prank on me. It worked too. I didn't discover it until I came dragging home late one evening. When those gals doubled over with laughter, I knew I'd been had. Nearly knocked a jockey off his thoroughbred out for training exercise early one morning when it bucked at the sight of it."

"Sounds like quite a woman," Magee said.

"She's a rum 'un." Anson parked the car in front of the house. Vivianne's rusting metal bells hanging from the porch rafter chimed on a sudden breeze as the two climbed out of the Delta, giving Anson a sense of familiarity. He was feeling better now, nearly convinced he was recovering from his sun stroke episodes. *Racing the Delta must have cleared the cobwebs.* He hopped up the steps to the porch with renewed vigor and led Magee into the stuffy house. He flipped on the swamp cooler and headed for the kitchen.

"Pardon the mess." He nodded toward the sink full of dishes. "Vivianne says we both need a wife. She's probably out reporting on the Future Farmers of America's pig contest or the like."

"What about you?"

"What do you mean?" Anson stooped in front of the refrigerator in search of something resembling a meal.

"I told you about the love of my life. Is Vivianne the love of yours?"

"Oh, that." He moved the milk and eggs aside to expose food items hiding in the back of the fridge. "In my opinion all women adhere to a strain of logic I have never understood, Vivianne among them. Women crave exciting careers as much as any man." Anson chuckled. "Well, for that matter, they crave exciting men too. As soon as they find one, their natural processes click in. They begin forming certain expectations of conformity. Don't get me wrong, I want to get married ... ."

"You just don't want to be tied down. And what is her perspective?"

Anson's mouth turned downward. "She thinks I want to marry her for legal conveniences."

"Oh, you want to take advantage of her U.S. citizenship, do you?"

"Have to admit I've thought about it."

"Why? What happened?"

"Well ... I was arrested while traveling through Texas on my way to a flying job in Louisiana. Bad luck, really. Border patrol agent boarded the Greyhound bus in the middle of the night, shook me from a dead sleep, and asked me my citizenship. I sleepily mumbled 'U.K.' without much thought, forgetting that my visa had expired."

Anson pulled out a plate wrapped in wax paper, a loaf of bread, iceberg lettuce, tomatoes, and an onion. "Would a cold tongue sandwich suit you? Tastes just like roast beef when you put a bit of horseradish on it. I have Colman's mustard too. Made in my hometown of Norwich, you know."

"That'll do. You were saying?"

"I was deported through Vancouver, Canada, in the end, but I sneaked back into the States with a driver's license the state of California issued to me along with a green card while I awaited the government to decide what to do with me. That took nearly a year, I might add. Basically, I'm here illegally. I'm in debt up to my eyeballs, and I need to accumulate enough flight time on various aircraft in order to work in England where the rules are much more rigorous."

"I, too, used Canada as a revolving door, only my destination was England."

"Why were you so desperate to get back to the U.K.?"

"My father's family in Pennsylvania came from money, you see. Their lives were the antithesis to my life in England, where all we had were our studies. I had a jolly time in the States horseback riding, sailing, carousing at night, all of which ran up quite a tab for my poor aunt who played hostess to my rabble-rousing. I admit I enjoyed every last penny I spent." He sighed. "In time, though, I came to resent my rich, spoiled acquaintances, every one of them seemingly right off the pages of *The Great Gatsby*, so frivolous in their expenditures of time and money."

"Most of the locals here remind me of characters in *Grapes of Wrath*."

"I missed that one, I'm afraid."

"It's about the Oklahoma refugees who fled to California during the Dust Bowl of the 'thirties. This was the epicenter of the Dust Bowl, you know."

"Read about it but didn't give it much thought."

"People around here still talk about the dust storms. Vivianne says that the farmers, with their new tractors, overplowed the topsoil and displaced the native grasses that normally trapped soil and moisture during drought and high winds. Much of the loose soil turned to black dust blizzards that rolled across the country."

"Dreadful stuff," Magee said, shaking his head.

"As I was saying, I rather appreciate that stoic pioneer spirit and self-reliance the Okies embody. They had to do everything they could to survive. Don't see ambition like that in England these days with so many on the dole."

"The England I knew forty years ago had an innovative spirit, or we would never have survived the war." He accepted the sandwich Anson made for him and seated himself at the little kitchen table. "So why don't you stay here until you get all the flying hours you need?"

Anson opened two bottles of beer and handed one to Magee as he seated himself. "It's not that simple. I'm probably good for only one season here. I've convinced the boss to pay me cash but he doesn't like it. He's a regular standard-bearer for morality and doesn't tolerate breaking the law. Don't know how long I can keep it up."

"I see." He took a bite of the sandwich. "You are a daredevil, aren't you? Where does that leave Vivianne?"

"Says I'm not 'marital material,' says she wants to meet my parents first, talk to my friends in Norwich, that sort of thing." Chewing on his own sandwich, he laughed at the memory of her coming home one day and announcing: "When you introduce me to your mother, I want you to say, 'This is America,' the way Prince Edward introduced Mrs. Simpson to his mother the Queen." It was something she'd heard on Paul Harvey's "The Rest of the Story" radio show.

When the two finished their sandwiches, Magee pulled a tin of Player's Navy Cut cigarettes from his pocket. He offered one to Anson.

"Cor! Just my brand," Anson said. Lighting both their cigarettes with his chrome Zippo lighter, he inhaled deeply and exhaled with a sigh of relief. "I was dying for one of these." He took another drag and spoke as he blew the smoke away from his guest's face. "I have a genuine Spitfire fighter pilot sitting in my kitchen and we're wasting it talking about women."

"What else is there but love?" Theatrically, Magee placed a hand over his heart and began reciting:

"Always there will be loves that drift, as ours;
Beautiful faces, touched by fresher winds
Change suddenly—and soon are blown away;
Passion forgets her few, ecstatic hours
Soon after, in new hearts, and other minds
—And finds enchantment for another day!"

"Yours as well?"

Magee nodded. "It's an immature verse written in youth."

"Seriously," Anson persisted. "I'd like to hear about your flying and war adventures, why you became a pilot in the first place."

"Ah, you want the romance."

"No, I want the grit."

"That's just it, you see. Flying is romance, isn't it? Love drove me to write poetry, but I soon learned how poetry could enable a young man to grapple with his conscience, his stance on war, his religious views, his quest for self. When I became stuck in America, away from my beloved England, my inspiration, the only way back was through flight. My restless imagination drove me to the skies."

Tears flashed in Anson's eyes, for he wasn't entirely insensitive himself. He, too, nurtured a creative ember deep within his soul, which he expressed by spreading his wings across the air currents. "Like Icarus."

The older pilot raised his eyebrows. "Ah, precisely!" Although Anson was already familiar with the Greek myth, he let Magee describe how Icarus's father—Daedalus—constructed wings of wax and feathers for his son to escape the labyrinth, which he also designed for the king to house a Minotaur. Daedalus warned Icarus not to fly too close to the sea nor too high to the sun, for excessive moisture or heat would destroy the wings. Through his complacency and hubris, Icarus did not heed his father's advice and plunged into the sea.

"That burning quest for unbound freedom that takes one too close to the sun, that leap into the unknown that requires blind faith and surrender to the delicate balance of the laws of physics, which enable one to defy gravity and death itself—yes, I'm intimate with those desires." Magee swallowed the remaining drops of his beer and set the bottle on the table. "So you see, to understand my plight as a would-be poet is to understand my flying ambitions and vice versa. One does not exist without the other."

Anson raised a hand. "Then, by all means, carry on!" He wasn't opposed to listening to the man's reminiscences as long as it didn't take all day. His history as a pilot was far more interesting to him.

Magee nodded. "I take you back to England, October of 1938."

Something about the heat, the alcohol, or the cadence of Magee's words as he told his story lulled Anson into another sort of spell. The harsh edges of the farmhouse's white kitchen began to fade, and he was instantly transported to another time and another place on the wings of Magee's story. He only wished Vivianne could be here to hear it.

7

A SECRET TO MY SOUL

THE VILLAGE OF Rugby, England, was abuzz with a harvest festival, at the center of which stood a modestly-sized Ferris wheel. Headmaster Lyon released the students from Rugby School early on a rare Friday afternoon to attend the festivities. "And when you see that mechanical contraption," the headmaster warned the students in Hall, "try to forget that seventeenth-century Bulgarians called them 'pleasure wheels,' lest you fall off and break a leg trying to impress the fairer sex." He looked directly into young John Magee's eyes when he said it, as if he guessed his scheme.

John didn't shrink away from the charge, for he did hope to see Elinor Lyon, the headmaster's daughter, and he wasn't ashamed of it nor did he attempt to conceal it. He assumed that his adoration for Elinor was already known by everyone.

That afternoon John spotted Elinor in queue at the ticket booth conversing with several of her giggling female mates. He sighed at the sight of her. She was a statuesque young woman of perfect posture, with finely chiseled yet soft facial features and an easy-going smile. True to his assertive nature, he stepped in line in front of her just in time to purchase tickets. "Two please," he said to the agent.

Startled, Elinor pivoted toward the sound of his voice. "What are you up to, Ian?" In the Magee family tradition, she called John by the Scottish version of his name.

"Why, nothing," he said with a feigned look of the falsely accused. He extended an elbow to her. "Would you give me the honor of accompanying me on the pleasure wheel?"

"Beg your pardon?" Elinor's smile betrayed her sternness. She'd had a proper upbringing but she wasn't above playfulness herself.

"Mr. Ferris's wheel, my love. The vertical roundabout. You deserve the Graydon Wheel at Earls Court or the *Grande Roue de Paris*, but both were demolished years ago. I'm afraid this is the best our empire has to offer."

"That would be lovely, Ian, but I have my friends."

"Go ahead, Elinor," said the girl with ginger hair.

"Then, I would be honored." She allowed John to escort her to the bottom-most gondola just as it came to a stop. Once seated, the operator pushed a lever and they were away.

"I enjoy the anticipation of the ascent, the breezes, the view from the zenith," she said. "It's the descent that gives me a tickle in the pit of my tummy."

"Like life," John said.

"Oh, Ian, how banal."

"Not a'tall. We are forced to live in the carriage we are placed in whilst we are obliged to go round and round *ad nauseam* until the wheel comes full stop."

"Whatever do you mean?"

"All who ride the wheel are equally bound to it. I could be rich, I could be poor, but no matter what, I am committed to my position and must obey its properties. Each seat has its proverbial ups and downs but they all endure the same sunshine, storm, or dark of night. Most of the time we can enjoy the ride and watch the people on the ground. Not everyone can get on the wheel at the same time, you see. They have to wait for their turn, purchase a ticket."

"Can we leave the wheel?"

"Only when it stops, silly." John tapped her arm playfully with his elbow.

"Can we get on again?"

"Did not Job ask the same question? 'If a man dies, shall he live again?' The Bible leaves that a mystery."

"Is it destiny, Ian, or divine will that dictates a certain position on the wheel?"

"One's position in life could be utterly random or utterly deserved for all I know."

"But there's a flaw in your premise. I, as an American-born divorcee, might fall in love with a king and persuade him to abdicate the throne. I've switched gondolas, you see."

"Ah, but maybe that wasn't out of the realm of possibilities for your particular perch on the wheel. And besides, love trumps fate."

Elinor nodded her approval. "And what about you? What is your perch?"

"That remains to be seen. I'm the son of a missionary yet not a pauper, for my father's family in Pittsburgh is wealthy. Of course, you wouldn't know it with my frugal mother's penchant for buying my clothes second-hand."

"And yet you always look smart, Ian."

"All for you, my love. And I've discovered that if I exert enough will power to dig it out, I have a fairly good imagination and can just about express it on paper. That's me, a small life in a plainly decorated seat."

Elinor grabbed his shoulder. "Humility doesn't suit you, Ian. Father says you have the genius to become a brilliant poet who could surpass his own skills in time."

"Headmaster Lyon has spoken to you about my poetry?" It touched John that her father discussed his efforts with her.

"It's no secret you're one of his favorite students. I suspect you already know that, or you wouldn't spend so many holidays with our family, would you?"

"I appreciate his taking me in hand, with my own father in China on his missionary business and mother busy with my younger brothers in Kent." John became pensive. "Even so, it was you who inspired me to verse in the first place."

"*I* did?" Elinor placed a hand on her chest, taking her turn to be surprised. "Oh, you're much better than I."

"Don't be so swift to judge." John paused, wondering if he should divulge a secret he'd been carrying for months. He decided to leap right in, despite the consequences that were sure to come. "Listen to the music in your own words:

"The sleepy sun lies glowing in the west,
His hot head sinks upon the ocean's breast,
The night pursues the day's departing glow,
And shadow casts on all the world below."

Elinor reddened. "How did you...? You must have gone through my personal things to find that poem."

"It was so long ago, I don't remember how I came by it," he lied. Her sister had shared it with him while they holidayed together the previous summer. "I think I remember the rest:

"The day of my life shall not set so soon!
My sun will not yield early to the moon,
But in the slow glory will I sink and die,
And then in content I will shadow lie."

John raised his eyebrows, "Rather steamy, don't you think?" He was teasing her now.

"You're such a cheek, John Gillespie Magee, Jr. I couldn't have been more than fourteen when I wrote that. I doubt I knew what I was talking about, although I may have been right."

"Oh, some part of you knew, clearly. Here's another one, a self-portrait perhaps?

"She has nothing in the world of her own
But beauty, which makes all the world her throne;
For the sky is not as bright as the colour of her eyes,
The sunbeams are paler than her hair,
The happy happy birds hush their singing when she laughs,
And she is freer than the mountain air.
Her words are precious as a prince's jewels,
Her thoughts are worth the gold of kings;
The moon watches when she dances,
And the stars listen when she sings."

"Not a self-portrait. More a character study for little stories that come to me. The last two lines are worth all the rest put together."

John's eyes lit up. "So that's what goes on in that pretty head of yours."

"Sometimes."

"T'would explain the poem about the young boy who was executed for not giving up military secrets to the enemy. 'And after the shooting they saw with surprise, a kind of triumph in his young dead eyes.' Or the ethereal epic poem about the knights roaming across the moor: 'All round the knights moved strange, transparent fancies, the weird and coloured company of Dreams.' Quite nice though a bit masculine for a girl."

"It's all right-ish. Childish, but with some good points. I would like that last line if I could be sure it was mine."

"Shows enough promise to put me to shame. When I first read them I felt I had to become a poet myself to impress you."

"No need to impress *me*."

"You really should allow me to publish some of your poetry in the *New Rugbeian*."

Elinor looked taken aback. "Why, so that the entire school can laugh at me?"

"No, so that you shall torture more hearts than you already do."

She arched an eyebrow in skepticism. "I don't attend this school, anyway."

"Very well, then. I promise you I won't let up."

She pressed her lips into a brief smile, showing that she would not be budged. John was familiar with that look.

The Ferris wheel came to a stop when their chair reached ground level. "Come on, out you go," whined the ruddy-nosed carny.

John steadied the swinging gondola with a firm grip for Elinor as she stepped out of it. "Will you walk with me?" he asked, as confidently as he could muster.

"It would be rude to abandon my companions."

"I suspect they will survive. Do you even know where they are right now?"

"Off with the lads, I suppose."

"Quite." John stepped back and sliced the air forward with his hand. "After you."

"Perhaps for a few moments," she said.

Hearing reluctance in her reply, he suddenly became aware of his heart pounding profoundly in his chest. In his experience she was just as likely to refuse him as accept his invitations.

She added, "There's something I'd like to discuss with you, now that you've given me opportunity."

"And what is that?" he asked. Now he felt hopeful with an admix of apprehension. He pushed his hair off his forehead, wishing that he'd visited the barber the previous weekend. As meticulous as he was about his dress, he always felt disheveled next to her comeliness.

She didn't answer, and John knew she was stalling for just the right opening in their conversation to tell him what was on her mind. They fell silent for a few paces. He tried to distract himself by focusing on the green-into-red and gold colors of the foliage surrounding them. Autumn was his favorite season—the crisp, shortened days that signaled death or dormancy in the plant and animal kingdom enlivened his senses. Even so, he was feeling quite nervous with her and he tried to conceal it.

"Where do you find your inspiration, Elinor?"

"I have found the bathroom at school to be quite productive."

John laughed and stopped abruptly when he saw that she wasn't laughing with him. "You are serious."

Her eyes twinkled, and the corners of her mouth curled upward. He bumped against her hip with his own.

"I walk the grounds in the small hours of the morning when I can't sleep," he said after a pause. "I find this to be the best time for writing poetry."

"All of nature inspires me."

"Ah, not just the bathroom." He sighed. "Inspiration is not hard to find when the moon is sailing above the clouds at midnight. Words can't describe the sensation of standing by an open window watching the moon when 'all this mighty heart is lying still,' when the only sound is the stirring of the wind through the elms on the close."

Elinor nodded. "When I feel restless I steal from the troubled house to the quiet world outside by the light of the moon's unquenched lamp. The stars burn so sharply I can almost hear them sing."

"Only poets hear star song," he said. He felt a wave of shivers wrap around his shoulders like a quilt. The sensation soon faded, but it left him feeling more connected to Elinor. "I sometimes wonder why were made to sleep at night. The night shouldn't be wasted, for it is a time when something strange, something in-describable is abroad … something that the powers of man can't attain or even begin to understand, and I won't be satisfied until I have found out what it is."

"What song do you hear from the stars, Ian?"

"Very well." He grinned at her invitation to recite something he'd been working on. He drew in a breath and launched from memory:

> "I stood alone
> And stared into a starlit sky,
> Hearing only the hum
> Of distant worlds, whirling
> Silently through space; and suddenly
> I knew! Adumbral Truth
> Took shape before my eyes, appearing
> Out of nothingness,
> Glimmering through a world of dark,
> Chimeric fancy. Its voice
> Re-echoed down the ages, wave
> Upon wave of swelling sound,
> Until the stars
> In their gigantic unison
> Took up the strain, and all the sky
> Was filled with a deep,
> Pellucid chorus … then it ceased,
> And all the thrill of revelation
> Sank into the obscurity of
> Reason … ."

Elinor pointed her face toward the clouds with eyes closed as if to visualize the nightscape he had painted with his words. She turned back to him and looked into his eyes, nodding and smil-ing slightly. "You see? You are the better poet."

"I disagree, but I won't argue." Heartened, he held out an elbow to her and she took it. They strolled past the clock tower on their way off campus.

"I remember when you climbed up there and tied a tag bearing your name around the hour hand," she said.

"I was practicing mountaineering. Your father locked me in the tower room to think about what I'd done."

Elinor gasped. "He would never."

"Carved my initials there to prove it."

"You're so brazen."

"That from a girl who writes about soldier children being shot."

"Fair enough. I suppose as long as my characters lead exciting lives, I don't have to worry that mine's so drab."

"Drab? I wouldn't say that. You want for very little. On holidays, you're given the run of a lake or a mountain."

"Point taken." She dipped her chin with a hint of deference.

"And I will concede that climbing the tower might not have been one of my more glorious moments. I'm here to tell you I've matured since then." John presented his signature grin showing the tiny lines around the corners of his mouth, proven to warm the coldest of hearts despite his antics.

"Matured? You were once top of your form. I hear you're falling behind in most subjects."

John's smile dropped. "Ah, your mission revealed at last."

Elinor shrugged. "Father expressed his concern to Mother over supper last night. He plans to write your father about it."

"Oh, dear," he said. "May I tell you something in confidence?" John asked in a serious tone.

"Certainly. You know that." She had never betrayed his secrets in the nearly three years they'd known one another.

He bent to pick up a stone from the footpath and threw it effortlessly into the nearby bushes, flushing a bird. "I have for some time been a little dissatisfied with the system at Rugby, whereby everyone works for material reward whether as a prize or a high mark or a move into the next form. So in true Faustian spirit, I have decided to renounce that system and work for what I consider to be my own good, without regard for competing with myself or others."

"Faust?"

"I'm reading Goethe on my own. That's my point."

Elinor stopped walking and studied John, shaking her head. "You have always been two people to me."

"Whatever do you mean?"

"You have such a soaring mind yet you are so undisciplined and rebellious—sometimes to your own detriment."

"Ah, I see." John smiled. "That cuts to the heart of it. To thine own self be true and all that."

"Aren't you simply attempting to rationalize … laziness?"

That's what he loved about Elinor—always so forthright. "Laziness toward doing things that seem foolish can be a great virtue."

"To the daughter of a headmaster that's blasphemy."

John laughed. "Let me try to explain."

"Please."

"It's merely that I find it illogical to thrust a boy at his most impressionable stage into one of the hardest battles of his life. Just when he is trying to form good habits, he is exposed to bad ones."

"Isn't that how character is built? I don't see what that has to do with your studies."

"Yes … but … a young man goes to a school such as Rugby, which in itself may be admirable, but which simply turns a lot of sausages out of a machine proudly called 'public school types.' Here a boy's emotions, desires, and hopes get swallowed up in the great quest, however constructive and abysmal. That's what I mean by bad habits. Youth gets squashed down by the whims and wills of Age in the shape of a fat old man with a mortar board and gown."

"That's how you view my father, is it—a heavy man in costume? When did you become so pessimistic?"

"Your father is quite fit. But don't you see? This is the time when life is, at its best, untainted by the sordidness of age. Why can't a boy have time to enjoy the beauties of nature? If I were to die tomorrow, how much of Beauty would I have seen? Pathetically little." He paused to frame his argument further in his mind before he spoke. "When shall I ever be happier or more appreciative or more able to see a thing in its natural beauty, without having to think of its position with regard to *autres choses*, its significance in life, etcetera? And how do I spend my time? Sitting before a pile of books, trying to concentrate on Demosthenes to the exclusion of all the thrills I might have at beholding something beautiful, something real, something natural. School consists of the worship of man and the things he has made, his books, his letters, his thoughts. Plenty of time, we say, for Beauty afterward. Suppose there is no afterward?"

"These are the 'other things' you think about? No wonder you can't sleep."

"I suspect you think I'm mad or unable to control my emotions."

"No, I don't think that," she said. Rain began to drizzle on them, and Elinor indicated that they should start back for the festival grounds. The discussion, it seemed to John, was closed.

"I want you to know that I am going to Switzerland next term. I will be leaving directly after the winter holidays."

Sudden sadness gripped him. "I shouldn't be surprised. Your lot always sends their daughters to finishing school abroad before university."

"I should like to write you and enclose some poems if you don't mind. See what you make of them ... as long as you're not too harsh. You truly are more gifted than I."

"That would be lovely," he said, feeling as if she'd handed him a consolation prize. If he couldn't have her heart quite yet, he thought, at least he would have what she dared to put on paper.

When they arrived at the festival grounds, Elinor stood on tiptoe to kiss him on the cheek. "I sincerely hope you reconsider this academic experiment of yours," she said. "Structure is good for a boy your age, and I fret over what might happen to you without it. You must train that genius mind of yours. I only want the best for you." She turned and walked away.

There ... she'd said it, he thought as he watched her disappear in the mist. She still saw him as a "boy" though she was a mere ten months older than he.

John wished he could spend more time with her, but he knew it would take more than bravado and wit to win her heart. She was fond of him—he had no doubt about that—but her actions confused him. On some occasions she touched his hand or smiled sweetly at him or spoke in ways that promised something deeper than mere fondness, while other times she closed him off completely. This ebb and flow of affections drove him mad. The previous summer, after she'd refused to play tennis with him, he'd sent her a packet containing a razor blade with a note saying: "Why don't you come and do it properly?" The memory of it still made him wince. He would not retaliate this time.

———

Inevitably, John could not sleep that night. Images of Elinor wafted through his mind, intermixed with legitimate fears about what his future might hold. He was not at all concerned about Elinor's warnings of repercussions should he fail his courses, for there were other things occupying his mind, things that were so much larger than his education. He tried to resume reading *Lost Horizon*, but James Hilton's prophecy regarding an approaching dark storm that promised to wipe out all of civilization was all too close to the truth. He had yet to find his own Shangri-la to wait it out.

The dark storm that brewed wasn't all in his mind. He worried about the safety of his missionary father in China, where the people lived in constant fear of the Japanese soldiers. He worried about what that chap Adolf Hitler was up to in Germany, annexing Austria and parts of Czechoslovakia. Would he also devour England? Would the Japanese and German aggressions merge? *Would I be called to defend England? What difference my studies then, dear Elinor?*

Grateful his roommate was away for the weekend, John left his bed and turned on the small light on the writing table. Often, when these spells came on, he'd compose hopeful love sonnets to Elinor like this one: 'If, when we walked together in the rain, did neither of us see that this was ... Love?' Instead, he wrote:

"This is a monstrous night!
It presses in my ears, my eyes,
As if to crush out
My very soul. I hear no sound
Except the urgent
Ticking of a clock, and some busy whisper
Of the wind. Above, the stars
Have hid their faces from my eyes ... ."

John rested the pencil on his desk. *Get hold of yourself!* He gazed at the photo of his family taken when they lived in Shanghai, and he thought about his brave father. The previous

December, without thought to his own safety, he had escaped the Nanking Safety Zone to help rescue who he could during the Japanese massacre of hundreds of thousands of Chinese soldiers and civilians. He had filmed the atrocities the Japanese army had committed upon the Chinese villages—beheadings, rapes, and babies lying next to corpses. John picked up a May issue of *Life* magazine and flipped to his father's uncredited photos, ten stills captured from his hours of film footage. The images were so horrible, John could barely look at them, yet he realized that if his father could bear to photograph them, the least he could do was gaze on his heroic work.

The first photo showed a heavily bandaged man folded into a fetal position and placed into a wicker basket for transport by neighbors to medical help. Similarly thousands of victims had sought help after being bludgeoned, burned, hacked, or otherwise mutilated by the Japanese, and were still showing signs of life. There was another of a man whose entire head had been burned to a cinder after being tied to a hundred fellow countrymen and set afire. He'd lived only a few hours after the filming. One photo showed a deep indentation in the neck of a woman who had been hacked with a machete yet survived. A man had been struck in the back by an ax, and a boy was beaten in the face with an iron rod. The final two images showed the streets littered with human corpses in such a manner that they looked like debris. The adjoining text explained that the photos had been contributed by an American missionary whose name was concealed. Only close friends and family members knew the photographer was his father and namesake, John Gillespie Magee.

John's father had written a personal letter to him about the orgy of terror that followed the entrance of the Japanese into the city. He'd confessed that the massacre had given testimony to his faith, just as it had unified the war-torn country and had reversed its fortunes. He'd managed to protect 500 people in their missionary houses alone, and not one missioner was killed. On Christmas they'd baptized a dozen adults and children. "In spite of the terrible situation in the city and the uncertainty of life and security, we could rejoice in the old, ever-new story of Christ's birth." The massacre had increased the numbers interested in his mission.

John flipped through the remaining pages of this issue of *Life*. One boldface headline boasted how Vienna had celebrated Hitler's birthday with a military parade marching through the Hofburg Palace gate beneath a prominently-displayed swastika. On the next page some Florida gentlemen, called "crackers and oldsters," were shown sitting in the sun while "waiting for something to happen." Overleaf a pilot took an aerial of the "tower of silence" in India, where bodies were placed in the open so that vultures could come and pick their bones clean. The following double spread illustrated how explosions on the sun's surface launched flames 600,000 miles into space.

The photographs in the magazine made him feel small and his problems insignificant in the scheme of things. People die horrible deaths on earth and life goes on. The wheel turns with each chair carrying its own particular set of experiences. The sun releases explosive gases and knows nothing of what transpires on earth. *All is well,* he thought. *All is well.* A calm came over him. He stared out the window and watched the glow of the moon peeking through the trees. He returned to his poem and continued writing:

... Above, the stars
Have hid their faces from my eyes. The aspen moon
Slips silently behind a cloud
As if afraid to shine; and somewhere in this thick,
Unfathomable gloom, there is

Reality.
Its shape, its form, its depth
I cannot know; incomprehensible,
A feeling, not a thing; but this I know:
A hand stretched out to mine. I heard a Voice
Whispering a secret to my soul ...

8

BRAVE NEW WORLD

SIX MONTHS LATER John Magee stood on the rugged edge of North Devon's Morte Point peninsula and leaned into the gale winds blowing off the bay. Waves surged through the cliff-side shelves and crevices nearly 300 feet below him, flushing birds every time the water crashed against the rock. He noted that the outcropping was called Death Point for good reason—she had conspired with a daughter stone splintered from her bosom to rip the bellies out of passing pirate ships for centuries. On approach from the south, the peninsula looked like a sea creature, raked and sculpted from grayish-purple slate by Neptune's trident. The creature's talons stretched into the bay, and a thousand armor plates stacked vertically on the tor. John tried to imagine the tremendous forces that must have caused the rocks to be heaved upward and stood on end like that.

It was a savage and beautiful place, and he never felt more exhilarated and alive than when he was here. Yet he fought the subtle impulse within himself to jump off the cliff. He was taken aback by the urge, for it couldn't be further from his intention. Possibly nothing more than a passing sentiment influenced by Elinor's poetry, he thought.

The trigger might have been a sonnet she had enclosed in a recent letter from Switzerland, and it came back to him now:

Whisper, o waves, that I may remember
A story I heard long ago,
Sing your faint tunes, you exquisite sea-shells,
Tell me the secrets you know.

Let the arms of the coral and sea-weed enfold me,
Until I am sinking to sleep,
Then may the strong arms of the waves come and take me,
And carry me down to the deep.

John understood from the poem that Elinor was homesick, if not melancholy, and was trying to cheer herself by composing poetry and shrouding her feelings in landscape metaphors. *What agony of beauty*, John thought. He pulled a small notebook and pencil from his pocket and, squatting, began jotting down ideas as quickly as they came to him:

A crazy sweetness fills my head until
the mind is swamped with the fullness of the soul ...
How will this beauty, at the time of death,
come sweeping back, come flooding over me?

"Sketching the scenery?"

Slightly annoyed, John glanced up at a mustachioed young man a couple of years his senior and held up an index finger as a silent request to wait for a moment. He knew he wasn't being cordial, but he needed to finish his thoughts. Returning to his notes, he wrote:

We found the nadir we had shunned in dreams
falling from the cliff among the shrieks of gulls
reaching the crags below before we woke ... .

Without reviewing what he'd written, John returned the notebook to his pocket. "Pardon me," he said. He stood and pushed the fringe of his thick hair out of his eyes. "In a manner, I suppose I am sketching the scenery."

"Bernard Browne." The man extended a hand. "We met last night."

"Yes, of course." John shook the man's hand with embarrassment. He'd been invited to an informal reading group hosted by a professor from Trinity College while he visited his granny in Mortehoe, Devon, over Easter holiday. He suspected the invitation to be another of Headmaster Lyon's schemes to set him on the scholastic straight and narrow, although he welcomed the opportunity to rub shoulders with intellectuals beyond his age. "Sorry for my rudeness. I'm entering a poem in a contest at Rugby, but it's nowhere near completion."

"Needn't apologize. I understand." Bernard wore a tweed jacket, cheese-cutter hat, and Wellington boots. John had dressed for the seashore and felt a pauper by comparison, wearing a rumble-sale rain slicker over a threadbare jumper. He wished he'd thought to have worn the sleeveless sweater he'd purchased in Mortehoe the previous day, but he didn't expect to meet anyone on the trail.

John looked over the edge of the cliff. "Tell me ... what is it about human nature that makes a person, who is otherwise mentally intact, fear that he will ruin himself?"

"Why do you ask?"

"I possess neither a fear of heights nor a death wish, yet I entertain a subtle anxiety that I will throw myself off this cliff against all reason. Why is that?"

Bernard shrugged. "Perhaps it's an early-warning alarm from the nervous system designed to protect the body. We never know what the mind will convince us to do. I feel that way too sometimes."

"Ah. It gets the adrenalin pumping, this feeling of being so close to death." John suddenly lifted his pencil to paper again to catch the next verse:

> How many generations loved this place,
> And, passing, left to us this privilege?
> Soon, soon you too will pass ... .
> All men go out at the End as the flowing of water
> Carries the leaves down ... .

John appreciated that Bernard waited until he closed the notebook before he spoke again. "What's the theme?"

"We've been given a title to work from ... 'Brave New World.'"

"After Aldous Huxley's satire on utopian novels involving psychological manipulation and baby factories?"

John laughed. "Rugby School is hardly ready for anything quite so modern."

"Then it is an allusion to Shakespeare's *The Tempest* in which the heroine, raised in isolation, mistakes drunken sailors for civilized men of refinement and ironically proclaims: 'O brave new world that has such people in't.'"

"We weren't given anything specific, but the sentiment is the same. If we survive the impending global war, we would indeed live in a brave new world, would we not?" John cleared his throat and straightened his shoulders. "I'm striving to portray the aspirations, disillusionment, and subsequent re-encouragement of a central figure I call 'Youth' in a conversation with voices of the dead and a chorus of angels."

"Oh, is that all? Slacker!" Bernard seated himself on the ground, pulled a pipe from his pocket, and began stuffing it with tobacco from a pouch. "I, too, sometimes wonder about this calamitous world in which we live. The idea of war permeates my dreams. Rumor has it that conscription will be reinstated and that men aged twenty to twenty-two will be called up."

"I've heard as early as seventeen." John squatted next to his new acquaintance.

"Not even our government is that heartless."

"How old are you?"

"I'll be twenty soon enough." He lit his pipe, cupping the flame as best he could in the wind. "And you?"

"Seventeen in June." John didn't want to admit his age, so eager was he to be accepted, but he felt truthfulness was required.

"I will have another year of Rugby to endure after I return from America this summer."

"Let's hope you'll have a school to return to. I'm willing to wager England will be involved with war by this fall. Why, just this past month, Germany has occupied Czechoslovakia and clearly plans the same with its take-over of Romania."

"I try to avoid the news as much as I can these days. Reading *Lost Horizon* for a second time. Saw the film not too long ago."

"Oh, I know it. A pilot hi-jacks an aeroplane and delivers his passengers to a mysterious monastery called Shangri-la. Intriguing story. How do you think the movie holds up to the novel?"

"Follows the general plot with a few different characters and twists, but it glosses over the details of Tibetan Buddhism that are in the book. I find that part most interesting because my father is a missionary in China where Buddhism is one of the major religions."

"You could always get that from *National Geographic*, as the novelist did," Bernard added with a smirk. "Would you say the author is pitting the West and East against each other, the British ideal of action against the Oriental pull toward the inner life?"

"I think Hilton wants us to blend the two."

"That isn't the prevailing thinking."

"Well, Father Perrault, the character who founds Shangri-la and becomes its high lama, is a Jesuit when he comes to the valley of the Blue Moon. He discovers the secret to longevity, which gives him many centuries to hone his mental and meditative skills. Through his influence, the Latin *Te Deum Laudamus* and the Sanskrit *Om Mani Padme Hum* are chanted equally in the valley temples."

"You might have a point." Bernard puffed on his pipe.

"Furthermore, the high lama establishes a culture of moderation, which is both a Buddhist and a Socratic ethic."

"Hmm, I hadn't thought of that."

"As I understand it, the story of Shangri-la is based on a Buddhist myth about great cycles of creation and destruction, much like *Genesis* in perpetuity. Shangri-la is at once the Garden of Eden, where all desires are so satiated that the inhabitants are no longer bothered by them, and a sort of Noah's ark, where they secret away the best art and music of western culture so that they can re-emerge when the dark storm of war passes."

"An apt topic for Easter week of the Resurrection," Bernard offered.

"Indeed, plenty of inspiration."

The two fell silent and took in the landscape.

"I say, is that a lighthouse on the next peninsula?" Bernard pointed north.

"The Bull Point Lighthouse."

"Think I'll head over there. Would you care to join me? That is, if you're not tethered to the ground here by your pencil."

"My pencil is mobile. Lead the way." They both stood, and John led Bernard along the knife-edged path that followed the meandering North Devon coastline. "Pity it isn't summer," John said. "We might catch glimpses of migrating whales in the Bristol Channel out there."

"Pity indeed. No matter … this place is made more beautiful by the wintry storm thrusting waves against the rocky shore. Cor, now you have me talking like a poet."

"There are worse things."

"Tell me, would you want to live a long life?"

John pondered the question a moment. "There would have to be a point to it. I'm not convinced I'd want to live in Shangri-la surrounded by so much beauty for so long. How numbing."

"Don't the inhabitants learn to cope with boredom and suppress their desires through meditation?" Bernard asked.

"Sounds like a waste to me. I recall the author saying that once the strong have devoured each other outside of Shangri-la, the Christian ethic may at last be fulfilled, and the meek shall inherit the earth. The meek and the lazy as well, apparently. One of the Tibetan characters in the story remarked that slacking was a virtue rather than a vice as the English regard it. I've experimented with it and have found it productive."

Bernard laughed. "Did not Milton say we must 'scorn delights, and live laborious days,' if we are to survive the Armageddon. Seriously, I feel it is our Christian duty to be pacifists during the war, if possible. I suppose that would make me a slacker too. Tell me, John, do you think a Shangri-la truly exists?"

"I should think we have to develop it within ourselves, perhaps through contemplative prayer and practicing, as you say, the Christian ethic."

"What do you believe in?"

"Simple things ... the earth beneath us. I trust the sun will not abandon the seasons, the stars will always be there on a cloudless night. I believe in truth and true beauty."

"Do you even know what that means, truth and true beauty?"

"Only what the poets describe," John said. "But I'd like to discover them before I die. How about you? What do you believe?"

"I believe in the will of God."

"Is not war the will of God?"

The question took Bernard aback. "I will have to think on that one. Can't imagine sitting in a foxhole and shooting blindly into opposing trenches and wondering whether my bullets pierce enemy bellies."

"Yes, but consider this ... in that moment, in the brutal holocaust of war, the young soldier is forced to contemplate his soul.

Perhaps that is the divine purpose of war. Where, then, is the bravery in *not* fighting?"

"I would ask you where is the bravery in dying? The soldiers keep their pride and fight courageously yet they pay for it with their lives. Some are in shock or disbelief, some are quick to battle, some eager for adventure, some don't want to appear weak. They walk bravely into hell for Country. The generals and rulers make killing their business, but they're really just bored. In an instant all their lofty ideas and visions can be hurled into nothingness."

"Mind if I use that?" The man's disdain carried the perfect pitch for poetry in John's opinion.

"Not a'tall."

"What will you do?" John asked when he stopped writing.

"I'm considering applying for an exemption by getting married."

"I trust you have a willing candidate?"

"Not yet."

"Oh. Well, perhaps I shall follow suit."

Bernard slapped John on the shoulder. "Wait until you're a bit older. War might be over by then. You're lucky you're going to America. Might think about staying there."

John blushed. He wanted his new companion to consider him a peer. "Most of us know when we'll die, and I believe that we must find out the secret before we go to our graves. So, you see, it doesn't matter whether one is twenty or eighty if the truth is left hidden. For after death, it is too late to discover the secret that the living must unveil."

"You should write that one in your notebook."

John smiled in agreement and dutifully complied. "What do you suppose the secret is?" he asked a moment later when they resumed walking.

"If I knew, I'd be a happy man." Bernard sighed. "I suppose that all that is asked of us is trust and hope. Without either, man is an animal."

"Trust and hope through religion? Wouldn't you say that religion is just an anodyne?"

"I don't agree with Marx that religion is the opiate of the masses." Bernard stopped and faced John. "Here is the secret. We must discover faith before we go to our God, for without these we as humans are nothing more than algae."

John considered this a moment. He had been confirmed into the Church of England the previous year yet, truth be told, he was beginning to question religion. His father wrote that his faith had saved him and many others during the Japanese raid on Nanking. Did this mean that his father could now die a happy man having discovered and reveled in his faith? No, there had to be something more, he thought, and the discovery had to be different for everyone.

John gazed at the bay. His eyes settled on the beach formed by a cove in the cliffs between the two points and saw that the tide was receding. He noticed from their vantage a small animal clinging to a narrow strip of sand between water and rock. "Looks like a lamb is trapped down there," he said.

"I believe you're right. Any way we can get down and help it?"

"By one of the sheep trails leading over the hill, but the last bit to the beach is steep. Not too dangerous." John grinned and winked. "Follow me!" He skedaddled over the grassy mound to the cliffs and started squeezing himself downward between the boulders. At one point he noticed that Bernard had lost his footing, and he watched him cling to a natural finger-hold in the rock until he regained stability and could continue.

John landed on sea level with a final jump. From here he could see that the bleating lamb was stuck in the mud, and he ran to scoop up the tiny creature in his arms. "Now, now," he crooned. "Where's your mother, eh?"

Bernard caught up, panting. He reached out to pet the lamb. "Looks fine for the wear. Don't see any injuries."

They heard sudden shouts from the cliffs. A barefoot boy wearing knee-length pants and a brown woolen sweater scampered down the rocks. "Oi! That's our lamb," he shouted.

John headed toward him and handed him the lamb when they met on the beach. "We noticed he was trapped and climbed down for the rescue."

"They're liable to do that," the boy said. He wrapped the lamb's body around his shoulders and headed back up the cliffs. "Ta," he called out, as if an afterthought.

"Well, that's that," Bernard said.

"We should nose around while we're down here."

"I could use a rest before climbing back to the top."

John sat on the sand, stripped down to bare feet, and stuffed a sock in each shoe. He tied together the laces and hung the shoes from his neck.

Bernard didn't need to remove his rubber Wellies. "I'm glad I doubled the socks to take up the slack, or I would never have made it down the cliffs."

"You did all right."

The two began combing the beach, picking up shells, and toeing rocks. They soon drifted apart on their own scavenger hunts. John discovered a small pool of water enclosed by jagged boulders. He sat on one of them and began mesmerizing himself by tossing pebbles into the water and watching the radiating rings they created. Lines of poetry soon churned again in his mind, and he poised pencil and paper to ensnare them as quickly as they came in:

You I would have flow over me like water

As some cool wave upon sun-dried sand—
Here is a soothing rest for the troubled mind
In evening's coolness, fingers of the wind …
For here, in this freshening hour of breeze and night-birds
Here is the source of our constant sanity.
Another wave of words quickly followed:
And from that Fount of Sense Untenable
There springs the Source of Life and Happiness
A cool oasis in the Desert of Life
Where all that lives spreads out from the hands of God
In wider circles through the Lake of Night
In which His hand has dropped the stone of Life.

John's skin turned to goose flesh. What was it about poetry that made one feel intoxicated and invincible as a writer? Under such a spell every line reads like a masterpiece, he thought and wondered if the illusion served a biological purpose in propagating the species or perhaps a role in contacting the Divine.

A more treacherous thought burst into his mind, and this time it spewed self-doubt and loathing. He did not question its litany but merely sought to record it. At this late hour he was forced to use everything that came to him, or the poem would never be completed. He would cobble the verses together later.

You think you are a poet, —preen yourself
On the obscurest reveries of the inward gaze
Lifting a wordy mirror of your affection
To some poor common girl you made a goddess … .
It was not hard to produce these lover's poems
Praising a woman's beauty with a pencil
Confident in the continuance of your living
Believing that you would meet with lips and hands
In some cool-scented paradise together … .

"Elinor!" John exclaimed out loud. He thought he could escape her for the holiday while he kept his mind busy, but regrettably he could not. His feelings for her always weaseled their way into his most sublime thoughts, even when she wasn't the subject. He half considered nipping behind the upended boulders and exorcising the tension welling up inside him, no one the wiser.

As if to mock him, the words continued to stream into his consciousness:

You thought that Love was all there was of pleasure
But now they search the avaricious features
Seeking a sign of the old remembered feeling
But finding nothing left of the love that was there
—Sixpence the price, it seems, for a change of passion
Cupid astride a compact—powder puff—
Smoking a cigarette … .

These are the lures of women, harlot-habits
Who, half alive, invite to a fuller life
And never loving would be loved by them
For now the love of vanity persists
Each striving to outdo the other's attractions
Fantastic clothes (if any) entice and kindle
The smouldering flame of desire in the other sex
They try to stir to new affections hearts
Already purged and drained of all their love
Invoking a world of passion … .

John re-read his last entry and pocketed his writing tools. The poem, it seems, was taking a sinister turn, or perhaps its intent was to appease his unanswered yearning all along. And yet if his love could be realized, would he still search for the answer to life's mysteries in the long after-years of love? Frustrated, John threw a handful of pebbles into the pool, disturbing for a moment a couple of seagulls. He swore they were laughing at him.

Blended in with the surf and bird chatter came the spasmodic growl of an aircraft approaching from the north. His enclosure within the high cliffs limited his view of the sky, but he could discern that the plane's spurting and skipping engine was having trouble. His eyes scanned for Bernard along the shore and saw that he'd heard it too. The two ran toward each other pointing wildly toward the sky.

At last a medium-sized, double-propped plane crested the cliffs with black smoke pouring from the exhaust pipes. It wore the insignia of a German commercial airline called Deutsche Luft Hansa, but none of the passenger windows showed signs of life. It swooped down over the beach at an alarmingly low level, disturbing groups of seagulls in its wake. It flew so low, they could see the pilot's blond hair through the fishbowl nose of the cockpit. The pilot stared back at them like a hawk eyeing its prey and then, as if to boast his vantage point, waved to them. John returned the wave enthusiastically. For an instant, an instant that nearly shocked him down to his bare feet, he saw his own face peering at him. In that same instant the poetry of flight began to bud in John Magee's heart.

The two watched as the aircraft flew south until it was no longer visible. They could still hear the engine long after that. As far as they could tell, it stayed airborne despite its malfunctions.

The episode harkened the familiar dread about his own mortality. He lifted pencil to paper again and scrawled the theme of his sonnet: "We were but a day in Eternity ... still, we believed."

9

LETTERS FROM AMERICA

"**I RETURNED TO** Morte Point on leave after my homecoming to England as an airman," Pilot John Magee said, bringing Anson's attention to the Oklahoma farmhouse kitchen some forty years forward in time. "I packed a notebook and pencil, but my muse had long abandoned me. All I could hear were the gulls crying, 'Elinor, Elinor!' Her face was everywhere."

"Yes, yes, but what was the aircraft you saw from the beach?" Anson asked. He was eager to keep Magee on point, but he wasn't so impatient that he hadn't noticed how different the man appeared to be. The fighter pilot now looked younger than he'd first thought, his hair far less gray and his face far less creased with lines. He chalked up his previous powers of observation to the heat stroke he'd been suffering. *The man is remarkably preserved for his age*, he thought.

"Ah. I later learned it was a Heinkel He III, affectionately called the 'wolf in sheep's clothing.' In disregard of the Versailles Treaty, the Germans created it ostensibly as a transporter but commissioned it as a spy plane prior to the war and then as a bomber during it. That it could fly up to 22,000 feet made it ideal for aerial photography. This one must have been snapping pictures of the docks at the head of Bristol Channel just northeast of Morte Point. Obviously, his engine trouble and covert mission made it necessary to fly so low."

"Did you report it?"

He shook his head. "Should have done, but it didn't occur to me. Too much on my mind, I suppose. I won the poetry contest, by the way."

"What?" For the life of him, Anson couldn't think what Magee was talking about.

"The sonnet I was composing at Morte Point, 'Brave New World.' Won the Rugby poetry prize."

"Congratulations." Anson didn't quite understand why such a schoolboy achievement seemed to be a highlight in the fighter pilot's life.

"It did mean a lot to me, you know," Magee said. "For a time I thought I might be following in the footsteps of a poet admired by most of England. Foolish and vain, I know but … there it is."

"Who was that poet?"

"Rupert Brooke, of course. Surely you've heard of him."

He couldn't recall whether he had heard of him or not, but he was hopeful this leg of Magee's story wouldn't take them too far afield. All he wanted was to return to the airport and get a proper look at the Harvard. He waited patiently for a break in the man's story, for it would be poor form to interrupt him. "Why the interest?"

"Rupert won the same poetry prize at Rugby in 1905. Friend to Churchill, Henry James, and Virginia Woolf, troubled by love the length of his short life, published numerous sonnets and prose, including *Letters From America*. Enlisted in the Royal Naval Division during the Great War and died en route to Gallipoli of blood poisoning from a desperate mosquito. He was only twenty-seven."

"Pity." He hoped he sounded genuine, but the death occurred decades ago.

"Rupert was most famous in his day for his war sonnets. 'If I should die, think only this of me: That there's some corner of

a foreign field that is forever England.' He was buried on the
Aegean Sea island of Skyros, and 'Forever England' was engraved
on his headstone. I wrote a sonnet eulogizing his life. 'A short
time dearly loved; and after—slept.'"

"You did have a preoccupation with death, didn't you?"

"My generation didn't expect to live past our twenties."

"And yet you carried on."

"Oh, yes, and eagerly so. When I was in Canada awaiting
flight training school, I learned that a close mate of mine had
died in a car collision with a tree. None of our friends had any
regrets because we knew that a spirit as irrepressible as his could
not be quenched. Metal and wood are purely relative and cannot extinguish the absolute of the spirit. I knew that somewhere
beyond time and space—or within them—the wooded hills re-
sounded to his laughter and singing. I knew that I would someday be there to join the chorus."

Metal and wood cannot extinguish the absolute of the spirit,
Anson repeated to himself, suddenly caught by the notion.

"But it made me wonder what would be said of me if I were
to suffer an untimely death," Magee continued.

"Excellent point," Anson said, realizing he'd never thought
about his own death before now.

Magee gestured theatrically. "Eulogies might say of me: 'A
voice raised in joyous song has been silenced.' Or: 'A star has
fallen out of the literary heavens, leaving a shining peace under
the night.' How utterly hilarious and almost Rabelaisian in its
absurdity. How about: 'The young flier converted by journalists
into a sort of worshiping Dante, starry-eyed over his Beatrice,
his Holy Grail?' That's why I hoped that if I died, it would be in
circumstances violently heroic so that they would never know."

"Violently heroic? Sounds severe. What did you not want
people to know? Your fear?"

"Fear?" Magee laughed in a way that made Anson regret his question. "I wanted no one to know I was besotted with a certain young English woman and wrote all my poetry for her. Lest you think me a complete idiot, I'll have you know she wasn't my only grand passion. There were others."

Anson's ears perked up. If he wasn't going to hear about flying, he'd at least hear about the sexual exploits of a WWII fighter pilot. The man was obviously a looker and quite charismatic. "Do tell... ." He loved gossip as much as the next man.

"Coming to America changed my perspective on everything!"

A chuckle erupted in Anson's throat. "Yes, yes," he said in a cracked falsetto. "Happened to me too. Women here are so much more ... what's the word? Self-assured?"

Magee grinned. "Willing to take the first step, let's say. Remember, I was only seventeen when I came to this country, and I barely had a clue having been raised in an all-boy's school. My obsession with Elinor began to fade as soon as I set sail on the Queen Mary that August of 1939. There was an all-girl music group on the ship, and I chatted up a different girl every night. Don't know how many times I became engaged after I graduated from Avon."

"Wait a minute, I'm confused. I thought you attended Rugby School in England."

"As I mentioned earlier, my parents took advantage of my inability to return to England at the onset of war and sent me to Avon Old Farms School in Connecticut for my final year. I had no choice but to acquiesce, though not without launching a robust letter campaign against my poor father in China pleading for my emancipation and subsequent return to Britain."

"I thought the U.S. opened travel to Britain after a couple of months."

"Not for me. In a sense I was a man without a country, having been born in Shanghai and raised in England and living in America without a passport. I was here only because my father was keen on my seeing that America was far more democratic, both idealistically and practically, than England or any other country. He also wanted me to see that American technology was far more advanced, especially in applied science and medicine."

"I would have to agree with him, for the most part," Anson said. "Except perhaps for the Harrier Jump Jet."

"Jump ... jet?" Magee looked clueless.

"The aircraft capable of vertical takeoffs and landings?" Anson found it puzzling that a veteran fighter pilot didn't know about this British innovation from the late sixties.

"Oh, yes, of course," Magee said after a moment's hesitation. "I readily acknowledged that America was the appropriate place to finish my education, but I retorted that England preserved everything that held both intellectual interest and spiritual attachment for me, and by spiritual I meant personally as opposed to Godly. The impassioned love for poetry I discovered in England was accompanied by a sort of awakening of interest in life and people and things. This could, I suppose, have been ascribed to adolescence rather than environment, but I knew, deep down where it hurts to know, that I needed to return to that certain stimulus, which I found wanting in America. Though it was a great and noble and up-to-date country, and though it held wealth and prosperity and democracy and everything that is considered fine and virile—in fact, all the qualities historians could declare as being the essentials of a great nation—none of these were what I was looking for in life."

Anson began wondering what this all had to do with aviation, but he kept this to himself.

"It is important for you to understand why I would have done anything to get back to the other side of the Atlantic. To express myself properly in my correspondence to Father, I resorted to Plato who wrote that one's first duty is toward the tendance of the soul. I told him that we should, by reading, thinking, and conversing with intellects, reason for ourselves the most profitable way to live—profitable, that is, for the soul. If I couldn't learn from others or discover these for myself, then I would take the best of human reasonings and embark on them, as one who risks himself on a raft, unless I could be carried more safely on a surer conveyance or some divine reason. Now, I was certainly not endowed with divine reason, so to my mind the only way I could live was to think out my best course and never allow myself to be satisfied but to think endlessly in the hopes of attaining a more logical conclusion. Didn't the Oxford Group Doctrine say that one should start with oneself? Goethe would call this 'divine discontent,' which is the term he gave to his continual seeking for the truth that Socrates so urgently advanced."

Anson empathized with the younger Magee's point of view. He had charted his own life's course through theorems he'd drawn himself, and he was well aware that few would agree with his conclusions. "You threw the great books at your father, didn't you?"

Magee laughed. "A sense of humor is the essential virtue when one's very existence is swirling in a maelstrom of uncertainty. Yes, I quoted from the best works I could find. I had taken to drinking tea and reading the classics in the private library of one of the masters at the school. I'd resigned myself to making the most of Avon, and this resolution produced results my parents, as Christian missionaries, could not have fathomed."

"How so?"

Magee's tone of voice became more energized as he spoke. "I was exposed to a liberal dose of cynical skepticism. I was introduced to Bertrand Russell's *Why I Am Not a Christian,* to Georg Brandes's *Jesus, a Myth,* and to Lucretius's *De Rerum Natura.* I began to see that the Christian faith had undergone a metamorphosis since Christ began it. I became concerned with whether reason and faith could coexist. I saw that there was something defeatist about casting your problems upon the deity as things being too profound for human solution. I did not particularly want to find peace of God, for peace and contentment are death according to Goethe. Then I met Emerson who wrote: 'Within man is the soul of the whole; the wise silence; the universal beauty, to which every part and particle is equally related, the eternal ONE.' And I saw how Socrates went to his death in the calm and absolute belief of a life to come. If Socrates, the wisest of all philosophers, believed in an afterlife, then I would deem myself foolish to believe otherwise. To say the least, I was at odds with my religious upbringing and, more importantly, with my father."

"Sounds like you were confused about your beliefs." Anson could relate to some of the anguish his guest had experienced in rejecting religion. Although the concept of spirituality rarely entered his mind, he never fully discounted the idea of a power working behind the scenes, responding to human pleas for help and manipulating events. He could also relate to the man's rebelliousness against the regimen of a strict education, having himself run away from home and school at the age of fifteen. "Sounds to me like your American education did you a service."

"I was not convinced of that at the time. Except for a generous teacher and an enlightened schoolmate or two, I felt I was a fish out of water wallowing in an intellectual backwater after the rushing stream at Rugby. I thought I was going mad with yearning, the vain and insistent groping to go back to where the wind blew in my face on the cliffs of Morte Point and all was ecstasy. I occupied myself as best I could, attending dances and conversing with friends in smoking sessions on the school rooftop. I learned the printing trade and hand-published several copies of a book of my poems, even submitted one to a New York publisher, which was roundly rejected for being too much like Rupert Brooks. And, no, the irony was not lost on me. I felt that Americans had no poetry, but truthfully the poetry was dying in me. I could write barely more than a few verses, being so far separated from the source."

"When did you enlist in the Canadian Royal Air Force?"

"I equivocated on this point too. I'd told my father that when I returned to England I would not fight because I was a pacifist and could not because I was an American. But when the Battle of Britain began in July of 1940, I became feverish with the idea of doing what I could to help save England. Thrashing about for a solution, I wrote a letter to the Canadian Secretary of War in August and received no reply. Inspired by recruitment adverts, I enlisted in His Majesty's Royal Canadian Air Force the following month. I was eighteen by that time."

"What made you decide on aviation?"

"Oh, the thrill, the adventure, the appeal it might provide to the opposite sex. That, and I saw a film called *Dawn Patrol* starring Errol Flynn and David Niven about the Royal Flying Corps of the Great War. Many of the new recruits had undergone only a few hours of training before they were required to fly what amounted to little more than kites made of fabric and plywood. Pilots of that war had short life expectancies, but they lived by a code, a sense of *noblesse oblige* and camaraderie."

"Sounds romantic," Anson said.

"I was the perfect target audience."

"So you started your training on the Harvard?" Anson hoped his question would steer the story to the aircraft sitting on his runway this very moment.

"No, the Harvard was the intermediate trainer for the Spitfire. I learned to fly in the Fleet Finch, a tandem biplane, ubiquitous in the RCAF that year. Actually, my first so-called flying machine was a Link Trainer—just a toy plane mounted to a control panel. Much harder to fly than a real plane because it went into a tailspin rather easily. I wasn't very good at it."

Magee stubbed out his cigarette in an overflowing ashtray and stretched his back against the chair by raising his arms toward the ceiling. Anson realized the pilot was probably feeling stiff after sitting for an hour. "I'm not being a good host. Can I show you around?"

"Look, I suspect you're keen on seeing the Harvard. I need to refuel and get on my way. Shall we?"

Anson hopped up from his chair, disappointed the fighter pilot would be leaving soon yet happy to be getting back to the matter at hand. "By all means."

The light shining through the windows suddenly dimmed, and a deafening crack of thunder reverberated throughout the house. Anson looked out a window in time to see the cattle bolting away from their water tank near the pump house. Unaware that a storm cell had stealthily built above them as they talked, Anson felt deflated. He knew a deluge would soon follow, which was confirmed in the next instant. "No use going down to the hangar until the rain stops."

"You're probably right. Might as well sit back with another beer."

Anson fetched two from the fridge. "It's usually a good show from the front porch, our major source of entertainment around here."

10

THROUGH ADVERSITY TO THE STARS

VIVIANNE'S RICKETY CHAIRS were not made for lounging, for both pilots tilted their slated backs against the stucco wall of the house and elevated their legs. The torrential rain echoed against the porch's concrete floor, and the scent of wet soil carried on the cooling breezes. Anson slipped into a relaxed, alcohol-induced state while Magee continued pelting away at his story of becoming a fighter pilot in the poetic manner only he could deliver.

"I faced many obstacles learning to fly right from the start. I was grossly underweight and was forced to eat bread and donuts for a couple of weeks to qualify for the RCAF. I was crushed, for I was looking forward to strutting about town and looking at my militarized and be-uniformed reflection in shop windows. Alas, the Canadian Air Force was terribly congested and disorganized. Took several months just to get into initial training."

"Where did you live in the meantime?"

"My unit was first stalled at a manning depot near Ontario for a month and further staged at a base near Trenton for another month. Now, Trenton was the largest military aerodrome in Canada, with hundreds of aeroplanes, mainly Fairey Battles, Lockheed Hudsons, and the like. Of course, the Avro Ansons were there as well." He shot Anson a quick smirk. "The whole place throbbed with activity day and night. We slept in a large hall with some 1,500 men in double-layered berths, and the food was terrible—all of it mashed, no, beaten to a pulp. This was just the *ardua* to be undergone before the *astra* came in sight."

"Ardua, astra, what?" Anson asked.

"*Per ardua ad astra* was the RCAF's motto, 'Through adversity to the stars.'"

"'No pain, no gain,' the Americans say."

"How fitting." Magee nodded approval and continued. "At Trenton I was put on sentry guard duty, graveyard shift. I sat in a sandbagged post behind a Lewis machine gun armed with 500 pounds of incendiary ammunition. From my vantage point, I could have raked the entire aerodrome. Above me the stars, in all their brittle intensity, seemed to watch with me through the long night's vigil. It was so bitterly cold, I felt that a frosty grave was opening its mouth for me. Other times I examined passes at the main gate of the aerodrome under the magnificent and baronial tutelage of the aurora borealis."

"I would have gone mad, being so close to the aircraft yet prohibited from flying them," Anson commiserated.

"Yes, and add to that the apprehension of going into air combat when it was all said and done. I had become one of a group of men who were all, to the very last one of us, resigned to death and even anxious for it—or if not for death, at least for the chance to show our mettle. We were all desperately hoping to get overseas for the spring offensive, but talk of the war was *verboten* among us. We spoke only of the past and the present. The future for us did not exist. We compared notes on shows, books, women, and all the lovely, trivial things of life. It was no good trying to talk rationally to any of us. We were deliberately living in a sort of grand, illusory, yet terribly precious fool's paradise. The interminable wait was hard on us all. I felt generally ennui with the military existence. I grew tired of all the conventional virtues—nobility, patriotism, manliness, and courage. Still the old lie—*dulce et decorum est*—ran through my mind, reminding me of the high ideals with which soldiers were supposed to be infused."

"Dulce ... what?" Anson continued to feel daunted by the breadth of the man's education, which clearly out-classed his own.

"A Latin saying quoted often during the Great War, made famous by Wilfred Owen's poem of the same title: 'It is sweet and honorable to die for the Fatherland,' or so goes the poem. Owen was vehemently against war, and his verse was saturated with horrific imagery and condemnation."

"You sound as if you were conflicted about war. I thought you said you were a pacifist."

"I found it strange that the old lie had got hold of me too, that they had made a soldier out of me. Really, I couldn't get over it. Too fearfully jolly for words. I was hardly what Cicero would have called *naturaliter ferrovialis*. In my heart of hearts, however, I was glad to be suffering for the country I loved so well. Hardly 'sweet,' but at least 'honorable.' Whereas, in reality, serving one's country was not a glamorous crusade, nor any golden fleece, but inevitable duty. Still it seemed rather fatuous to be discontent with life when I had invited myself to this misery as a means to England."

"Sounds like you were just bored."

"Out of my skull!" Magee dropped his front chair legs, stood, and strolled to the edge of the porch. He extended a cupped palm into the rain. "Will this last all day?" he asked.

"Nah. Should blow through in less than an hour."

Magee wiped his wet hand on his trouser leg and continued. "Finally, finally, I began initial training the end of December, and elementary flight training followed in February at St. Catherines, Ontario. My excitement was quickly deflated when we learned that nearly eighty percent of the preceding class was gone with the wind, washed out in a period of three days. You had to be a born and flawless pilot to succeed. I didn't know St. Kitts had the reputation for being the toughest station in the whole of Canada. I'd chosen it because it was only nine miles from Niagara, and I'd imagined myself walking across the border on leave and meeting women in the bars there. I soloed in six hours, and that cheered me up a bit."

"You were gifted, were you?" Anson said. He had been equally gifted in his flight training, but he kept that to himself.

"That, and I used money my uncle sent me for private lessons while we waited to begin proper instruction. Now that I'd been bitten by the flying bug, I wanted to go balls to the wall."

Anson laughed at the pilot's use of old steam-engine slang. "Full throttle, eh?"

"I mistakenly thought the harder I pushed my flight training, the sooner I would be sent to England."

"One must follow a scope and sequence, but I suspect you tried to circumvent the system."

"You know what Sir Isaac Newton had to say about gravity, don't you?"

"What goes up must come down?"

Magee grinned facetiously. "After my first solo flight, I begged my instructor to show me how to put the aircraft into a spin so that I would know how to recover from one."

Anson was put through the paces in flight school himself. "Full opposite rudder, stick back, then forward and full throttle.

"Many pilots were lost during the previous war because they didn't know how to recover."

"Until a few recovered accidentally," Anson said.

"The instructor soon taught me how to do it and was pleased with how quickly I picked it up, but he warned me to never purposely put my aircraft into a spin without an instructor aboard."

Anson saw where this story was headed. "You didn't listen to him, did you?"

Magee shook his head. "Frankly, it was a ghastly and terrifying sensation ... and I couldn't wait to do it again! That night I realized that they held a sort of morbid attraction for me—possibly because it was so frightening when the engine was cut off and all I could hear was the wind screaming in the struts."

"You do have a death wish!"

"Well, I discovered a love for excitement. The very next day I was told to practice making steep turns at 3,000 feet for my second solo. On the way up a voice kept telling me that I could easily do a spin if I got out of sight of the aerodrome, and nobody would be the wiser. When I resisted, that vicious little voice taunted me for being afraid. I fought it during the long climb skyward and finally, in a fit of impatience, I decided to do one. So instead of leveling off at 3,000 feet as instructed, I continued climbing for another twenty minutes until I was above 6,500 feet. When I thought it safe to try, I let her go."

Anson suspected that Magee's escapade wasn't going to end well.

"As soon as I went into the spin, I knew immediately that something was wrong, for I was upside down and could see the ground whirling beneath me. My safety belt snapped, and my head hit the cockpit cowling. Meanwhile the plane hurtled like a corkscrew toward the earth in an inverted spin, which is exactly what the flight manual warned against in heavy, black type."

"Did you recover?"

The pilot shook his head. "I applied full opposite rudder, which made the plane spin all the faster. By this time my eyes were bulging out of my head, and my ears were blocking up."

"Red out!"

Magee plopped into his chair and pulled an imaginary stick into his belly with both hands. "Frantically, I heaved on the joystick, but I didn't have enough leverage to pull on it hard enough to make a difference because of the busted safety belt. I fell unconscious for a moment. When I came to again, I made one last effort. It worked. I was pressed back into my seat as the nose came up. The altimeter needle trembled between 700 and 800 feet, which meant that I had dropped nearly 5,000 feet in about twenty seconds! As the ship leveled out, I relapsed into a state of semi-fogginess. When I regained full use of my senses, I headed straight for home, circling the field twice before plucking up the guts to land."

"Saved by angels." Anson was being sarcastic, but he didn't rule out the possibility of certain forces intervening in such scenarios.

Magee shrugged. "I was beginning to think that I was being preserved for something big by the Fates." Magee paused, studied Anson, and then continued. "My instructor met the plane and gave me a good going over. He'd watched the whole thing from the tower. Before I could fall out of the plane, he climbed into the rear seat and took me straight up again. He immediately put me into two consecutive spins."

"You had to get back on the horse, so to speak." He recalled Vivianne using the adage after he'd made her airsick.

"When I finally staggered out of the plane, the instructor put an arm around my shoulder and said, 'Laddie, you've got what it takes.' I never admitted that I had purposely spun out."

Anson suddenly had the distinct and sickening feeling that he had experienced the same harrowing episode in an aircraft himself, though he couldn't quite remember when. Maybe the details were different here or there, but the gist of the story was overwhelmingly familiar. He shuddered and chalked up the sensation to Magee's robust storytelling.

"I soon learned the loop the loop, the slow roll, the half roll and loop out, a stalled turn, a chandelle, and an Immelmann turn."

"Had to master most of those maneuvers myself for spraying. Learning them is one thing, putting them into practice is quite another."

"We found ways, believe me. Two of us had one magnificent dog-fight during our first cross-country solos in our respective Fleet Finches—strictly against regulation. I got a going over from the CO when we arrived at our destination. On the return trip, I looped over the other student pilot and sat on his tail from about fifty yards behind, pouring imaginary tracers into him like the devil. Out of the blue, a Harvard dived down between us in a yellow blur. My mate went on home, but I stayed to grapple with the Harvard despite my aircraft's disadvantage of speed and maneuverability." Magee was on his feet again, suddenly animated and using the porch as his stage. "He outflew me most of the time, but whenever he turned around me, I turned inside his path and drilled his plane. Finally, when he came down on my tail, I rolled onto my back and looped out. I held her in the dive and pulled out at 500 feet going 180 miles per hour. When my vision returned, he was circling a field to land. I landed and taxied to him."

"Wanted to have a good look at you, did he?"

Magee grinned. "It was mutual. He turned out to be an officer from the service flying school where I'd hoped to go eventually, and he complimented me on keeping him in my sights as long as I did. On takeoff he skimmed the farmhouse at the windward corner of the field, yanking back on the stick before he reached the fence and zooming upwards at a terrific speed. I followed suit, but if he missed the house by five feet, I missed it by two. We dived on the unfortunate inmates again and again. When I'd had enough, I dipped my wings to him and headed back to my aerodrome. The ceiling was dropping rapidly by then."

Anson shook his head in amazement. To crisscross the sky at will, dog-fighting pretend enemies—what better life? "Did you get away with it?"

"Er, no. Upon landing I was told to report to the chief flying officer immediately. Apparently the poor benighted farmer had lodged a complaint against me. The Harvard was going too fast for him to get his number, but he got mine. What could I say in my own defense? It was useless to plead engine trouble as they obviously knew I had been deliberately low-flying, the greatest crime you can commit in that outfit. I was quite open about it and described the whole incident without divulging the name of the Harvard pilot. The CO said he was probably going to wash me out, but he decided to check my ground school exam scores first."

"Were you nervous?"

"Shivering in my boots. I sat in silence with the chief flying instructor, who was just civil enough to offer me a cigarette. The CO returned ten minutes later, slapped me on the back, and said, 'Sorry, laddie, we haven't a hope of washing you out. You came in first in ground school!' Thought I'd flunked all the technical portions, but I escaped by the skin of my teeth. I'll never forget what the CO said to me before shooing me out the door. 'And for God's sake, remember that the crime is not in the doing but in the getting caught!'"

Anson laughed along with Magee. "The bit over the farm sounds like crop-dusting. Do you ever get over feeling light-headed when you're flying aerobatics?"

Magee nodded. "It is a good thing to keep talking to yourself and keep an eye on the instruments, but they're marvelous for the thrill they give. Flying upside down feels strange—when you're hanging in your safety belt, it's hard to keep your hands and feet on the controls. Learning instrument flying was also disorienting. We'd sit in the back cockpit with our heads covered so that all we could see were the read-outs telling us exactly what was happening."

"I didn't get into instrument flying. Crop-dusting isn't performed at night or during a storm."

"No, I wouldn't suppose so. Well, I finally finished elementary flying school that March. Our group got through in record time. Rather than graduating to fighter or bomber training, the RCAF decided to guinea-pig us with an additional fifty hours of formation flying and advanced aerobatics to give us the advantage when we joined more seasoned squadrons."

"Obviously they didn't want to repeat the mistake of using inexperienced pilots in Europe."

"Quite right. The British Commonwealth had recruited thousands of potential pilots by then, all to be trained in Canada's expansive airspace, which President Roosevelt called the Aerodrome of Democracy. Not only that, England was now focused on purging Germany in occupied territories. They could well afford to take their time."

Magee took a break from his story to light another cigarette. Anson accepted one from him and sat back to watch the rain puddle in front of his Oklahoma home. He wished it would clear up so they could get down to the runway. "Sodding weather."

"The bane of every pilot's existence. We were grounded whenever the weather was deemed 'non-serviceable.' It snowed nonstop in Canada over winter. Not gentle, friendly Christmas-card snow, but driving icy matter that burns the skin and clutches at the very soul with freezing fingers. By spring the fields turned to mud. You can't take off or land in a sticky field—the planes turn over in the muck or throw clods that break the propellers. So we'd start flying before dawn when the ground was still hard from frost, but then we'd have to turn back if the engines froze."

"How was it to learn formation flying?" Anson asked.

"Difficult but a great deal of fun. The slightest jerk on the stick is enough to throw you into the next plane only a few feet away."

"I can't imagine the conflicting sensations such a feat must invoke," Anson said.

"I enjoyed the challenge. One day we flew out of the clouds on some army maneuvers near Niagra-on-the-Lake, scattering the troops and causing tremendous havoc. By the second pass, they had their AA guns out, and if we had been enemy planes, they could have shot us to pieces. We decided to drop little paper bags of flour on them the next time."

"Did you?"

"Didn't get a chance. I was finally transferred to the flying school at Uplands, Ottawa, in late April to train on the Harvard."

Yes! Anson thought. *At last ... the Harvard.*

Magee grinned. "Starting on the Harvard meant I was being trained to fly the Spitfire in England. If I had started on the Avro Anson trainer, I probably would have become a bomber pilot. Whereas the idea of long bombing trips over Germany by night had its appeal, I personally preferred to revel in the speed and independence of a fighter."

"Ho, I would too!"

"You have no idea how fast, noisy, and generally terrifying the Harvard was to me at the time. They carried between eighty and ninety instruments plus bomb-racks and mounted cameras where machine guns would normally be. I didn't take long to solo in it, and soon I was off on my own adventures across the Canadian blue."

"Bet it was beautiful." Anson glanced skyward, trying to imagine the freedom and thrill of flying such a machine, going wherever his fancy took him.

"Yes, it was indeed. I got hold of a Harvard one afternoon and started north to have a look at the mountains in the Gatineau district. Within minutes, I noticed someone on my tail. I went into my Immelmann and rolled down out of the loop to put myself on his tail, but he had disappeared. I looked over my shoulder and found him still behind and above me. I throttled back until I flew alongside him. The plane turned out to be a stubby, Yankee-made Grumman Wildcat belonging to a fighter squadron in Ottawa. I had never seen one before. Soon we were at it again and must have maneuvered for an hour at least, he of course getting the better of me most of the time."

"Just when you think you've mastered one class of aircraft, another shows up to challenge you."

"Such is life. Things didn't go so well the following week. I got lost, and having misjudged my petrol supply, I was forced to land near a tiny town where there was no telephone. Took me three hours to hitchhike back to Ottawa. I was severely reprimanded for three separate crimes: getting lost, not watching my fuel gauge, and taking too long to return to the base. The next day I was put on charge for failing to show up for night flying—didn't hear my alarm. I thought I was doomed until it came to light that I was top dog in my class for a commission, with recommendations from the CO at St. Kitts. That would have been good news except that a charge on my record, which is nearly as bad as a court martial, would potentially disqualify me for the commission, something I desperately wanted. I loathed the idea of returning to England as a sergeant pilot and forced to salute my school mates."

"Don't blame you." Anson sipped his beer. "With all that breakneck flying, it's a wonder you didn't crash."

Magee frowned. "I was coming to that. A few days later I misjudged a night landing and cartwheeled a Harvard on the runway."

"That's incredible! Were you hurt?"

"Not even a scratch, though the $35,000 aircraft was demolished. I might have felt better if I'd hurt myself because I thought I'd shattered my chances for getting the commission."

"How did it happen?"

"I came in one night after flying routine circuits over the airfield for an hour and a half and feeling about ready for bed. Everything seemed fine until I approached the end of the flarepath and noticed I was going about ten miles per hour below landing speed for a Harvard. I put my nose down a bit to gain the necessary speed, but what I didn't know was that I was already practically on the ground. If I'd remembered to hit the throttle, I would have been okay, but in the thrill of the moment I forgot. Instead, my immediate reaction was to pull the nose up. The aircraft lifted upward again and stalled about twenty feet off the ground. A wing dropped and the tip hit the runway. There was a terrific jar, and I was thrown out of my seat as the plane cartwheeled around the wing-tip and dug her nose in. I landed on my face feeling very silly and angry, while the plane continued to grovel on the ground—it was nearly laughable. Then all was still, and I sat and swore silently for about a minute."

"Bad luck," Anson said, shaking his head.

"The flight officer for that night, who happened to be my instructor, came dashing out to the accident scene with the fire truck and ambulance. It was too dark to identify the foolish pilot who'd wrecked the plane, so I called out to him. He laughed and said, 'I might have known—you've certainly been having yourself a field day, haven't you?' I crawled into the back of the truck and cried like a baby, feeling rather mortified over what started out to be such a promising career had to go and spoil itself like that."

"What a shame." He reminded himself that Magee was still just a teenager at the time.

"After typing up all the reports, it was a very tired, angry, and thoroughly disgusted Magee who crawled into bed just as the bugle was blowing in the morning. I slept until noon and spent the rest of the day going from brass hat to brass hat and getting all the callings down you can imagine. I barely escaped being put on charge again for my negligence in misjudging the flare-path."

"I'm assuming you weren't washed out."

"No, incredibly, but I received every manner of punishment—restricted privileges, pack drill, and plane washing every day for a week. I resumed night flying before long. I should have been frightened except that I'd had so much bad luck, the law of averages demanded that I get a good break once in a while ... or so I thought."

Are all pilots superstitious? Anson wondered.

"It came time to test on the Harvard. I did well on my written exams, but I stank all the way through the instrument test. The only consolation was that I wasn't having my wings test that day, when suddenly a corporal announced that Magee was wanted for testing. My heart fell into my boots because all pilots know that we can fly well one day and not the next."

"How did it go?"

"I was panic stricken when I climbed into a Harvard for the last time. It was so hazy you couldn't see the ground from a thousand feet, and there was no horizon. To add to my despair, I'd drawn the flight lieutenant rumored to be the toughest marker on the station. But it so happened that I missed the highest standing in my course by one point. It all goes to show that you gain on the swings what you lose on the roundabouts."

"You got your wings, then?"

"Not just my wings! On the last day of leave with my family in Washington, D.C., a telegram arrived stating that I had been gazetted as an officer two weeks prior."

"Ho, brilliant! You must have been astonished."

"To put it mildly."

"And you were shipped to England?"

"I was at last returned to that country to pursue my heart's desire."

Anson nodded and sat back in his chair, feeling satisfied for the man. He'd been so engrossed in the story that he only just noticed the sun peeking through the breaking clouds. He figured the rest of the day was going to be sticky and hot.

Magee stood. "What do you say we get down to your hangar?"

11

THE HARVARD

"AH, THE NECTAR of the gods," Magee said as he pumped aviation fuel into the tank opening on the Harvard's wing. When the plane had its fill, he removed the hose nozzle and handed it down to Anson on the ground.

Anson returned the hose to its hook on the fuel tanker and parked it next to the hanger. He thought he'd reconcile the bill with his Boss later, if he could figure out how such transactions were conducted.

"You're as giddy as a boy on Christmas morning," Magee said when Anson jogged back to the Harvard.

Anson hated being a cliché more than he hated hearing them expressed by others. In this case the assessment was true. He'd noticed a definite upbeat in his own stride.

"Come on up, then," Magee said. "Have a look."

"Aye, Captain." Anson climbed upon the wing and helped Magee pull back the canopy. He poked his head inside the cockpit, taking note of all the dials, read-outs, and switches. The two rudder pedals straddled a hole that revealed the plane's innards and, alarmingly, the concrete runway below.

"It's all here, isn't it?" He turned to Magee. "Except ... where's the floor?"

Magee grinned. "Military trainers don't need such luxuries. Just don't drop any FOD."

"FOD?"

"Foreign objects and debris that can jam the controls and kill you. Go on, get in."

Surprised, Anson turned and faced him. "You're joking."

"Be my guest. Oh, but wait, you must wear this." He brought forth a relic RAF parachute seemingly from nowhere.

"Whatever for?"

"We're taking her up."

Before he could react, Magee was helping him strap into the chute. Anson stuffed his keys, wallet, and lighter into his baseball cap bearing the Union Jack patch and shoved it inside his shirt. He then pulled on the leather cap and goggles Magee produced from some compartment in the back.

"You're set. Now step into the pulpit." Anson started to climb into the rear seat. "No," Magee said. "You're taking the front seat." Delighted, he climbed into the front seat and strapped in.

Magee donned his leather pilot's cap and goggles, leather flight jacket, silk scarf, and chute. Anson wished he could wrap a scarf around his own head to filter out bugs and dust he knew he'd consume while flying.

"All right, Avroe?"

"Affirmative, Captain," Anson responded with a thumbs-up.

"I want you to do the preflight and takeoff."

"Me?"

"This is what you do." Magee began ticking off the preflight procedure, but Anson was steps ahead of him, checking the trims at ten and two o'clock and stroking the oil pump. When the pressure raised, he started pumping the primer with the other hand. He flipped the battery switch and engaged the starter, then counted four blades before turning on the mags.

Magee nodded approval and climbed into the rear. The engine burst into action and a fireball shot down the right side of the plane.

"You've over-primed!" Magee shouted. "Just keep cranking until that fire is out."

Anson complied. He felt a little dazed—not by Magee's instructions but by the fact that it all seemed so familiar. He felt he'd done this before, and many times. "Oil pressure is up," he shouted.

"Good. Keep her running steady and don't move the throttle. Push the prop to 'fine pitch,' and let her idle at about a 1,000 rpm until the temperatures come up."

"Check," Anson yelled once the temperatures responded, holding his thumb high in the air again.

Magee tapped him on the head, signaling it was time to taxi to the runway.

Anson opened the throttle. The plane reacted with popping and belching sounds.

"The prop is still in coarse pitch," Magee yelled. "Pull the throttle back, push the prop up, and try again."

Anson followed instructions and the engine steadied itself. He pushed the joystick forward to unlock it and pulled it backward into steerable mode. He let it idle up to around 1,700 rpm then cycled the mags and the prop.

"Now run the flaps, and don't forget to put them back," Magee instructed. "Do you want the canopy open or closed?"

"Open," he yelled. He pushed the manifold pressure to thirty-six inches and revved up the engine to 2,250 rpm. The growl told him the propeller tips had gone supersonic. He pulled on the throttle, and the Harvard rolled forward. View of the runway was blocked by the plane's large nose and high wheels, so he had to feel his way onto the pavement. He stomped on the rudders with all the force he could muster, struggling to keep the ship centered on the runway as it picked up speed. Once he felt the wings lift, he pulled back on the yoke. Airborne, he retracted the wheels and started to power back on the manifold pressure, the prop, and the rpm. The plane felt heavy and glided like a brick.

"Well done, Avroe!" Magee shouted. "I'll take it from here."

Anson reluctantly let go of the controls to lean back and enjoy the ride. The plane leveled off at 1,500 feet and cruised at about 180 miles per hour. The landscape transitioned from flat farmland to craggy prairie to flat-topped mesas cut deep with arroyos. The vegetation transformed from cornstalks to earth-hugging junipers. Soon they were flying above the mountains, whisking just above the tips of cedars, pines, and aspens flickering silver in the light. *What agony of beauty*, Anson thought, quoting Magee's prize sonnet.

Two peaks not more than ten feet apart appeared directly in front of the plane, but Magee didn't bank or climb to miss them. "Watch out!" Anson yelled, throwing his hands above his head to signal imminent danger. With no response from Magee, the plane continued on its fatal course.

At the perfect moment, the Harvard rolled to its side and flew between the rocks as smoothly as threading a needle. Before Anson could protest, a massive lake spread before him, so clear and blue he could see fish swimming in its depths. The Harvard swooped over the lake and skimmed its surface. It pulled up sharply, turned, and rolled lazily above the water several times before heading toward a mountain on the opposite side of the lake. The plane spiraled up the peak in circles and banked at the summit. It shot straight down a towering precipice, leveling off once more just over the water. Magee then performed several more aerobatic stunts, which were clearly designed to scare the piss out of his passenger. Anson was both alarmed and amused.

The Harvard climbed another peak and headed toward flatland. Much to Anson's dissatisfaction, Magee didn't circumvent the storm cell that loomed ahead of their ship. Amidst streaks of lightning, the thundercloud poured buckets of rain on them and pelted his face with hail, causing him to regret his decision to leave the canopy open. The plane suddenly bounced on choppy air currents, and Anson thought he would lose his lunch. Before he realized it, the Harvard was back on the ground at Texhoma, taxiing for the hangar. It was the flight of his life, though he wondered where there was a mountain-top lake so close to the Oklahoma Panhandle.

12

IF YOU HAVE NOT CHAOS

ANSON LEANED OVER the glass front of the jukebox at the TO Lounge, deposited a quarter, and selected the song he knew would best describe his flight of fancy in the Harvard. Steppenwolf exploded from the speakers, blasting out "Magic Carpet Ride" in growling vocals and a lively hard-rock rhythm. Although it was mid-afternoon, the light emitting from neon flamingos and beer advertisements fused into a pinkish glow in the windowless room. The lounge was empty of patrons—even the bartender was absent from his post. Anson assumed the man who usually presided over this shift was taking a delivery in the back.

He stepped behind the bar to pour a couple of celebratory brews. Having worked here a few hours on the odd Sunday for cash, he knew where the essentials were stored and felt comfortable, if not entitled, to help himself until the bartender returned to collect the tab. "That was one hell of a ride." He handed Magee a mug.

"Cheers." Magee accepted the draft and took a sip. "Least I could do for your hospitality."

"Didn't think there'd be enough fuel to fly all the way to the Rockies or wherever it was we went. Felt like we were gone for hours."

Magee folded his hands and stared at him. "I don't know what you're talking about. We were hardly in the air for more than ten minutes … fifteen at most. Didn't want to waste the fuel or risk getting lost."

Anson shook his head. "Don't be daft. You squeezed the Harvard through two rock spires and flew some crazy stunts over a lake."

"You're mistaken," Magee said. "My flight instructor treated me to just such a flight in Canada, but you and I merely circled the airfield here a few times."

Anson knew the flight he experienced was real, but now he was beginning to distrust his own sense of reality in the context of Magee's behavior and the blackouts and memory shifts he'd been having. Not only that, Magee was undergoing a metamorphosis right before his eyes. In the perpetual twilight of the lounge, he looked even younger than he had earlier that day. When Magee had first climbed out of the Harvard, he looked to be about sixty years old, which would coincide with the age of a WWII fighter pilot in 1980. Then, in the diffused, appliance-white light of his farmhouse kitchen, he noticed the man's hair was not as gray and his wrinkles not as pronounced as he previously thought. Now he looked a full twenty, thirty years younger, closer to Anson's own age. *Flying must be this man's fountain of youth*, he thought.

"This is turning out to be the rummest day I've ever had," Anson said aloud. He reached for another mug to pour his own beer, tilting the glass at an angle to control the foam as he filled it under the tap. This simple act reminded him of Vivianne.

———

Steppenwolf's "sound machine" abruptly transported Anson to a different drinking establishment, where amber light from stained-glass windows and incandescent bulbs danced off the varnished bar. He knew instantly that he was standing on the service side of his beloved pub in England. To his shock Vivianne stood next to him, expertly pouring an ale the traditional way by pumping it up from the cool cellar with one of a dozen long, wooden handles mounted on the top of the bar. He remembered teaching her to tip the glass at just the right angle for just the right amount of foam on the top. He remembered teaching her the technique in that very pub, yet the timing didn't make sense to him. If all their things were still in the house back in Oklahoma, when did they go to England? The confusion made him feel dizzy again as the visual aspect of this memory faded.

Although Anson no longer saw anything, he heard his own voice shouting angrily into the void as if he was being broadcasted on a badly-tuned radio channel. He heard Vivianne's disembodied voice sounding defensive and sad. He perceived that they were having an argument, but he couldn't pick out the words nor discern what the row was about or where it was taking place.

At once, he teased out one thread of the argument. Vivianne was flatly refusing to marry him, something he emphatically argued for her to accept, though he could not think why.

"What is love to you, Anson?" she asked him quietly.

"It is us."

"Then why don't you say it?"

"I don't need to," Anson responded.

———

"Avroe! Can you hear me?"

Anson alerted at the sound of Magee shouting at him in the Texhoma lounge. "Wha ... what?" His right hand was still holding the mug under the tap, and beer was running over the rim of the glass and pooling on the bar, his shoes, and the floor. "Bloody hell!" He fetched a wet rag from the sink and mopped up the spillage. "Sorry," he said. "I've been having these lapses all day. Don't know what's wrong with me."

"You'd better come around and sit. Maybe knock off the beer for a while."

"Oh, this is watered-down stuff. Can't get drunk on it. Believe me, I've tried." Even so, Anson staggered around the bar and leaned a cheek on a stool.

"Tell me about these ... lapses."

Anson removed his cap and padded the sweat on his forehead with a fresh bar towel. "It's hard to explain. I have dizzy spells, black-outs. Do you know what lucid dreaming is?"

Magee looked at him thoughtfully. "I assume it's the sense of self-awareness and control during a dream."

"Yes, only I'm having lucid memories, as if I'm reliving the original event."

"That must be interesting. Like time travel, I suppose."

Anson felt foolish. "I'm also having *déjà vu* experiences."

"Déjà ... vu? Already lived?"

"As if I've done this all before. Take the Harvard—it was so familiar to me."

"That's easy to explain. I reckon certain models of modern aircraft descended from that design."

"But I *knew* how to fly it. I could actually see myself flying it. The only explanation I can come up with is sun stroke and heat exhaustion. Except ... ."

"Except what?"

"You're going to think this strange," Anson said.

"Try me."

"I don't know whether these visions are premonitions about the future or memories from the past. If the visions are memories, then either they're out of sequence or ... ."

"Or what?"

Anson rubbed his face with his hands. *There's no other way to say it,* he thought. He blew air through his lips. "I'm not supposed to be here. It's the present moment of time that's out of sequence."

"What do you mean?" Magee asked. Anson was grateful that the pilot didn't react to the absurdity of what he was saying.

"Well, for instance, I sold the Delta, yet it's sitting in front of the bar. More importantly, I think that Vivianne and I packed all her belongings into her Volkswagen Bus and parked it on the side of her parents' house in Albuquerque. I don't remember the details, but it seems we then boarded a jet and flew to England."

———

"She's mine," Anson announced to the customs agent inside a terminal at Heathrow Airport. He had already gone through the queue designated for U.K. citizens and was now assisting Vivianne as the agent for foreign visitors addressed her, whether she wanted his support or not.

"Is it true?" asked the middle-aged man with a Scottish brogue, his tone and demeanor accusatory. "Are you his?"

"No, we're not married or even engaged," Vivianne stammered. "I have to see what he's about in his own country. Marriage is a big decision. I've already been married once. Still trying to sell a house my ex and I own jointly … ."

The agent raised his hand. Anson figured he was thinking that if Vivianne still owned property in the U.S., then she was a woman of means with ties to her home country. The agent stamped the passport with a six-month visa.

———

Magee eyed Anson. "You just experienced another one, didn't you?"

He nodded and shrugged.

"So, you're saying you left Vivianne's possessions at her parents' house, yet they were furnishing your house today. Do you know where she is now?"

"Haven't got the foggiest. I do have a vague impression I'd gone somewhere else for a flying job. Some hot country where the people don't speak a language I can understand. The Sudan, perhaps Kenya. I'm not really sure."

"So what you're saying is your memory is intermittent and incomplete. You remember some events so vividly you feel you're actually there. On the other hand, you're experiencing things that never happened to you but are a sort of, I don't know, bleed-through from someone else's life or, rather, my life. And then you have a bit of amnesia about certain other events more closely associated with the present time. Now here you are in Oklahoma."

"You must think me a nutter."

Magee looked at him abstractly, saying nothing.

"There's more. I have a terrible notion that something awful has happened, maybe even fatal. Something that has to do with Vivianne, but I just can't put my finger on it." *Where the bloody hell is Vivianne?* He suddenly felt more desperate than ever to solve this piece of the puzzle.

Magee nodded without changing expression. "You are having a rough time of it, aren't you?"

Anson exhaled audibly. The pilot was not being helpful, but that wasn't his fault. This was all happening inside his own mind. "I hope I'm not going mad."

"Well, if you are, it won't matter. However, it isn't entirely unlikely that you're having some kind of spiritual breakthrough. Why don't you just let it play out? Fly by the seat of your pants."

A spiritual breakthrough, eh? That was almost laughable to Anson. "Rather an existential crisis, I should think."

Magee nodded. "Goethe said: 'If you have not Chaos in your mind, you cannot give birth to a dancing star.' Perhaps all this memory hopping means something. Goethe also said that 'Nothing is worth more than this day.'"

Anson snorted. "Sounds like something Boss always says: 'Make hay while the sun shines.'" He had to admit, the pilot made some sense out of what would seem nonsensical to most people. He rested his elbows on the bar and held his face in his hands. *Bloody hell.*

"Why don't I tell you about what happened when I finally returned to England? Give your mind a rest."

Anson looked at the pilot. "Go ahead."

Magee's face lit up in triumph. "I learned to fly the Spitfire."

"Yes, but did you see Elinor again?"

"Now you're beginning to understand." He gripped Anson's shoulder. "I finally arrived in England at the end of July in 1941 as a newly commissioned pilot officer."

Anson relaxed against the bar, slipstreaming into Magee's life story as if he'd lived it himself.

13

Take Me to That Far Hill

SOMEWHERE IN THE hedge-rimmed fields below his wings, John Magee hoped he would find Elinor's family. He flew over what he determined to be Kemerton village at the base of Bredon Hill in Worcestershire, England, and continued north up the slope toward an Iron Age rampart at the summit. Near the ancient encampment stood an eighteenth-century tower, which he'd heard the locals called "Parson's Folly" after the man who built the monument to himself. He fretted his own mission today would be Magee's Folly. Feeling lightheaded with excitement, he banked and headed toward the village having confirmed his navigation.

The prospect of finally seeing Elinor made his heart thunder in his chest. He had dreamed of this day as he performed aerobatic stunts over the forested mountains of Canada and crystallized it in his mind's eye when he won his wings and at last received his orders to return to Great Britain. Remnants of a poem Elinor had sent him a few months earlier came back to him now:

> You stood on the hill, where the trees were sombre,
> Tall and dark overhead,
> The cool air flowed down after the thunder,
> The sky was calmed of dread.
> Still and kind hung the clouds, caressed
> By the weary touch of the air;
> Silent I waited, until quite suddenly
> You turned, and saw me there.

John let out a breath of longing. *Is Elinor's poem about me? Did she yearn to see me on the hill?* He was determined to find the answer. As it happened the poem dovetailed with one he'd written, though he'd never sent it to her:

> Always you come, a precious ghost, to haunt
> The days, the nights; —in sudden, waking dreams
> I find your face; you smile, you beckon; —flaunt
> Your lovely self before my eyes; it seems.
>
> To love is pain! But did you really care?
> Have you forgotten? —Is it all in vain
> To breathe out sonnets to the midnight air,
> —To long to touch your hands, your lips again?
>
> I know that some day I shall find you
> Alone, and in the evening shade of trees;
> Twilight, and hills, and quietness behind you
> —A scent I shall remember in the breeze …

Only just this morning he'd crawled out of his bunk at RAF Llandow in Wales to be tested on his flying aptitude in a Miles Master I, an intermediate flight trainer for the Spitfire. John questioned the reasoning behind such an exercise after his rigorous training and testing in Canada despite it being two months since he'd last flown. He dutifully performed a few "circuits and bumps" for Flight Officer Beck, who was nearly his own age though in possession of far more spots on his face than John. Upon landing he ignored the flight officer's signal to disembark and beckoned the man to come to him. When the FO reluctantly climbed upon the wing, John pushed his goggles to the top of his leather cap, leaned through the cockpit window, and lowered his voice in a conspiratorial tone. "There is a woman."

Beck's face turned bright red. "You got me up here for that?" He started to jump to the ground.

"Haven't seen her in nearly three years."

"My sorrow. Look, I don't have time for high tea with you. Get out of the aeroplane for the next pilot, eh?"

John refused to comply. "For reasons beyond my control, I was stranded in North America, and it took me nearly two years to the day to return." The officer yawned but John continued. "I spent nine months training in the Canadian RAF and the last month in a convoy across the pond with little to eat but Bully Beef on sea biscuits. Then there was the twenty-four-hour luxury tour from Scotland to Bournemouth on a train that was so crowded, I was forced to sleep on the luggage rack, which, I might add, broke under my weight."

"That is unlucky, isn't it?" FO Beck said, with the perfect mix of courtesy and sarcasm. "Why were you, as you say, stranded?"

Encouraged that Beck had taken the bait, he explained his long ordeal, ending with what he hoped would be the crowning argument. "Eagerly, I enlisted in the RCAF just so that I could return to fight for this beautiful country of yours and take a shot at Jerry."

Beck executed a mock salute. "On behalf of the king and all British subjects, I thank you wholeheartedly."

"Not a'tall," John said. "But … ."

"Out with it, man. What do you want?"

"Now, this woman … Elinor … she was in Switzerland and had been for several months when I left for the States, so we didn't even have a proper good-bye. If I don't see her I will lose my mind, and then I will certainly be non-serviceable for flying."

Beck started to launch another barb, then stopped himself and frowned. "You may have a point. I would be useless if I were you. Where is she?"

"In the Cotswold hills of South Worcestershire."

"That's, what, a day's journey by train, all told? Not a chance, mate. I needed to have you qualified on the Spit yesterday. Can't have you tramping all over the country after a woman."

"It's near an RAF Station in Defford, no more than thirty minutes away by air." John flashed his most charming smile and silently counted to ten while he dug his fingernails into the palm of his hand.

Beck flipped through the pages on his clipboard. "Says here you've an excellent flying record, but it's tainted with mishaps and bad decisions." He looked around the busy airfield, visibly resigning himself to the inevitable. "You can take this boat. I want it back by mess tonight. I don't want to see a scratch on it, and I don't want to hear you've run out of juice. If you commit either of those sins, I'll report you." He added with a wry smile, "You understand, Maggie?"

"Yes, sir. And it's Ma-gee."

"Not anymore, Maggie." Beck hopped off the wing and signaled to the ground crew to let the aircraft take off.

John roared over the fingerling village of Kemerton again, lower this time and more slowly to announce his arrival with spasmodic belches of the engine. He could see people waving from the gardens and orchards below. He thought he spotted Elinor but he couldn't be certain. When he reached the southern end of the village, a journey of interminable seconds, he banked and landed in a nearby field. Yes, he had told the FO he'd land at RAF Defford, but that was a few miles away, and he didn't wish to delay his reunion another minute.

John climbed out of the cockpit and looked at his watch. Just gone eleven. He grabbed his knapsack and secured the canopy on the plane as best he could. Starting for the village, he approached the first stranger he met, a round, red-faced, middle-aged woman. A green scarf was wrapped tightly around her head and knotted under her chin. "I say, is that Kemerton?" he asked.

"Yes, i'tis. You've landed in our field." The woman didn't appear to be angry.

"My apologies. I hope I didn't cause any damage."

"Laying fallow this year. No harm done. Would it be all right if the grandchildren have a look?"

"Go right ahead. Mind they don't climb on it. The flight officer will have my neck if he sees any new scratches. I'm looking for the Baldwin home."

"They're on holiday," she said. "They do have guests staying there, a middle-aged couple with three beautiful daughters and a son."

"Sounds like the Lyon family I'm here to visit. Mr. Lyon is the headmaster of Rugby School. Secretary there told me they were in Kemerton on a fruit-picking holiday."

"Oh?" The look on her face indicated her delight in being able to share a bit of news in the village. "That road next to the field is Kinsham Lane. Follow it to the right and then turn left. It's the second black-and-white at the bend in the road."

He stood in the middle of the lane minutes later, staring at a cottage with black timber frames and white wattle-and-daub panels. The Tudor-style dwelling, with its steep thatched roof, snuggled behind an overgrown garden that made it look all the more medieval and daunting. A rare moment of emotional inertia set in. If he were to knock on the door, he thought, the entire family might answer. He wasn't prepared to see all of them quite yet. Or worse, they were all in the fields, and he'd be forced to wait in the garden for hours and use up his leave. These worries merely masked his real fear. *What will I say to her?*

A woman peeked from behind a garden wall across the road. He waved at her and she disappeared. Knowing he couldn't stand there all day looking daft, he thrust himself toward the wrought-iron gate. The squeaky hinges betrayed his presence.

The face that had haunted his dreams, both asleep and awake, appeared suddenly in the doorway of the cottage. Her expression turned from shock to joy as her eyes teared up. She ran down the garden path to him, threw both arms around his neck, and squeezed. "I'm never letting you go," she said. Tingles rushed up his spine and his stomach fluttered. A warmth caressed his cheeks, now scarlet for sure. *This, this is worth the two-year exile and the return across the Atlantic.*

"How are you here?" she shouted. "I can't believe you're here!"

"I arrived in England just last week."

"You should have rung," she scolded.

"Didn't know when I could come, and I wanted to surprise you."

"Let me have a look at you!" She stepped back, holding his hands in hers. "You're much taller now … and much thinner. Are they feeding you?"

"Barely," he said.

"We'll fix that right up. Come through." She grabbed his arm and pulled him into the house. "How long do we have you?"

"Just a few hours. I need to leave around three."

"That was you overhead, wasn't it?"

"Why, yes." He smiled.

"I might have known. Must have thrilled the neighbors." She led him through the cottage into a large country kitchen. "Everyone's out picking berries. I nipped home to make sandwiches."

"What's on right now?" He set his knapsack on the table.

"Well, we're too late for gooseberries, but we've most of the other berries as well as currants, plums, and apples. The conservatory is filled to the rafters with fruit." She put a fresh loaf of bread on the cutting board, sawed off a generous slice, and slathered it with butter and preserves. "Try the strawberry. Not set up quite yet but still edible."

John accepted the slice and gobbled it greedily. She continued cutting more slices of bread. When she turned back toward him, she lifted a corner of a tea cloth to one side of his mouth and dabbed gently. "You left a bit here," she said.

"Sorry. When you're forced to eat alongside hundreds of other men in a limited amount of time, you don't stop for manners. There's a reason it's called 'mess.'" He stared at her, not believing he was standing within kissable distance of his beloved and not doing anything about it.

"Well, you be as messy as you wish here and take your leisure." She returned abruptly to her kitchen chores as if aware of his thoughts. "How about a bit of ham to go with the next slice?"

"Yes, please. Eggs and baked beans too? And chips?"

"Full English i'tis." Elinor began bustling around the kitchen, lighting the stove burners and filling a tea kettle with water. She reheated potato slices on a pat of melting butter in a cast-iron skillet. She cracked two eggs and slid them next to the potatoes and added a coagulated lump of baked beans. A rectangle of ham floated in the middle like a culinary life raft. "Try the Worcesterberries next?"

John nodded and leaned on the counter to appreciate how she'd matured into a beautiful woman. She wore a pair of wheat-colored dungarees cinched at the waist by a thin belt, with a pink button-down blouse beneath the bib. He'd been among men in uniforms and work clothes for so long, he'd forgotten how a girl was supposed to dress. "Blimey, woman, what are you wearing?"

She posed like a model for a glamour magazine. "All the rage in London these days. Fabric is rationed along with meat, dairy, and sugar. We have to glean what we can from the countryside, and of course we must dress for the job. 'Make do with less so they have enough,' as the posters say. Father and Mother started a Victory Garden at Rugby. We're here to stock preserves for the school."

He frowned feeling guilty. "I'm taking your food."

"Nonsense. You're putting yourself in harm's way every day for us. You need your nourishment." She added a couple of tomato slices to sauté with the mix.

He started to tell her that it was all for her when the kitchen door burst open and in walked Headmaster Hugh Lyon, his wife Nan, daughters Barbara and Jill, and son Christopher, each carrying a basket brimming with fruit. "John Gillespie Magee, Jr.!" the headmaster bellowed. "We thought that might be you flying over the village."

"Yes, sir."

John stood to shake his hand, but his former mentor and surrogate father gave him a bear hug instead. "We've never stood on decorum," the older man said.

"Yes, sir. How did you know that was me?"

"Who else would try to take out the chimneys?"

The women embraced John and pecked both his cheeks with kisses. Elinor delivered a full plate of food to his place at the table. Barbara ferried a tea-service tray, and Mrs. Lyon followed with the stack of sandwiches Elinor had assembled. Everyone joined John on the benches and chairs, making him feel so at home and such an abundance of familial love that he thought he would burst.

Before he tucked into his meal, he shifted his bag from the table surface to his lap. "I come bearing gifts." He began pulling items out of the bag to the oohs and ahs of those who would love them the most: chocolate for the younger ones, American coffee for the older ones, pipe tobacco for the headmaster. Placing eyes on Elinor, he said: "Finally, *le pièce de résistance* ... ." He handed a small, flat, pink box labeled DuPont to Mrs. Lyon, sensing it would be inappropriate to give such an intimate gift to Elinor directly. "I trust you will parcel these out judiciously." She carefully opened the box cover and gasped. Inside the tissue chrysalis lay four pairs of stockings.

"Oh, my goodness!" Barbara reached for them first and brushed the material with her fingertips. "Doesn't feel like silk."

"Made from a new material called nylon, fifty-one gauge," John said. "Or so I'm told."

"Oh, we can't get silk anymore because of the conflict with Japan. I read that nylon will be redistributed to the military for parachutes and the like if America enters the war."

"Don't you want to save these for your best girl?" Mrs. Lyon asked.

"You are my best girls." He winked at Elinor.

"How thoughtful." Elinor smiled in her usual reserved fashion. "Thank you."

"Yes, indeed, John," Headmaster Lyon added. "Now eat, man, before it gets cold."

John complied, certain he was not to eat in peace.

"How are your parents?" Mr. Lyon asked.

"Very well, thank you, sir. Father is settling in his new parish in D.C. They'd moved to the States where it's safer."

"Frightful business, him getting caught up in the Japanese genocide raid on China. We're glad he's safe."

"Yes, sir. He lives to serve, and he's quite resilient."

"How was your trip here?" Mrs. Lyon asked.

"Long and roundabout, ma'am. Our ship sailed via convoy, with a two-week layover in Iceland. We managed to make do with hiking and picnicking on local fare and kicking our heels around some hot springs."

"Life of Riley, eh?" Mr. Lyon said.

"I was so restless and frustrated by the snail's pace of our progress, I could have swum here myself."

"Where are you stationed?"

"The number 53 Operational Training Unit at Llandow, newly formed to train fighter pilots on the Supermarine Spitfire."

"Have you flown the Spitfire yet?" Christopher's pupils grew with excitement.

"I should be airborne in that aircraft starting tomorrow."

"Spit-spotting has become a popular sport ever since the air invasion," Elinor said.

"I'm up to forty-nine," Christopher said. "I'll show you my chart later."

"Is that so? I daresay the Hawker Hurricane was as much the champion of that battle as the Spit, if not more so, though fewer Spitfire pilots died," John said. He rolled his eyes skyward as if joining the ranks of admirers. "But the fast and agile Spitfire has superseded it as the primary fighter."

"Its maneuverability has to do with the wasp-like, elliptical wing design, does it not?" the headmaster asked.

John nodded with enthusiasm. "Yes, sir! It made sense to create the thinnest possible wing to reduce drag and provide a higher top speed whilst being thicker near the fuselage to carry heavy guns and retracting wheels. The RAF frequently issues improved models."

More questions began pouring in from all sectors of the Lyon family, and John answered each one between bites: "Yes, I think I will be happy at Llandow for the short time I'm there, though our living conditions aren't particularly luxurious. We sleep in one hut, walk half a mile to the bath hut and even farther to the mess then a mile or so more to the airfield. At least I'm getting some exercise for a change. How was the flight training? Only three of my whole bunch managed to get on fighters—the rest are on bombers." His heart sank when he realized the family would stay as close as cats rubbing his legs for kippers, no doubt part of a cosmic scheme to keep him separated from Elinor. It was just as well, for he knew he would simply make a fool of himself reciting love sonnets and devising desperate attempts to whisk her away on his lap in the Miles Master. He enjoyed the attention nevertheless.

John spent the next few hours with the entire family in the fields picking fruit. It felt wonderful to be doing something ordinary and productive. All too soon he was saying good-bye, most wistfully to Elinor. He powered up the aircraft and set course for Wales.

Recharged, John jumped out of bed the next morning and arrived at the airfield before dawn. After some hurried instruction with a flight instructor on the Spitfire, he performed his first solo in that plane. He spent as much time in the air as he was allowed, to him a glorious one hour and fifteen minutes, then returned to Kemerton. Flight Officer Beck was not on duty this time, and he thought that everyone who saw him take the Miles Master would assume he had permission. He did make sure the plane had enough fuel so as not to invite the wrath of Beck.

"I could rhapsodize for days about the Spitfire," he told Elinor later that afternoon. He was so excited about the morning's training exercises he could barely contain himself. "It's at once a thrilling and terrifying aircraft. It took off so quickly that before I recovered from the shock, I was sitting pretty at 5,000 feet."

"You do seem on top of the world," Elinor said. She was perched on a ladder in her beige dungarees, which John found endearing but not all that flattering. The upper third of her body was in the tree, and her face was hidden by leaves and branches. She tugged at plums and dropped them to the ground for John to gather and place in the basket.

"Exactly the way it feels. When you're up there and surrounded by sky and cloud, you don't even hear the roar and throb of engines nor the buffeting of slip-streamed air … you are swept into an endless space."

Elinor snickered.

"A laugh at my expense?"

"The poet in you has found expression as a pilot."

"Nothing that I can put down on paper."

"I don't mean it that way. Flying is your art now, the plane is your brush, and the sky is your canvas. You've thrown yourself into it with full knowledge of the hazards that go with it, as if you are joyful in that knowledge."

"It is exciting," John said. "I like flying. I want to make a career of it after the war is over."

"We've endured so much with the bombings in this country, I can't tell you how wonderfully reassuring it is to find you so full of life and ready to enjoy everything that happens to you. You've always been that way. But I do hope you'll carry on with your academics and your writing after the war."

Elinor's caring remarks encouraged John to start confessing his feelings toward her, but she never gave him a chance to say anything revealing. She kept climbing down the ladder and repositioning it for better access, only to re-ascend and pluck fruit—as well as topics—as quickly as she went. *Doesn't matter*, he thought. Her sisters were within sight working nearby trees.

John continued chattering about what he knew best. "I shouldn't tell you this, but we always fly with the guns loaded so that if Jerry comes our way unexpectedly, he is sure to get his head bashed in. If we get a nice day with mild weather and cloud cover, a bunch of us are going to run across to the French coast in the hope of finding something small and badly armored to initiate ourselves upon."

"Oh." She poked her head through the leaves and grimaced. "I suppose that's the nature of war. Does the thought of actual combat frighten you?"

"Sometimes I get queasy—my mouth goes dry and my hands clammy, and my knees feel as if they are about to give way. That soon passes. Most of the time I feel a certain inexpressible thrill and ecstasy at the prospect. There is no telling what I will make of myself in this great game I've gone into."

"The thought of you getting killed in action frightens me."

That Elinor worried about him at all warmed his heart, but he wanted to reassure her. "Picked up the *Times* the other day and scanned the active service column. I happened to notice a friend of mine listed as missing, believed killed in flying operations against the enemy. He was an air-gunner."

"I am so sorry to hear that," she responded.

"Don't be. It's the most hopeless news a family could ever receive but the greatest thing a man can have written about himself."

"Please, be careful. It isn't news I'd like to hear."

"Sweet Elinor, I will have had hundreds of flight hours by the time I see action. I am well trained."

"It wouldn't do to be too brazen."

"No?" John begged to differ, for how else would he work up the courage to fight if he didn't feel invincible?

Elinor descended her ladder and kneeled on the ground next to a picnic basket she'd brought. John rested on his side close to her. She unscrewed the lid of a preservative jar full of water and drank half of it in several gulps. She offered the other half to John and he downed the rest. She scooted backwards against the tree trunk and pulled the handkerchief from her neck to dab perspiration from her face.

They were in an orchard about halfway up Bredon Hill. It was an enormous, gently sloping hill, broad enough to nestle a dozen villages around its perimeter. "Lucky we have a clear day. The view is exquisite." John felt his pent-up energy relax. "Do you remember the holiday we had in the Lake District?"

"I remember everything we've done together," she said. "Lake Windermere ... 1935, I believe."

"That's right. Do you recall finding the row boat hidden in a rocky alcove and taking her out?"

"I remember finding a weathered dereliction that almost sank with us in it," she said.

"That's because the stop had been removed."

"At age fourteen or fifteen, you'd think we would have known better."

"We found the stop under the bench along with the oars."

"Then the mists came in, and we got lost on the lake."

"Which led to the discovery of the ruins on an island. I remember imagining that it was a castle." He moved to share the tree trunk with her. "When you feel frightened for me, think of me in light of that trip. Danger is everywhere, but each predicament leads to some kind of ingenuity to get us out of it, which almost always leads to a discovery of something unique, something new meant just for us."

Elinor stretched her legs in front of her and wiggled her feet as she pondered his point. "Those were such innocent times. Who could have foreseen ... this? Are you still writing poetry?"

John frowned and sighed. "Barely a word. Most of my creativity goes into flying, as you perceived so descriptively. The rest goes into letter writing, and even that has become more prosaic than prose-like. How about you? Are you able to concentrate or find inspiration for your writing?"

She seemed genuinely delighted he asked. "It's taken a rather grim turn, I'm afraid, but I don't question it."

"How so?"

"I wrote a short story entitled, 'Eyes of the Dead.' It's being published in a November edition of the *New English Weekly*. I didn't want to tell you because of the title."

John sat up and faced her. "How marvelous! I'm so happy for you. You should know by now that I don't feel squeamish or superstitious about death. I've given it so much thought the past few years, it practically has its own persona in my imagination. What is the story about?"

"It's an odd tale about twin brothers who died in consecutive years and were buried separately, one in the family garden and the other in the churchyard. Because it was the only decision they had ever disputed, they took their argument into eternity, each instructing that an enormous eyeball be carved on their tombstones. "The tombstone of the first twin to die read, 'Look at me, Brother.' The second twin ordered that, when the time came, the words 'I see you, Brother' be carved on his tombstone."

"Ingenious! So, what happens?"

"I don't want to spoil the ending for you. I'd rather you read the published version."

"Dearheart, all we have is now. I can't wait that long."

"Very well. The two gravestones, each bearing an eyeball, faced each other across the valley line of sight. On the anniversary of their deaths, which happened to fall on the same day of the year, an energy stream formed between the two and bored like a gigantic gimlet clean through whatever got in the way— houses, trees, boulders, anything solid. The deadly stream barely missed living beings by less than a foot. After several years, the family turned the stones in opposite directions so the eyes would no longer look upon one another."

John belly-laughed. "You astonish me, Elinor! Whatever made you think of that story?"

"Oh, I don't know. Just came to me."

John shook his head. "What an interesting mind you have."

She smiled, obviously pleased. In this light her eyes were as translucent as aquamarine gemstones. He'd forgotten how pretty she was—delicate like a primrose, the first breath of spring.

She caught him staring at her. "What are you thinking about?"

"Primroses," John said, plucking grass a blade at a time.

"Ah," she said, and began reciting:

"Now the bright morning star, day's harbinger,
Comes dancing from the east, and leads with her
The flow'ry May, who from her green lap throws
The yellow cowslip and the pale primrose."

John scrunched his brow, failing to remember who wrote the verse. His brain was now filled with such things as the physics that keep him airborne and not getting himself killed.

"Milton, silly. I'm going to feel guilty reading Milton at Oxford this autumn when most of my closest friends are putting their lives on the line."

"Never you mind. Someone has to hold down the intellectual castle. For whatever else am I fighting? Isn't that what Churchill says?"

"You're a dear, Ian."

He was close enough to her now that he leaned to brush her cheek with his lips.

She accepted the gesture then pulled away ever so slightly. "What time is it?"

He looked at his watch. "Half past three. I suppose I should be going." He felt rebuffed but not defeated. This prim-and-proper rose would take time to cultivate.

"Sovra is Gaelic for primrose," she said.

"Is it?"

"Wouldn't that be a lovely name for a heroine?"

"Yes, I suppose it would. You know what Shakespeare says about primroses, don't you?"

"Refresh my memory."

"I think it goes something like this:

"Do not, as some ungracious pastors do,
Show me the steep and thorny way to heaven,
Whilst like a puffed and reckless libertine
Himself the primrose path of dalliance treads,
And wrecks not his own rede."

"Are you saying I should practice what I preach?" she asked.

"If the halo fits." He grinned.

"Humph!" She packed up her wicker basket and handed it to John to carry for her. "Race you!" she shouted and started running down the hill.

"Oi! That's not fair." He chased after her and didn't stop until he reached the Miles Master. She finally caught up to him and collapsed into his arms, winded. The basket he was carrying landed in the grass, and a hardbound notebook fell to the ground, its pages flirting with the breeze.

"What is this?" John asked. He flipped through the journal. "Hmm. Dare I ask if it contains some of your blessed poetry?"

"Never you mind." Elinor tried to grab the book from his hands, but he held it high above his head and beyond her reach. He opened to a random insert and began reading aloud, his mouth running ahead of his mind:

"A milky phosphorescence hangs
Above the apple-trees,
Pale as the gleam that haunts the foam
At night, in shallow seas.
Shepherds made love in Arcady
Beneath such boughs as these."

John winked at Elinor and grinned. "Shepherds made love in Arcady?"

She feigned annoyance. "Represents contentment and innocence."

Before she could further protest, he continued:

"Till day revive their dreaming flame,
Let human longings sleep;
The apple-blossom gleams, the trees
Standing in enchantment deep;
And all above, a million stars
Eternal vigil keep."

"Why, that's lovely." His face warmed with deepening fondness for her.

"Thank you." She reached for the notebook.

He knew he shouldn't, but he continued reading to himself.

"From the first night until the last
Our creamy branches sway,
And lovers' whispered words remain
Endless as night and day,
These are the old, eternal things,
That will not pass away."

These are the old, eternal things that will not pass away, he repeated. *I didn't know she had such longings.* He looked up to see her blushing, and her eyes pleading with him to relinquish her book. In the back of his mind he wondered if she was writing from imagination—or experience.

Not finished with tormenting her, he feigned returning the journal and then jerked it away from her hands. Flipping through the book, he came to a two-page spread displaying a pair of poems. One was titled "Reverie" and the other "Reverie Fulfilled." *This looks delicious*, he thought. Realizing he had only seconds, he scanned the lines without reading aloud. In "Reverie" he caught:

"Take me to those far hills, where toil and time,
danger and loneliness, can touch us not.
Oh set us free those shadowy paths to climb,
and let me hear his voice among the streams."
He turned to "Reverie Fulfilled":
"High in that windy haven—
That hilltop—we are there,
though all unseen, unrealized,
our bodies made of air
…There we rest forever
After the hard climb.
…There our hearts have harmony
In each other still,
For an eternal second
On that windy hill."

The intensity of her words stunned John as his poet's heart detected a veiled romantic encounter enshrouded in the imagery of death. He gazed into Elinor's eyes for a long moment, searching for answers there, for some kind of clue that she'd either found love or was merely being inventive. She, being Elinor, retreated within herself, resolutely silent if not seething beneath the surface.

"You've much improved, my lovely Sovra," he said. He closed the book and handed it to her, trying against hope not to let his face reveal his emotions.

"Now I simply must fly home." He brushed her left cheek with his lips and climbed on the wing of the Miles Master.

She pulled him by his sleeve, her face full of contradictory emotions. Betrayal, fear, worry—he wasn't sure what he was detecting. "You mustn't take my poetry seriously. Sometimes I aim for the stars, but I hit a tree somehow."

"As do I," he said. He climbed into the cockpit. "I'll return, rain or shine." As soon as he closed the canopy, his head began spinning with confusion. All he could think about as his plane took to the air was the childhood game of ripping petals from daisies. *She loves me, she loves me not.*

He flew over Kemerton in a Spitfire the following day, fully recovered, having swallowed deeply the tonic of rocketing through high clouds and rays of sunshine. He didn't touch the ground this time. Instead, he performed aerobatics over Kemerton like a lovesick hummingbird diving and looping above a desired mate.

14

There Flies a Nobler Heart

THE NEXT STORM to set in over Wales turned the airfield at Llandow into a mud lake, rendering it non-serviceable for several days and affording John an overnight leave to Kemerton. Though the distance to south Worcestershire was relatively short, sporadic scheduling, delays, and multiple transfers made the trip by train intolerably long for someone used to unhindered speed. He finally arrived in the late afternoon at the Ashchurch train station near Kemerton and caught a lift on a hay wagon to the cottage.

Just in time for tea, everyone including Elinor was happy to see him, though she stayed at arm's length. He suspected that she was still licking her wounds from his taking liberties with her poetry journal, yet she respected him enough as a would-be war hero not to throw him out of the house. In turn, he didn't push her into being more sociable than she wanted to be. Otherwise the mood in the household was cheerful, and he kept up his end of the lively conversation.

Mrs. Lyon arranged for him to occupy a bedroom to himself for the evening. On Headmaster Lyon's suggestion, he perused the library shelves for something to read while everyone else preoccupied themselves with their evening chores and ablutions. He pulled several leather-bound books from their slots and seated himself in an overstuffed chair next to a lamp to refine his selection.

He started to set his first discard on the lamp table when he spotted Elinor's poetry journal on its surface. He could tell by the cover that this was the very same journal he'd teasingly thumbed through when the two of them raced down Bredon Hill the previous week. He was curious, but he didn't wish to pry. More specifically he didn't want to be caught prying. Even so, he hadn't forgotten what he'd read either. The lines that had hinted at a secret love affair worked on him the way the tongue worries over a chipped tooth. He left the book in its place and went upstairs to ready for bed.

He returned to the library an hour later and noticed the book hadn't moved from where he'd first found it. He went outside to puff a pipe in the chilling breezes as his mind mulled over the options. It was possible, he thought, that Elinor had mislaid or forgotten the journal. On the other hand, he told himself, she may have left it there for him to find as an innocent and gentle means of letting him know she was attracted to someone else. The lights upstairs dimmed one by one, and the household settled. His heart overruled his head, and he decided that he had to know the contents of the journal, never mind that he felt like a voyeur or thief. He slipped back into the den, turned off the lamplight, and tucked the journal under his sweater. He only hoped Elinor did not feel inspired to go looking for it in the night.

The journal was not a workbook for Elinor's ongoing compositions per se, for verses do not always flow from the mind like water from a tap without strike-outs, margin scribbles, or thorough rewrites. Rather, this notebook was a record of precisely 127 poems to date, each carefully numbered and copied from other sources. The poems generally followed a chronological order, with occasional inserts from previous years as they were likely found on scraps tucked away in a schoolbook or some such manner. He noticed she'd added comments at the bottom of nearly every entry, and he envied her organizational skills.

The first page contained a heading: "Herein are inscribed poems composed in sudden moments of youth and foolishness, by Elinor Bruce Lyon." She'd started two lists: those that were for public view and those that weren't. The indirect request for privacy didn't intimidate him in the least, and he began flipping through the pages.

The first entry was written in 1934 when she would have been twelve or thirteen. He recognized a few of these early poems shared with him by her sister. He was struck by how enamored she had been with adventures of yore and knights in shining armor. Part of him already knew this about her, for why else had he fashioned himself into an aeronautic Lancelot? She had invented a fantasy world through which she could escape from tedium and difficulty. She also strained to find inspiration in nature—hills and sunrises were recurring themes with her—though he felt this avenue was not always fruitful. She had been young and merely needed more time to develop.

That's when his eyes rested upon a poem about a festival composed in October, 1938. She'd written the poem through the eyes of some poor sap who thought he was in love with the heroine, someone for whom she might have felt pity:

"All night my lady looked at me, her smile was sad and
    sweet;
Though parted now forever yet our eyes are free to meet,
And all the night I followed her, and loved her from afar,
As a lonely heartsick wanderer will press towards a star."

The verse took him aback. He had attended just such a festival with Elinor in October of that year, and it was the last time they were alone together before they each launched on their respective journeys. He recalled with fondness their ride on the Ferris wheel, their exchange of philosophies, and their walk together in the gentle rain. He also recalled, in flashes of memory that still stung a bit, how she'd admonished him for neglecting his academic responsibilities. He wondered if she'd written the poem about him, for he was certain she knew about his infatuation for her. After all, she was the daughter of a headmaster of an all-male boarding school—the heartsick wanderer could have been any of a number of her long-suffering admirers. Then again, the character might merely have been a figment of her vivid imagination.

He turned next to a series of poems composed beginning in February, 1939, when she was in finishing school in Switzerland. She'd mailed one or two of these poems to him. For the most part, her Switzerland phase portrayed a general unhappiness and homesickness that seemed to shroud her entire time abroad. The first stanza of one poem read:

> "The far hills of my childhood,
> Beyond the horizon lie;
> Their green grey-shadowed shoulders bare
> Will haunt me till I die."

Ten stanzas later, she'd written:

> "… And even now, when sometimes
> I stand still in the rain,
> I shut my eyes, and hear the wind—
> And I'm a child again."

As with most of her poems, she'd penciled in a footnote of criticism: "I could go on like that forever, but it's silly to mourn for happiness." The final line of another poem read: "I long to be in England, but England's far away." John's heart went out to her, for he more than anyone could empathize with this sentiment.

A dozen or more poems continued in this vein for another year. Then something shifted in the spring of 1940 when John was just graduating from prep school in America. Elinor's poetry took a cynical turn:

> "No rest have they who love,
> All is for them confused,

A bitter longing fills their soul,
With passion's light diffused."

John turned the pages, and his eyes fell on this embittered yet practical composition:

"The fool who thought that love
Was a thing of stars and laughter,
Of happy music, and calm
Expectancy of happiness after
For ever; of heart meeting heart
In love and answering love—
This fool had no thought of pain …
… In pursuit of this he calls Love!"

Elinor's footnote to this poem read: "There *are* fools like that. I'm not one of them." John thought Elinor wasn't being truthful with this declaration, given its context. In another poem entitled "Reality," she continued with the now familiar theme:

"Nothing is real; this life is but a dream;
Its strangest things, and gravest, do but seem;
Nothing assaults the heart, or enters deep
All transience but shows us that we sleep.
Then what is love? A dream within a dream?
Or the reality's undying theme?
Love is the slayer of this gentle sleep;
Dreaming, we smile and sigh; awake we weep."

She'd made a sound point, he admitted. Life did seem surreal at times. Elinor had scribbled below the poem, "Better to be awake, all the same, as long as we can remember the best parts of the dream." With that remark she'd thrown herself a life preserver.

In November of 1940, when John was in Canada still awaiting initial training to commence before he started flight school, Elinor wrote:

"Into the grave
My heart I gave,
That now a heart have none,
And so I feel no happiness
To see that sorrow done."

In January, 1941, when John was learning to fly, she had written a poem about soft blue curtains shutting out the rainy darkness. In her footnote she wrote, "You can't shut it out. If you do,
it's much worse when it gets in. Better to face it all the time." She
underscored her opinion in verse:

"Such agony is in the heart
That longs for love again—
Peace! What has love to do with me?
I will not hear the rain!"

In March, 1941, she wrote about all the lovely things "we
have missed together," in memory of something that happened
to her the previous summer. A subsequent poem in May spoke
of weeping for a vanished year and a dark-eyed narcissus that had
caught the dew:

"So heavy with weeping it scarce could stand—
'Oh flower, you're crying, you understand!'"

In June, when John had completed flight school and received
his officer's commission, she'd composed a beautifully sad poem,
parenthetically lamenting to "O traitor Time!" and "O traitor
Heart!"

Elinor's poetry notebook was a cave of crystalline thoughts
that slowly dripped sadness to the floor and formed immoveable
monuments to her grief, John thought. Her writings implied, at
least to him, that she'd fallen in love the previous year and had
had her heart decidedly and irreversibly broken. He decided that
she was mourning, though for whom—someone who'd died
or someone who'd loved and left her? "Don't worry," she

had written, "I'm walking with a year-old ghost … and his hand is cold in mine."

John looked up from the journal. *Oh, dear Elinor*, he thought. *Shall I ask her what happened, or shall I quietly shut the book and pretend ignorance?*

He continued reading against his better judgment, turning to the final entry from just the previous week when he'd barnstormed his way back into her life at Kemerton. She had titled the poem "Falling Stars," and the last stanza made his heart leap:

"Yet when the winter frosts are fierce,
And shattered stars spin down;
I think, there flies a nobler heart,
Through agonies to a crown."

The poem might have been written for fighter pilots in general, John reasoned. Or it carried a more religious meaning for a soul who'd passed into immortality and had become an angel. Even so, he couldn't dismiss the coincidence, and he wondered if the poem was meant for him. The footnote read, "I *do* mean this." Was she trying to convince herself of something? he wondered.

John closed Elinor's journal, feeling that he knew her now more intimately than ever before, yet she remained an enigma. He slipped from the room and tip-toed downstairs to return the notebook to its original place on the table. He stepped onto the terrace and looked up at the clear, starry sky. *Elinor is really a most inspiring woman*, he thought. *I am sure she is the one for me.* He could foresee hard work ahead of him to win her heart. He knew he faced competition, but the other chap, if there was one, was not a current fixture in her life. This was his chance, and he vowed to make good use of it.

15

ICARUS REBORN

AS JOHN SETTLED into the routine of Spitfire training in Wales, his life divided into three distinct worlds—the ground, the airspace over England, and the upper realms of flight. It was all he could do to keep those worlds from colliding.

The ground level of his life harbored his earthbound concerns, all the mundane necessities of survival—shelter from the rain, food, and distraction through entertainment and camaraderie. By necessity this lower sphere was where he was forced to deal with his fears of going into combat, of his friends being killed, of his feelings for Elinor, and of his stunted ability to compose a decent couplet let alone a cathartic letter.

He was grounded often, either from having too many hours on the Spitfire ahead of his flight mates or from the incessant rain that rendered both the aerodrome and the airspace above it non-serviceable. On those days he was at wit's end with restlessness, and so he was usually the first to notice a break in the clouds and sprint to the airfield to grab a Spitfire before anyone else had a chance. When he wasn't flying he set his attention to making model planes and playing squash or billiards with the other pilots. More often than not he could be found poring over a book he'd found called *Icarus: An Anthology of the Poetry of Flight*. These diversions enabled him to keep his mood elevated with moderate success, yet his muse still dug fox holes around herself with high berms to keep him out.

His ventures into the strata above the earth thrilled him. There he learned how to handle the Spitfire in formation flying, how to excel in combat maneuvers, how to shoot at the enemy on his tail, how to shoot his camera guns at a moving target while avoiding getting hit. On one occasion, he led a difficult flight formation up through stratocumulus cover. His unit stayed above the ceiling for an hour and then descended through a hole in the clouds, only to discover that a thin layer of haze stretched down to the deck. That time he and his fellow squadron members counted themselves lucky to have landed without mishap. Another day his group performed some camera-gun attacks, the results of which encouraged him greatly because he was the only person in the whole course who had the "enemy" aircraft on film for more than half the length. He pushed the limits of the Spitfire's capacities as well as his own, staying airborne as long as he had the fuel. The intense concentration it took not to crash the airplane allowed him success in keeping his emotions at a distance, especially those for Elinor. As long as he was flying, he was not grounded by his yearning.

It was in this middle space of his life where he put his genius on display, crisscrossing the English skies to perform aerobatics over the homes and schools of his family and friends. Once he grabbed an unmarked Spitfire, which allowed him to fly as low as he liked without anyone on the ground reporting his call numbers. First he "beat up" the Lyons for three-quarters of an hour, nearly touching the grass on their tennis court several times. After that he shot off to Reading and buzzed the home of his former Rugby roommate, then flew down to Mortehoe in Devon to "have a look at Granny." At the top of the hill he misjudged a pull-out and left some elevator fabric on a bramble bush. He thought it must have thrilled his grandmother, but the damage took some explaining when he returned to RAF Llandow.

As challenging and enjoyable as life in the middle airspace was to his mind and ego, it was the outer reaches of the atmosphere, the third sphere of his existence, that ignited his soul. He'd been to 20,000 feet where oxygen was needed for dog-fighting practice, but most of those times he was so focused on the exercises that he couldn't fully appreciate the heights. In rare moments he managed to escape the group and fly off on his own where he could forget, if only temporarily, the task of honing his combat skills and staying alive, where he could even forget himself.

On the eighteenth of August, as a mere eleven-day veteran on the Spitfire, he took his aircraft higher than ever before, even higher than Mount Everest. He was feeling particularly chipper because he'd called Elinor the previous evening on her birthday, and they'd had a pleasant conversation. She'd told him she was looking forward to seeing him on his next leave. If he couldn't make it back to the Cotswolds before her family returned to Rugby, she'd said, he was most certainly invited to visit her while she was attending university in Oxford. That had put him over the moon.

Whistling a tune, he lifted off from the runway the next morning and rocketed to 30,000 feet. As soon as he reached the vaulted clouds, the sun's rays shattered on his bubble-top canopy and torched his imagination. Performing somersaults within the lower reaches of the earth's stratosphere at speeds of more than 350 miles per hour made his heart pump adrenalin throughout his body. The pulling of G-forces caused his mind to dislocate, and he felt his own consciousness project outside of his physicality. At once he sensed a protected closeness to what he could only describe as a benevolent power. The sensation stunned him, and he marveled at the wonder of his expanded universe. He was Icarus who'd escaped the Labyrinth prison on make-shift wings and flew precariously close to the sun. He knew with certainty that he'd been given the gift of life so that he could discover this secret.

John's mystical experience reminded him of a few stanzas from a poem in the *Icarus* anthology, called "The Blind Man Flies" by Cubbert Hicks, which he'd been studying in his bunk:

"… I learnt from the air to-day
(On a bird's wings I flew)
That the earth could never contain
All of the God I knew.
I felt the blue mantle of space,
And kissed the cloud's white hem,
I heard the stars' majestic choir,
And sang my praise with them.
Now joy is mine through my long night,
I do not feel the rod,
For I have danced the streets of heaven,
And touched the face of God."

He reckoned that only a few hundred men, if that many, had ever experienced the jubilation of flying alone at such an altitude. Fewer still had experienced the truth that God was not limited to church or temple. God did not belong to any one religion, God could not even be contained on the planet below him. God was a power that was everywhere! John Magee, via the Supermarine Spitfire, was but a citizen of this celestial city, where he could indeed explore and dance the streets of heaven.

He felt indebted to Hicks for having shown him this truth, but the poem didn't go far enough in describing the ecstasy he had experienced. Upon landing he performed his post-flight duties as quickly as he could and rushed back to his bunk. He searched for any scrap of paper on which he could fill in the lyrics to the iambic-pentameter rhythm beating like a heart within his most inner being.

He began with his favorite line of the Hicks poem: "touched the face of God." This would be the crowning jewel of his sonnet, but he needed to show how he had rocketed to the pinnacle of his mind and then transcended it to enter the rarefied strata of divinity. Other poets in the *Icarus* anthology provided further lines of inspiration: "on laughter-silvered wings," "the lifting mind," "the shouting of the air," and "across the unpierced sanctity of space." His finished creation would not be entirely original, but he didn't think that mattered. What mattered was preserving the euphoria he'd experienced tens of thousands of feet above the earth so that he could remember it when he fell to the depths of combat hell.

With the encouragement of instructors and fellow students, he copied the polished sonnet for his parents on the third of September, 1941. "I am enclosing a verse I composed the other day," he wrote in a letter to them the next morning. "It started at 30,000 feet and was finished soon after I landed. Thought it might interest you." He hastily penned his sonnet on the back of a sheet of thin, blue stationary and called it "High Flight."

"Oh! I have slipped the surly bonds of Earth
And danced the skies on laughter-silvered wings;
Sunward I've climbed, and joined the tumbling mirth
of sun-split clouds,—and done a hundred things
You have not dreamed of—wheeled and soared and swung
High in the sunlit silence. Hov'ring there,
I've chased the shouting wind along, and flung
My eager craft through footless halls of air ...

Up, up the long, delirious, burning blue
I've topped the wind-swept heights with easy grace
Where never lark nor even eagle flew—
And, while with silent lifting mind I've trod
The high untrespassed sanctity of space,
Put out my hand, and touched the face of God."

———

Back in the TO Lounge, Anson Roe studied John Magee with furrowed eyebrows, trying to remember where he'd heard the poem before today. "Got it!" He snapped his fingers. "Television stations all across America sign off the air with your words. You're famous, mate!"

Magee shook his head and shrugged. "I'm glad something I wrote was of use to someone."

"I certainly found it inspiring. Well, sentimental but inspiring nevertheless." Anson looked at Magee with glistening eyes. "Go on, then. What happened next?"

"Well, I finished my Spitfire training mid-September, a full year after enlisting in the air force in Canada, and I celebrated my promotion from "pilot, under training" to "pilot, fully operational" with a seven-day leave. I fitted for a new uniform in London and stayed a few days at Reading and Rugby School with friends."

"Where were you stationed?"

"With the newly formed Canadian number 412 Fighter Squadron at RAF Digby in Lincolnshire. You will never guess what the airbase's motto was."

"Likely something heroic."

"*Icarus renatus*, Avroe. Icarus reborn."

"Now, that is ironic. Did you see Elinor again?"

"I visited her in Oxford in late October. Oh, and I bought myself an old set of wheels."

"Now you're talking," Anson said. "Go on, then. Tell me." Once again, he leaned back and allowed Magee's story to propel him down the runway of his imagination.

16

THE OPENING OF DOORS

"HELLO, WHAT HAVE we here?" John had just stepped off the train and was rushing up Hythe Bridge Street in Oxford to rendezvous with Elinor and his mate, George Abernathy, when he spotted a shiny, black motorbike leaning against a produce stall. The bike was accented by a gold and black gas tank, and a for-sale sign hung from the handlebars. John crossed the road for a closer look.

A bent, middle-aged man hobbled from behind the stall and lit a pipe with crooked fingers. "She's a beauty, what?"

"Looks old." He could see the paint had been scratched in places, but the wear didn't detract from the overall beauty of the machine. The word "Matador" was imprinted above a golden pair of stylized wings flanking a scallop shell. "Tell me about her."

"She was made in Lancashire by Bert Houlding and Sons. This is a 1925 model with a Bradshaw 350 cc oil-cooled engine."

"I see." John didn't know the first thing about motorbikes, let alone how to drive one. If he could fly a Spitfire, he reasoned, then he could certainly drive one of these, which would be preferable to riding the train or borrowing an aircraft to see Elinor. "Why are you selling it?"

"My rheumatism pains me too much to ride it, but she's been very good to me."

"How much do you want for it?"

"Forty quid."

John cringed. "Forty pounds? It's more than fifteen years old."

"What can you afford?"

That raised a flag in John's mind. "I need to see if it works before I decide."

The owner produced a key from his pocket, hopped onto the seat, and kick-started the engine. Coughing and spitting, the bike blew black smoke out the tail pipe.

"Are you sure you're well enough to drive it?"

"No worries," the seller said. He drove it off the sidewalk a few yards before it stalled. It took several more starts before he was able to return it under its own power. "Needs some work," the man said sheepishly.

Despite all logic, John had to have it. If he could get it back to the RAF station, he reasoned, he might persuade one of the mechanics to overhaul it. "I'll give you twenty quid if you can make it run better. Ten when I pick it up and ten next month."

"You're serving king and country, so I'll take your offer. I can have it ready for you Monday. But I need five to show me you're interested."

"Done." John produced a five-pound note and shook the man's hand, not at all convinced he would ever see him again.

———

George had suggested they all gather at the Eagle and Child—nicknamed the Bird and Baby—because of its equidistance between Oriel College, where he attended classes, and Elinor's Lady Margaret Hall, both constituents of Oxford's university complex. John enjoyed stretching his legs on the brief walk across the canal under the October sky. He entered the long, narrow seventeenth-century pub and strolled toward the back past a number of hideaway tables in dark wood-paneled and heavily-beamed rooms and alcoves. Several male students and professor types sat sporadically in these recesses, smoking pipes and drinking ales behind piles of books and writing implements. John ached to be doing the same, but this was not his life now. Some of them glanced at him in his new officer's uniform, and he imagined they harbored similar yearnings for his profession. He ordered a pint of a local India pale ale and seated himself near the door at one of the forward tables flanked by wooden partitions that integrated stained-glass insets.

He celebrated his motorbike purchase by downing half of the IPA in one go, which started to ease the tension of the perpetual scramble-readiness he lived under but did little to relieve his urgency to see Elinor. He hadn't gazed upon her lovely face since he'd spent the night with the family in Worcestershire two months earlier. That was the time he'd gone on expedition through her poetry journal, and he still felt some guilt and trepidation for having done so. He was also eager to see George, his former Rugby roommate, though they'd spent time together while John was on leave in September. George had accompanied him to America in 1939 and had spent some time with him visiting family in Pennsylvania before the war started. He considered George a touchstone to his former self in England, and he felt it would be good to be in his company again.

John nearly failed to recognize the man who rushed through the door with his open-fronted academic gown billowing around him. George was not a man who ordinarily stood out in a crowd. He was of average build with medium brown hair and a fair complexion, yet he seemed to be enjoying a new vitality now that he was at Oxford. He ordered a pint at the bar then seated himself at the table and leaned toward John. "Right. So have you seen action since we last met?"

"Indeed, I have been in two or three operations against the enemy." John enjoyed talking about what had become a calling, but he kept one eye on the front door as he spoke. "I've yet to hit the mark. A sergeant pilot in our newly-formed squadron recently scored our first confirmed victory against a Messerschmitt BF

109E in an offensive sweep. It of course called for a tremendous party, which in no way improved our sensory faculties for the following day's operations." He chuckled as he spoke. "We have this game in which we hurl each other through the air to be caught on the other side of the room. I'm guilty of tossing a chap into the fireplace at our last soiree. Not sure it wasn't an accident."

"Spend a lot of time in your cups, do you?"

"I was apprehensive about joining the squadron as a newcomer, but the lads threw a celebration in my honor. Then I found out they'll throw a party at the drop of any old hat. If you muck up in some way, you're required to buy a round for everyone. Even if you clap out, the bar bill goes on your tab anyway."

"Clap out?"

"Killed in action, my friend."

George equaled John's frankness with a deadpan expression. "I see."

"Our squadron moved from RAF Digby to Wellingore a couple of days ago. I mess with a good bunch of officers in an old country cottage called The Grange about five miles from the aerodrome. It's the kind of place where you bump your head wherever you go."

"Well, at least you would," George said, referring to their difference in height, a standing joke between them.

John laughed. "The air force is rather casual. We wear battle dress, flying boots, and sweaters, much to the chagrin of the Penguins and Brown Types, or the non-flying air force and army officers. I sleep until half past eight every other day, unless a scramble is ordered, in which case I have to be ready for immediate takeoff. I alternate between dawn and dusk patrol. We only patrol when the weather is good unless on alert, and the weather is bad far more days than not."

"What do you do in the meantime?"

"Off duty we lounge in garden chairs, go to the pub, catch a film. But there's much to do while on duty too. Last week the RAF issued a dozen new Spitfires to our squadron, and we have to be qualified on the model as soon as possible. The Mark Vb has a Rolls-Royce Merlin supercharged engine. I'll be able to push it to 375 miles per hour and climb at a rate of 2,600 feet per minute. Carries two cannons and four machine guns."

"Sounds utterly daunting!"

"You have no idea how thrilling it is to have that much power at your disposal. When the weather is good, and we're not on readiness, we practice flying in air combat and formation attacks. The squadron is all-Canadian and rather new, even the crew. We're trying to improve our collective skills before we go on any real operations. Not long ago we had a week of maneuvers with the army in some low-level attacks. Of course it was all pretense, but it gave us some good experience and a bellyful of thrills seeing the countryside and camping in tents. One night four of us went into Salisbury and had a few drinks and danced. I met a clever, pretty woman from Boston."

"Ah ha!" George raised his eyebrows. "Anything promising?"

"Maybe I'll see her again in London." A group of cheerful students burst through the front door and made their way toward the bar in the center of the pub. He knew at a glance that Elinor was not among them. He returned his attention to George. "Most of the time we wait in the dispersal hut for a legitimate scramble and get bored and frayed. When the alarm sounds, those of us in our flying suits race to our aircraft already started by ground crew. We slip into a parachute left dangling from a wingtip, throw on a helmet and oxygen mask, and fall somehow into the plane's 'office.' We take off in any old direction and reorganize ourselves into formation once we're in the air."

"That would fray my nerves."

"Frazzles mine. One time the loudspeaker crackled, and another pilot and I ran to our planes in such a hurry that we hardly heard the controller's orders. We flew way out into the North Sea in search of a Luftwaffe torpedo bomber. Unfortunately, we got into some severe weather and had to call it off."

George shook his head as if trying to imagine his friend's surreal adventure. "Never found it?"

John shrugged. "Another time we flew in formation just above the water practically all the way to Holland. Must have looked formidable to the blokes on those naval ships we passed over." John checked the front door again.

"She'll be here, mate," George said. "Probably held up in a lecture."

John nodded. He resisted ordering another pint before she arrived so he could be relatively sober for her. He also wanted to wait before buying food despite his growling stomach. "We play cards every day to fly an open roundabout anywhere we'd like. I volunteered to air test one old kite nobody likes to fly after the crew had given it a thorough overhaul. Everything went well until I came in for a landing. Wouldn't you know, the damned wheels wouldn't come down."

"Good God, man! What did you do?"

"Performed a series of short dives and violent pullouts over the aerodrome until I thought the wings would come off. After failing a dozen times, I decided to have one more go before crash-landing it on its belly." John mimed his actions with a hand as he spoke. "I climbed to about two angels—that's code for 2,000 feet. I rolled the plane onto its back, pointed the nose straight down, and chopped vertically onto the aerodrome. I held the dive as long as I dared, and a little longer, and then hauled the stick into my belly as hard as I could, which effectively put on the brakes. When I heard a violent jerk and shudder, I thought, 'there go the wings.' Then I blacked out. When I came to, I realized the following points. One, the wings are still attached. Two, the wheels are down. Three, I am about to hit the hangar."

George laughed. "How terribly frightening."

"Oh, wait, it gets better. I taxied to the flight commander only to find the Duke of Kent standing there, come to inspect the squadron. The FO introduced me and said 'nice work' in that dry, British manner. The duke had watched the entire procedure and seemed duly impressed."

"What are you boys laughing about?" asked a feminine voice above their heads.

Startled, John looked up to see Elinor standing next to their table. Her academic gown hung regally from her shoulders, and she was smiling her queenly non-smile. Both George and John stood, but John got in the cheek kisses first. "You look lovely, my Sovra." She blushed as if remembering his new nickname for her. He pulled back a chair for her on his side of the table, feeling himself grinning like a fool. "Can I get you something to drink?"

"I'll have whatever you're having."

"Pint of IPA coming right up."

"Proper ladies only drink ales in half-pints," she said sternly.

John realized she was joking with him and sighed. "I need you to remind me what proper ladies are, obviously. George, what are you having?"

He nodded to his glass for a refill.

"I'm ordering fish and chips while I'm there. What about you two?"

"I'll have the same," George said.

"Whatever meat pie looks good," Elinor said. "I'm famished."

"John was just saying he met the Duke of Kent," George told Elinor when John returned with drinks.

"Oh? Is that so?"

"And his timing could not have been more propitious. His landing gear wouldn't come down, but he did some expert flying magic to release them. The duke happened to see it all."

"Sounds like you, Ian."

John loved it when she used his childhood name. "The saga continues. It soon came time to retest the same aircraft, and the mechanics guaranteed that the wheels would release this time. The plane had no markings because it had been repainted, so I took off gayly in the direction of Rugby and gave the old place a really good beating up. I have fleeting impressions of boys pouring out of classrooms and a former schoolmate leaning on his bicycle looking aghast. I think I saw your sister running out waving a blue handkerchief."

"I heard about that," Elinor said. "Apparently you were flying upside down at the time."

"Naturally." George chuckled. "He doesn't know how to fly upright."

"Thought about dropping something incendiary on that hideous monstrosity of a school chapel, but I'd probably be shot down for that. Back at the aerodrome, I found once more that the wheels were stuck in place. Mouthing harsh words at the flight mechanics, I repeated the same maneuvers as before. This time I flew a bit higher so I could be even more violent with the aircraft. After forty-five minutes of diving and jerking back the stick, I got the wheels down at the expense of two engine cowlings, the hood, and several bolts off the wing roots. I informed the engineering officer that if it happened again, I would bail out and let the plane fall into the sea."

Their laughter blended with the loud conversations and general merrymaking within the now-crowded pub. An orange-rose glow from the setting sun began filtering through the windows, making John feel at home in the company of his two most favorite people in the world. He didn't want to talk about the war anymore. He happened to look up when the front door opened to a man in a long, wool robe edged and cinched in the middle by yellow cording. Everyone else noticed him too and stopped their conversations to gawk.

"Who is he?" John asked after the man walked past their table.

"Oh, that's C.S. Lewis," George said. "One of the Inklings."

"What's that?"

"An informal literary group that meets in the Rabbit Room in the back of the pub," Elinor said. "Tolkien, who wrote *The Hobbit,* is a member. Lewis wrote an odd book called, *Out of the Silent Planet.* He sometimes broadcasts religious programs on the BBC during bombing blitzes in London."

"Well done, him. I can see I'm behind on my reading. I'll wager they're in line with your tastes, Elinor, after hearing about your soon-to-be published story."

"Oh? Am I in the presence of literary greatness?" George asked.

"She's having a story published in the *New English Weekly* next month. It's called, 'The Eyes of the Dead.' Elinor is a prolific writer."

Her eyes twinkled at the compliment. It impressed John that she didn't look down at her hands in false modesty.

"Congratulations, Elinor!" George lifted his glass to her and drank.

John felt his cheeks warm, which he attributed both to the beer and to Elinor's company. He felt he'd better change the subject for fear of confessing his intrusion on her journal. "Oxford is truly one of the most beautiful cities I've ever set eyes upon."

"The City of Dreaming Spires," Elinor said. "From a poem, 'And that city with her dreaming spires need not June for beauty's heightening.'"

"I would have to agree with that. Mind you, all I've seen thus far is from my train window and trek across the canal. There is such an air of peace and learning here, considering the country's at war."

"Why do you suppose Oxford hasn't been bombed?" George asked.

"No steelworks or bomb-making factories or political bastions here serving as targets."

"I heard Hitler has spared the city because he wants to make it his capital after he's won the war," Elinor added.

"He won't be winning," John stated resolutely.

"No, that's correct, of course not." She looked half embarrassed by her unpatriotic comment. "Did you two like America?" she asked as if to change the subject.

"Yes, until I was forced to stay there."

"I liked it," George said. "We went to the World's Fair. Had a wonderful time."

"Yes, but you were allowed to return to England after the war started. I had to come back the hard way."

"Perhaps you were meant to be stuck in America," Elinor offered. "Look at what you've achieved."

That she seemed taken by his flying cheered him. "Leave it to you to cut to the heart of it. Be that as it may, there were many times that first year in Connecticut when I longed to be roaming the hills of England with my only care being whether there were any chocolate biscuits left for tea."

"Maybe you'll attend one of the colleges here after the war."

"Oh, I'd love to, but it would be silly to waste the Yale scholarship. The provost allowed me to defer it."

"If you returned to the States for university, you might never come back." Elinor protruded her lower lip.

"I will have to think it through more thoroughly," John said. He sat back and stared at Elinor. *If I'm not mistaken, I may be making some headway with her.* He swallowed the last bit of beer in his glass. "Right. What's on tomorrow?"

"Come to lecture with me," George said. "I'm sure we can dig up a gown for you."

"I'm free in the evening," Elinor offered. "Let's meet for tea in my room, and we'll make plans then."

————

Elinor looked relieved when she opened her door to John and George the following evening. "I was beginning to wonder if you were still coming."

John removed his officer's hat and pecked Elinor on her cheek before entering. "Pardon us for being late. We had quite a time locating you."

"Fairly straight forward," Elinor said as she showed the men into the room.

"If you have the correct number," John said. The room, he noticed, was the feminized version of standard Oxford dorm issue, furnished with two small beds with peach spreads, two desks with chairs, and two peach-colored wingback chairs. A window flanked by brown drapery looked on the river that ran behind the college. A lit fireplace kept the room cozy.

"I heard T23," George said. "John insisted on H68."

"Neither of which is close to D31." Elinor scooped tea into a porcelain teapot and poured hot water into it from an electric kettle. She seated herself in one of the desk chairs.

"One of the young ladies we pushed in on directed us to the correct room." John seated himself in the wingback chair next to the window and George took the other. "In truth I was so excited by your invitation I'd forgotten the number."

"You're redeemed, Ian. What did you get up to today?"

"We attended a lecture on Goethe with George's roommate, who oddly wore a sports coat and rather a loud canary-yellow jersey beneath his gown."

"You've been away so long, you've forgotten about British eccentricity," Elinor said.

"Eccentricity isn't appreciated in the military," John said.

George laughed. "John was terrified he would be asked a question."

"When you masquerade as a student, you don't want to appear foolish."

"You're not at Rugby anymore. Can you believe he was actually taking notes, Elinor?"

"As I remember it, he wasn't all that keen on his studies."

"On the contrary. I've found Goethe's literary works most inspiring, but I hadn't delved into his theory of color. Just wanted to take it all in."

"After the lecture, we went into the hall and watched the 'One O'Clock Review' by undergraduates. We went backstage to meet the members of the cast who were surprised to learn that John was a fighter pilot."

"We had a funny little lunch in a snack bar and then went back to George's to retrieve my uniform so that we could meet you for tea. And here we are."

"I must provide my end of the agreement, then." Elinor strained tea from the pot into bone china cups, adding milk and a sugar cube to each. "McVitie's, Ian?"

"Chocolate?"

"Of course."

"Yes, please." He was glad she remembered chocolate biscuits at tea being his fondest memory of England. She placed a row of cookies and several small cheese sandwiches on a plate and served them to her guests.

The door opened abruptly and in walked a stunning strawberry blonde. Her cheeks were nearly as rosy as her hair, John noted. Both men stood. "You're just in time for a cuppa," Elinor said.

"Swell. I'm chilled to the bone." She removed a neck scarf and rain slicker and flung off the moisture in a manner that approached the theatrical. "Aren't you going to introduce me to your guests?"

"I was just beginning to do that," Elinor said in measured tone. "Eve, this is my long-time friend, Ian ... or rather, John. As you can see, he's a pilot officer in the Royal Canadian Air Force. This is John's friend George Abernathy. Both went to Rugby where my father is the headmaster."

"Pleased to meet you." Eve helped herself to tea and then sat in the empty desk chair. "What are you fellas doing tonight?"

"Eve is from America," Elinor said as if to explain her roommate's manner.

"My father is here on diplomatic service."

"Oh? My father is American, but I was raised in this country."

"Yet you're in a Canadian uniform."

"Long story, as it happens." John noted that Eve wasn't as pretty as Elinor, but her extroversion made her attractive.

"We were going out this evening," Elinor said. "John and I have much to catch up on."

Eve perked up. "I hear there's a swell play at the Oxford Theatre called, 'The Blue Goose.'"

"In Beaumont Street?" John said. "Yes, I passed by there yesterday. What do you say, Elinor? This is your night."

Elinor smiled and hesitated. John could not sense what she was thinking but reckoned her reticence had something to do with Eve. "I think it's a swell idea." In her own way she was subtly mocking Eve, he thought. "You will join us, won't you, Eve?"

"Just give me a minute to powder my nose," Eve said as she skipped out the door.

———

The crowded theater was a visual feast to anyone who'd spent months surrounded by foul-smelling men, noisy hunks of metal, open sky, and mud. Golden beams arched across the ceiling and everything was awash in an ocean of red fabrics. John and his friends found four seats together in the mezzanine at the end of a row. He nodded to the women to go first, but Eve insisted on a different arrangement. "George, you take the first seat, then me, then John, then Elinor."

George caught John's eye and shrugged. "As you wish." He side-shuffled down the row, and everyone else fell in behind him as Eve directed. She proceeded to dish out every manner of eye-batting, flirtatious smile, and fingertip brushing upon both gentlemen. John noticed a bit of jaw stiffening in Elinor's profile, showing disapproval that only he would detect. *Could it be she's jealous?*

Halfway through the second act, John became less interested in the play and Eve's overtures, though flattering, and more interested in making the most of his precious time with Elinor. He thought about their short visit in the pub the previous day and how pleasant she'd been this evening. She was laughing in all the right places of the performance, but there was no sparkle in her eyes, and lines were beginning to crease her forehead. He thought about her journal, about how heartbroken and sad her poetry seemed to be, month after month, verse after verse. He wondered whether the sadness was a genuine reflection of her well-being, or if there was something deeper behind Elinor's all too cordial demeanor. He decided to ask her about it.

"Are you content, Elinor?"

She faced him with a look of surprise. "Why do you ask?"

"You seem … preoccupied."

"I'm buried up to my neck in literary studies in the middle of a country that's at war," she said in a half-defensive tone. "I've had acquaintances die and dear friends put at risk. Difficult to be cheerful in times like these."

"Fair enough. Yet there seems to be something deeper that's troubling you." He didn't want to press too hard. "Something at the depth of your soul, perhaps."

"It is precisely my faith …," she said out loud, then modulated the volume of her voice to a whisper. "My spiritual beliefs keep me going."

He could see he'd touched a nerve. "I'm sorry. I don't mean to pry."

Several minutes passed before Elinor leaned toward him again and whispered, "You are perceptive, Ian."

Her compliment encouraged him, but he chose not to respond knowing she would speak when she was ready.

"There was a chap two summers ago," she whispered a moment later. "But that's over now. I was put off my stride, I must say."

John nodded. He already suspected this, but he wanted to hear it from her.

"Then I met another a year ago last summer, a temporary teacher at Rugby. He went into the RAF nearly as soon as I met him. We correspond sporadically, but I don't see him."

John already suspected something like this as well, and it did sting. He reminded himself that he was present with her while the other contender was not.

"How about you?"

"There have been a few promises here and there. Did you know I was engaged?"

"No!" she exclaimed. The man in front of Elinor shushed them without turning around. She put a hand over her mouth.

"We're being impolite," John mouthed. He signaled to George that they were moving, and George nodded his understanding. Eve pouted but before she could say anything, John urged Elinor to stand and escorted her to the last of several empty rows in the back of the mezzanine. They both flopped into the chairs.

"That's better," he said.

"Much. The play isn't very good, anyway. You were saying you were engaged?"

"To a Czechoslovakian girl," John said just above a whisper. "She married someone else, I think. There was also a French-Canadian woman who broke off our arrangement in a letter in French."

"How tragic."

John tossed his head. "Eh? *C'est la guerre.*"

Elinor smiled.

"That's what I want to see."

"What does it mean to be content?" Elinor asked and continued before he could respond. "I think humans are overly concerned with contentment, but I don't believe life is about happiness. I'd rather burn in anguish in this mortal fire. Contentment will come in heaven."

"You've answered your own question."

"I want to hear your answer. What do you think it is to be content?"

"I'm content here with you."

"I want a serious answer."

He looked into her eyes and wrinkled his brow. "I am being serious." She held his stare but made no concession. He exhaled and continued, resigning himself to the more profound aspect of the question. "I have to tell you, I am having the time of my life, flying by day, gathering with the lads by night."

"Sounds swell." Elinor smiled at her continuing jest at Eve.

"Do you think it's wrong of me to take such pleasure in something at the expense of whom we call the enemy, at the expense of even my own life?"

"That's a conundrum you will have to reconcile within yourself, I suppose."

"I can tell you that I'm most content when I'm behind the stick of a Spitfire. Flying is poetry in motion … no, it's more than that. Flying feels to me like a spiritual communion with what Emerson called 'the Oversoul.' You have no idea how terrifying and yet how marvelous it all is."

"Is it the flying or is it the danger that's so appealing?"

"Both." He didn't have to think about his answer.

"Careful. You may love it so much that the rest of the world will seem mundane by comparison when the war is over."

"Granted, the world does seem far away even as I sit here with you."

"You do know you're not invincible, don't you?"

"Ah, but I am, you see." He smiled broadly, flashing his dimples. Then his expression turned somber and his tone more adamant. "This may not be very sensible to discuss, but I have to take risks to be good. If that decreases my chances for a long life, then that suits me right down to the ground because I'd rather not be ordinary. I'd quite like to build up a score and get a decoration. Not for the recognition itself, but because it would mean that I was excellent at what I did … for the war effort, of course."

Elinor fell silent and turned her attention toward the stage as if she disapproved of his comment. *I suppose it is not a good idea to talk about life expectancy when trying to court a woman,* he thought. He leaned closer to her. "You'll have to excuse my outburst. I have been taking myself to task for being too apt to show my emotions."

"You've always had a poet's sensibilities."

"Politely stated, Elinor. However, I do recognize my inconsistency with anger, and such volatility is unbecoming of an officer."

"What do you mean … inconsistent?"

"I have developed a sharp distaste for petty emotional display, but one must choose righteous wrath over personal anger. We live under a pretty good nervous strain. It doesn't do to blow up at a fitter or rigger over a mechanical failure even if it might have caused a fatality. One should save that for the enemy."

"How mature of you," she said. He was genuinely touched that she no longer considered him a boy.

A moment later she added, "Could it be that you are so in love with life … that you're not afraid of death?"

John was speechless. *What an interesting paradox*, he thought. "Truthfully, I'm terrified of dying," he said. "But I'm not afraid of death itself precisely because of what I've learned about it by living at such a pace."

She gasped and faced him. "Oh, do be careful."

The urgency and tenderness in her voice tugged at his heart. He squeezed her hand and began whispering a poem he had written while he was still a schoolboy at Rugby:

"I will not die, while roses laugh in June,
When Beauty wanders through slow, secret ways,
And sombre winter leaps again to mirth …
And I must live, while sleepy summer days,
And You—and You—are lovely on the earth!"

She couldn't help herself but smile and that cheered him. "I have one for you I've been working on," she said. "It's called 'Hymn for an Airman.'"

"Let's hear it, then."

"Very well." Even in this dim light he could see her opalescent eyes beaming at him as she spoke.

"For thee no tears, no vigil,
No tomb, no frozen shroud;
But thou shalt soar far over
The vaulted sky embowed,
To life beyond the morning
In light that knows no cloud."

He started to say something in response, but his words caught in his throat. A deafening outburst of applause abruptly ended the moment. The actors bowed on stage and exited, the curtain dropped, and the auditorium lights brightened. John and Elinor caught up with Eve and George, and all four crowded into the mob of people flowing down the stairs and onto the street. The group began drifting back toward Lady Margaret Hall so that the women could meet their 11:15 curfew, though there was still time to catch dinner in a café en route.

Along the way Elinor did something out of character, at least to John. They were treading a narrow footpath that allowed for only two to walk abreast at a time. When Elinor stopped to answer George's critique of the play, Eve took the opportunity to grab John to herself and keep his attention. Some two blocks later, Elinor, who had been walking behind them with George, gracefully stumbled into John so that he had to turn around to catch her. Suspecting her motive, he held out an arm. "Hold onto me," he offered. She smiled and responded by interlocking her arm through his.

They never continued their conversation, although John suspected there was nothing left to say on the subject. They stopped for a bite to eat, then sang in the streets on their way back to the women's room, and Elinor promised to write a poem about their evening. She did show signs of relaxing just a bit, and for that he was grateful.

————

John returned to Oxford Monday morning on the 8:27 train after spending Saturday and Sunday in Devon with his grand-mother. By late-morning he'd finalized his purchase of the Matador Bradshaw and had acquired a license for it. He found Elinor in Hall having lunch with companions, and she invited him to join her. Afterward she walked him out to the quad where he'd left his motorbike. He'd hoped to stay another night and take Elinor to see a play starring Vivien Leigh. In the end he decided to give himself an extra day in the event the contraption broke down during his hundred-mile trek to Wellingore.

"This is it?" Elinor exclaimed when she saw the Bradshaw for the first time.

John couldn't tell if she was impressed or appalled. "Afraid so. I can get someone to work on it back at the RAF station. Now that I have it, I ought to be able to get down to see you more often."

"You're welcome anytime, provided I'm not sitting exams."

"I thoroughly enjoyed your company more than ever before."

"And I yours." She smiled and offered her hand. "To say 'take care' or 'be safe' seems so inadequate."

He took her hand and caressed it, lightly kissing her lips as he did so. "You are indeed lovely, Sovra, my primrose."

Her eyes glistened and her chin quivered as she struggled to hold back her tears. "Go before I break down."

He reluctantly let go of her hand and turned to throw a leg over the motorbike. With a kick on the starter pedal, the engine sputtered alive.

"Wait!" She handed him an envelope. "Don't read this until you settle for the night."

He put it in the breast pocket of his leather Irvin jacket, just over his heart where he knew it would be safe.

"And stop off to visit my parents at Rugby. They'll be happy to see you."

"Yes, dear." He pushed off and only drove a few yards before the bike died. They both laughed. He restarted it and rode down the road, waving a hand overhead without looking back.

John couldn't wait to read what Elinor had written him. At the earliest opportunity, he parked beneath an oak tree for a rest. He sat on the ground and leaned into a crook in the trunk. He found a poem nestled within the envelop.

> "Sometimes, suddenly, the doors fly open,
> Those drab dull-varnished doors,
> And the light we knew
> Before we were lost, quite lost,
> Breaks forth like trumpets to the soul
> With a glory transfiguring all things—
> Making fields gold, the sky a cloudy miracle,
> All sounds music, and men angels.
> In this light, strife is not;
> Rest is not, for nothing wearies;
> Dreams are not, for the reality
> We thought so cold, is the living warmth
> Of all dreams sublimated.
> To live in this light, is death,
> Since death is Heaven,
> And Heaven, the opening of doors."

John cradled his head in the folds of his arms and wept. She had given him a prayer of comfort and optimism though paradoxical, as was her nature. He liked to think she was saying that, though she struggled with her sorrow, the doors had flung open and the light was within sight. He liked to think that the pilot in her life, as an angel, had lit a votive within her and had shown her heaven on earth. He recognized his own grandiosity speaking, and he was growing familiar with that voice. In truth she was the light in *his* life, and he realized he might never reach the depths of her soul.

As it happened, John had also clandestinely tucked a note in Elinor's handbag during lunch. It contained a verse from a poem entitled "A Prayer," written when he was much younger and could not have foreseen his role in the war.

"When breath comes short, and tears come all in vain,
And in the silence I must realize
That I shall never laugh, nor love again,
May I find, leaning over me, —your eyes."

17

I Find Them Laughing Beside Me

"**I WOULD HAVE** given my eye teeth to know if Elinor had purposely bumped her roommate out of the way so that she could walk with me that night." John Magee stood and made his way to the back of the TO Lounge in Oklahoma. "How about a game of pocket billiards?"

Anson followed the pilot to the table. "You never asked her?"

"Never had the opportunity."

"Why not?" Sensing the worse was about to happen in Magee's narrative, he felt nervous for the man and wanted answers quickly.

Magee shrugged as if preferring to tell the story at his own pace. "In November, just a few days after leaving Elinor in Oxford, everything changed. I got my shot at Jerry, but I realized how foolish I'd been."

"Foolish?"

"I was certain I knew what combat would be like. You can train for battle, practice all the dogfighting you want, but you never really know what it's like until you actually engage the enemy." Magee started racking numbered balls on the pool table, alternating stripes and solids in ascending order. "The eightball is missing."

Anson checked the slot at the end of the table where the balls dropped after landing in the pockets. "Here it is." He placed the black eightball in the center of the racked balls. "What happened?"

Magee rolled the rack around on the green felt top, placed its tip on the dot, and carefully lifted it away. He positioned the ivory-colored cue ball at an angle to the triangular grouping and chalked the tip of his cue stick. He bent over the table to line up his shot. "First, I pranged Brunhilde." His stick slammed the cue ball into the cluster so hard, it broke into a starburst with a resounding *clack*. The striped nine and ten balls and the solid-colored number one landed into various pockets. "We're playing eightball. I call stripes, obviously."

"Who, er, what was Brunhilde?"

"A beloved Spitfire among the ranks." He slammed number eleven into the side pocket. "Named for the mythological shield-maiden and angel of death."

"Hope it wasn't a harbinger of things to come." Magee cast Anson such a stern look, it made him leery of what he'd say next. "How did the accident happen this time?"

"Failed to open the throttle and exert proper rudder control on landing, which caused the plane to bounce and the port wing tip to stick in the ground and buckle."

"That had to hurt. You weren't too good at landings, were you?"

"I wasn't hurt physically, but I was crestfallen. My CO, Flight Lieutenant Christopher Bushell—we called him Kitt—went easy on me. Shouldn't have done. In the accident report he generously wrote that I had shown above average flying ability up to the time of this accident, which he felt would eradicate any tendencies toward carelessness I may have had."

"Tendencies toward carelessness?" Anson asked. "I thought you were just a showboat."

"I didn't tell you … when I trained on the Spitfire in Llandow, the prevailing opinion was that I showed patches of brilliance laced with a tendency to be overly confident."

"You were distracted by Elinor."

Magee shrugged. "I took chances to better my skills, and such a strategy can create a convergence with the earth much sooner than one anticipates," he said. "But taking chances isn't the same as negligence."

"I understand," Anson said. "I just can't be bothered sometimes."

"I would have been grounded and recommissioned if it hadn't been for Kitt saving my arse. Kitt was one of the lads, a real friend and mentor to us. He had been appointed squadron leader only the day before my accident, and he was to lead us on Circus Ops across the English Channel just a few days later." Magee picked off number thirteen, far corner pocket. The ivory cue ball spun backward and bumped number fourteen into the opposite corner.

"Circus Ops?"

"After the Battle of Britain ended the previous autumn, the RAF turned to winning air superiority over northwestern France. Squadrons from all the main airfields operated together as massive fighter wings to lure the Luftwaffe into a war of attrition. In Circus Operations we'd send twenty or thirty bombers into Europe under the heavy escort of a dozen or more Spitfire squadrons as the lure, while more fighter squadrons hid at high altitude to ambush the enemy planes as they attacked the escort. It turned out to be an expensive, vain attempt and only marginally successful."

"The RAF underestimated the German prowess in the air."

"And Goering was on to us from the beginning." Magee walked around the table and aimed for a bank shot to pocket number fifteen. With expert precision he sank his target, leaving only one more striped ball on the table. Anson was beginning to think the fighter pilot was a pool shark. "Up to this point I had been doing little more than practice exercises and flying in the box in protected formation. This was to be my first real mission, and I had to admit I was a bit apprehensive."

Anson was half surprised to hear this admission, considering Magee's bravado.

"Kitt was wonderful about it. He took me in hand like an older brother. He said that my fear meant that I'd been properly trained. Told me to face the fear and allow my muscle memory to take over. Be aggressive but watch myself, that sort of thing. He made me his wing man in the Circus Ops, which meant I'd fly to his right and slightly behind him as Red Two. He was Red One and excited to be leading his first squadron, and of course I was excited and honored to back him up."

"Sounds like Kitt had confidence in your flying."

Magee showed no acknowledgment as he chalked his cue stick again and stalked the best angle to hit the purple-striped number twelve, which was boxed in by several solid-colored balls.

"For this mission roughly seventy-two Spitfires from six squadrons were to escort a dozen Blenheim bombers on a drop over Lille, France." Magee continued to circle the pool table, avoiding eye contact with Anson. "Three more squadrons were supposed to hover at high altitude just off the coast of France and ambush the Messerschmitt 109s as they attacked the lower-flying bombers and wing escort on their way back to England."

"I can see how that might work, but you're bound to lose a few."

Magee shot him an acerbic side-glance. "And so on Sunday, the eighth of November, my squadron of twelve took off from Wellingore and met two more squadrons in southern England. Now thirty-six Spitfires strong, we set course for France in Vic formation. My squadron flew at 22,000 feet, the next squadron at 21,000 feet, and the next at 20,000 feet stepped down into the late morning sun. We were to rendezvous with the bombers and the wing escort a few miles northeast of Dunkirk, France. It was a beautiful morning, with good visibility and no clouds above us. However, the air below us was hazy. I remember thinking how easily we could be spotted from above, like a murder of crows flying across a snowy field."

"Didn't it occur to the leadership that the wing wasn't suitably camouflaged?"

"Should have done, but the wing commander, though seasoned and older, had never led a mission of this magnitude before." Magee formed a bridge on the table with his free hand for the best angle of attack of the stick on the cue ball. "Problem was, we arrived at the rendezvous point about seven minutes too early." He sliced the cue ball with his stick tip, causing it to leap up and hit the twelve-ball into the side pocket. The ball rolled down the chute and dropped in the slot at the end of the table with finality. "That was our undoing," he said.

Magee leaned the stick against the table and turned toward Anson with a grave look on his face. "The wing commander made a tight turn to the left just off the coast of France, presumably to stall for time while the other six squadrons escorting our bombers caught up with us. But the commander cut so sharply that the three tiers of Spitfires fell out of formation, and most of the squadrons lost sight of their lead planes. The entire wing, orbiting at different altitudes, spun just off the coast like a vortex of migrating cranes whose formation had been disturbed."

"And as vulnerable," Anson said.

He nodded. "We were quite vulnerable indeed. Kitt and I turned left along the patrol line with the other two from the red section. That's when I looked up and saw a cluster of 109s swarming out of the sun. One of them came for me."

"They were waiting for you from above." Anson began to fear the outcome.

"I heard that an approaching Messerschmitt is so beautiful and mesmerizing that you're hit before you can react. Not this time. Adrenalin dumped into my body as soon as I spotted it, and I turned so violently that I spun down several thousand feet and got away for the moment. Then, before we could reposition, four 109s flew in from the north and individually chased each member of our red section." His hands became speeding Spitfires as he spoke, flying wildly over his head and diving to the floor. "When we turned around to attack them, heavy and accurate anti-aircraft artillery closed in behind us." Magee's fists shot at imaginary Spitfires across the lounge ceiling.

"I weaved back and forth and dropped behind, losing Kitt on the turn. An instant later I watched a Spitfire attack a Messerschmitt, which was attacking Kitt's Spitfire, all in line astern. I started to assist when a 109 came across my sights. I rolled and fired a four-second burst on him, amounting to 160 rounds from four machine guns." He gripped the button on his imaginary joystick and made a growling, buzzing noise with his lips. "The enemy target dived so rapidly, I couldn't see if I hit him. Then I spotted a 109 firing on a Spit, and all I had to do was turn in behind and fire at him, but another one pulled the same trick on me. When I saw tracers streak across the sky, I realized it was time to forget about my bird."

"Sounds incredibly chaotic," Anson said, shaking his head.

"That was just what was happening to my section. There were other battles ensuing at all altitudes around me—some even started for home. I was now several miles inland, and at this point I saw a Spitfire diving straight past me puffing white smoke before I lost sight of it. As I started to climb, a 109 dived on me in a quarter attack, and I banked right and lost it."

"So you don't know if you got the one you fired on?" Anson asked.

Magee shook his head. "We debated it for days. One bloke dared to suggest I claim it anyway."

"You found that offensive, no doubt," Anson said.

"It isn't useful to lie about a claim. Finally, I joined a group of Spitfires flying a thousand feet above the returning British bombers. Flak was intense but we stayed ahead of it. What was left of our squadron landed wherever we could back in England. I refueled and returned to search for survivors."

"Was anyone killed?"

"Of the nine squadrons sent up that day for Circus Ops 110, eleven Spitfires and eight pilots were lost, causing the RAF to suspend such operations until spring. The wing commander died. I saw one of the pilots in our section go straight into the sea. Another tried to bail out but his parachute didn't open. Nobody ever saw what happened to Kitt. I was the only one of the red section to survive."

"Kitt was the one who recommended you be retained in the RCAF after you crashed Brunhilde?"

"The very same," Magee said. "We all hoped he'd become a prisoner of war. His dog slept under his empty bed for days, reminding us of our loss. He was one of the grandest men I had ever known." He hunched his shoulders, pausing to remember.

"Must have been devastating," Anson said.

"It is indeed a weird and chilling thing to watch someone you know and live with go down in smoke. You can see all the *Hell's Angels* and *Dawn Patrol* movies you like, but it isn't the same thing. And, too, it gets you kind of mad. Our losses were the first we'd sustained and were pretty hard to take, but we needed some waking up."

"How were you able to recover from the trauma and continue flying the next day?"

"With an air of forced cheerfulness, but each of us nurtured our anger. I began to build up a real hatred for Jerry. If I didn't hate him, his bullets would get me before mine got him. I became determined to get a 'confirmed' before Christmas. I wrote several letters to friends and family members about it as much as I could without alarming the censors, and I used each letter to bolster my confidence. I told one friend that once you get over your fear of the Messerschmitts, you get to love it. And, really, I was loving the whole thing. Dodging anti-aircraft artillery fire was a little disconcerting at first, but great fun. And then I wrote a poem entitled, 'Per Ardua.'"

"Per ardua ad astra. Through adversity to the stars," Anson said. "The slogan for the Royal Canadian Air Force."

"You *have* been listening. 'Because my faltering feet would fail, I find them laughing beside me, steadying the hand that seeks their deadly courage.' I dedicated it to the pilots who died in the Battle of Britain."

"Must have felt cathartic."

Magee's shoulders straightened. "We did have some positive moments," he said after a reflective pause. "King George VI visited the squadron at Wellingore the following week despite inclement weather. He chatted with all the pilots and numerous other ranks during his tour of inspection, and afterward he attended an informal tea in the dispersal hut. There were pictures in all the papers in which one might have picked me out if they exercised a great deal of imagination. What the papers didn't publish was the king yielding the right of way to a bunch of geese the ground crew had herded onto the parade grounds for a laugh."

"That must have cheered you up a bit."

"It was a welcomed distraction. Soon after that my decrepit motorbike stopped working. The engineering officer promised to overhaul it in exchange for borrowing it for forty-eight hours, but he was unable to resurrect it. I auctioned it off and conveniently forgot to pay the seller the ten quid I still owed him."

"Did you ever get your confirmed kill?" Anson asked.

The fighter pilot, ignoring the question, returned to the table to finish off his round of pool. "Eightball in the side." He leaned over the table to line up on the white and black balls, which, Anson noticed, were already set up by his last shot. "No, I never got to claim one."

"Why not?"

Magee tapped the white ball, which bumped the black eightball swiftly into the side pocket. He stood straight and faced Anson. "I never claimed a hit, Avroe, because I clapped out."

18

Falling Star

"**I DON'T UNDERSTAND,**" Anson said, but something told him that he did understand, and for that reason he feared hearing the rest of the story. He broke into a cold sweat and his stomach roiled. "I don't think you should tell me right now. Not feeling so good." Anson groaned and covered his mouth.

"The story is the cure, not the cause. You will be fine."

"Out with it then and be quick!" He felt he had no choice but to listen.

Magee pivoted away to lean his cue stick against the wall. When he turned back he looked to Anson like a kid of maybe eighteen or nineteen years of age. His youthful appearance did nothing to diminish his presence.

"It happened on the morning of December the eleventh, four days after the Japanese attack on Pearl Harbor."

"*What* happened?" Anson was still feeling panicky.

The pilot squatted to pull the billiard balls from the collection bin and place them on the table. "We hadn't done much flying over the previous few weeks because of the wintry weather settling in, which was good news because the Luftwaffe stayed home too. So you can imagine how happy we were when the weather broke just enough for us to get in a sorely-needed practice on wing formation with another squadron thirty miles to the north. I say the weather had broken, but there was still a 3,000-foot cloud bank sitting about 1,200 to 2,500 feet off the ground. We practiced our formation flying with the other squadron above the cloud for about an hour before heading back to Wellingore."

In his mind's eye Anson could see himself behind the Spitfire stick, happily frolicking above the heavy cloud with his squadron mates mere yards away from his wingtips.

"Now, there are two ways to descend through cloud. One way is to perform an instrument let-down in stages, four planes at a time. This is often the wisest approach, but it can take some time and fuel. The other way is to shoot straight down through a sucker hole in the cloud if one opens up. We were running low on gravy, so guess which option we chose?"

"Since there were no aircraft warning systems or radio navigation aids in the Spitfires, I assume you shot through the cloud."

"We dived through the hole in single file a hundred yards apart, 'whip-cracking' our way as we descended to watch each other's blind spots while also putting the brakes on our rapid descent." He ordered seven balls into an S-curved line across the table. "I was the third Spit to dive into the hole, going about 400 miles per hour and dropping 600 feet per second."

Magee hesitated, drawing in a few breaths before continuing. The man's breathing sounded labored to Anson. He was terrified of what would come next.

"Suddenly, I heard a voice on the com yell: 'Miss that aeroplane!'" Magee gently rolled the eightball perpendicular to the line of balls representing the descending Spitfires. "In a split second, the first two aircraft pulled up and away." He pushed aside the bottom two balls before the black ball could reach them. "I dropped through the cloud and ran nose first into the fuselage of the approaching plane." He struck the black ball with his Magee ball. "The Oxford Trainer exploded into flames."

"Oh ... my ... God!" Anson shouted. "What did you do?" Surviving such a collision sounded incomprehensible to Anson, yet he must have lived, he thought. He was standing right there playing pool with him.

"I jumped. I pulled the radio cord ... ripped off my oxygen mask ... unbuckled the safety belts ... broke open the canopy. And jumped."

Anson's mind, horrified by the description, was assailed with every action, every sound, every sensation Magee described. It sickened him. It sucked the life from his lungs. As he started to pass out, he heard Magee's voice but couldn't make out what he was saying. All went dark.

19

THE SURLY BONDS

ANSON LAY FACE-FIRST in a pile of shattered glass surrounded by smoke and crumpled metal. He couldn't smell aviation fuel, but he was aware of its presence and danger of igniting. He tried to shout a warning but couldn't make a sound, couldn't catch his breath. An eternity passed before rescuers reached him. Amidst shouts of alarm, strong arms pulled him from the wreckage and laid him on the tailgate of a truck. Something blocked his airway and restricted his breathing. He tried to raise his hands to his throat, but they were forced away. Through swollen and bloody eyelids, he could barely make out the shapes of people leaning over him. Hands everywhere pressed on wounds where he assumed he was bleeding out. One shadowy figure, a woman, whispered encouragement in Arabic. He thought, *Vivianne!* He tried to shout her name aloud, but again no sound emitted from his throat. He wanted nothing more than to see her face right now. He drifted into blackness.

Anson heard Vivianne's laugh before she came into focus like a Wonderland Cheshire cat in reverse. They were both working the night shift at the Yardarm, his pub in England. The room was so crowded, many of the customers huddled in groups on the walkway outside the pub's front door. Vivianne was laughing at an anecdote a male customer was sharing with her. Anson pulled a pint and offered it to her, knowing the publican would not approve. "Shhh!" he whispered. "On the house."

Without acknowledging his gesture of reconciliation, she placed the glass in front of the man who held her attention. She was clearly punishing Anson for something he'd done, but he couldn't remember what sin he'd committed.

"Oi! It's almost time," someone shouted. Anson looked at his watch ... mere seconds before midnight. He cranked up the volume on the transistor radio behind the bar, and the deep tone of Big Ben gonging in the New Year sounded over the speakers. Cheers broke out among the drunken well-wishers who began hugging, kissing, and back-slapping each other in celebration. A patron at the other end of the bar shouted for service, but Vivianne ignored him, looking at Anson as if she were waiting for something from him. Finally she shook her head and moved toward the gentleman calling her.

———

"This may hurt," Anson heard someone say. He was back on the tailgate at the crash site, barely able to see and drowning in a sticky, metallic-tasting substance. He felt something sharp sink into his neck and throat and pierce his esophagus. It hurt like hell, but he didn't care. He gasped as air rushed into his lungs. He'd never felt more grateful for anything in his life. He blacked out again.

20

NEITHER HERE NOR THERE

ANSON REEMERGED IN the Oklahoma lounge, sprawled out on the pool table, hyperventilating, and thrashing about like a fish out of water.

"You can breathe normally, Avroe." The pilot sat on a nearby barstool, undisturbed by Anson's hysteria. "You're all right, mate."

Anson took in long, conscious breaths and let them out slowly. Tapping the front of his throat with his fingers failed to find the gaping hole he expected. The skin wasn't even broken. He explored his face and felt no obvious bloodiness or swelling. All systems checked out normal. He sat up and threw his legs over the side of the table, bewildered by how he got there in the first place. "What just happened?"

"You tell me."

"I think I was in an accident, a plane accident. What I don't know is ... when or where?"

"What do you remember?"

"Very little. It was bright, hot, dusty. People speaking Arabic-sounding words all around me."

"Does that sound like Oklahoma or England to you?"

He rubbed his forehead, hoping it would make him think more clearly. "I did take a brief side-trip to my Norwich pub, but the accident was in a desert I think. I remember nothing about what caused it or what happened to me except that I was hurt rather badly."

"How do you feel now?" Magee asked.

"Lightheaded but remarkably well considering all this jumping around, and the wreck... ." Anson stopped talking as a thought dawned on him. All this time he'd been thinking that his strange episodes existed in his own mind, but he realized he'd dismissed a major clue. *Where are all the townspeople?* The airport, the lounge, even the roads—all quiet. He'd discounted the stillness when he'd first noticed it earlier in the day, but its significance didn't register on him until now.

A pang of fear dropped into his stomach. He scrambled through the front door of the lounge into the stark sunshine and heat. No vehicles cluttered the parking lot. He jogged to the adjacent motel lobby and peered through the window. There was no one behind the desk. He ran out into the usually busy highway and searched both directions. As far as he could see, not a single vehicle threatened to mow him down. He was utterly alone.

Breathlessly, he re-entered the lounge and approached Magee who was still on his barstool waiting for him to return. He gulped, trying to speak through a parched throat. He found his beer mug on the bar and took a swig before facing Magee again. "Am I ... dead?"

"No, not exactly."

"Not exactly? That's hardly reassuring ... or even logical. But if I'm not dead, then the crash must be an illusion."

"No, the accident is quite real, I assure you."

Anson found that bit of news disturbing. "When did it happen?"

"I believe it is ongoing."

"Then, am I here ... or am I there at the site?"

"You are here when you're here and there when you're there. Technically there is neither a here nor a there, only now. Space and linear time are an illusion."

"That makes no sense."

"Only because you believe in hard-core corporeality." Magee had taken on a calm, ageless, professorial demeanor, and the cocky fighter-pilot youthfulness of the day had vanished. Apart from the uniform, he hardly looked like the same man.

"What's going on?" Anson asked.

"It will take some time to adjust. As I was saying, the physical body is finite, soul is eternal. The part of you that is you per se, the essential you, is tethered to wherever you place your attention. So if you are viewing a 'here,' you are here, wherever you are. Just so you know, your soul is still keeping the body alive while you project your consciousness here for our exchange."

"Sounds confusing."

"It isn't important to understand it, only to glean what you can from the experience."

A noisy dizziness started to roar back into Anson's skull. *Just breathe*, he told himself. Magee nodded encouragement. The sensation passed. "Why am I not … there?"

"Can you imagine a worse place to be, given the little bit you know about what the accident did to you? Might as well take a break and enjoy yourself."

That sounded reasonable to Anson, if reason still applied. "So why am I *here*?"

"Do you mean to ask why did you choose the Oklahoma Panhandle as your setting?" The corners of Magee's mouth barely twisted upward, but his eyes did all the smiling. "It's the best place you can imagine being."

"Why not England? I've been popping in and out of there all day long."

"Something about England won't allow your attention to stay there. Oklahoma, as you've described it to me, is where your life was beginning to come together. It was temporary though not perfect—you didn't mean for it to go on forever. But you met a nice woman here. You had an income, a roof over your head. You could finally relax and transition into the life you always wanted."

"I called it a 'stop-gap.'"

"An apt term."

A concept sprang up from his childhood religious training. "So this is Limbo?"

"You might call it that. More like a waiting room or intersection without the religious encumbrances."

"That implies a decision, a change in direction."

"Yes."

Interesting, Anson thought. "A decision about what?"

"That remains to be seen."

Another idea occurred to Anson. It made sense now that he thought about it, the way the fighter pilot had grown younger throughout the day, the way he'd stepped out of the Magee persona altogether. There were other clues that he'd only vaguely noticed or had chosen to ignore. The magical mystery tour of a mountain-rimmed lake in an antique plane should have provided a hint—he could see that now.

"Are you ... dead?" An Englishman rarely asked such a blunt question, but Anson figured the dead weren't so easily offended.

"No need to be squeamish. My physical life as an American-born, English-raised, Canadian-trained pilot came to an end. My soul exists as we speak."

"How did it happen?"

"When my plane hit the Oxford, I jumped but my parachute failed to open in time."

"That had to have been horrifying."

Magee shrugged. "Those last few seconds were rough, but it was over in a heartbeat. I'll spare you the details."

"Lovely, cheers." Anson shook his head. He couldn't believe he was being subjected to this odd turn of events.

"You have to understand—this experience is happening because of you, not me."

"Me? Why?"

"That will probably start revealing itself soon."

"Are you an angel?"

"Heavens, no."

"Then, what are you?"

"Suffice it to say I am an echo of who I was on earth, and yet I am the greater part of myself. You can continue to think of me as John Magee."

"But you are dead." Magee's cryptic responses weren't providing answers quickly enough for Anson.

"Just to set the record straight, no one truly dies."

He had no choice but to accept the premise. There was no explanation for any of this, and all evidence—such as it was—seemed to ring true. "Let me try one more question: Why have you come to me?"

"That is a good question. I assume it's to tell you John Magee's life story."

Admittedly Anson was becoming curious now about how it worked, death. "Tell me, what was it like?"

"I experienced a similar transitional period. The setting for me was Shangri-la, from the novel I'd read, *Lost Horizon* by James Hilton. Had a profound effect on me."

"Oh, yes. You talked about that." Anson hadn't been interested when Magee first discoursed on it, but it interested him now.

"Shangri-la, you'll recall, was the Tibetan haven of immortality and serenity, a place to hibernate among the world's cultural treasures while the war and destruction passed. That's all I had wanted in life, a quiet corner of the world where I could exercise my intellect and pursue the woman I loved. England was just such a pastoral place, but it was under siege, and its imagery was damaged for me as a postmortem sojourn."

"You say you craved a quiet intellectual life, yet your tendencies ran to the contrary. You actually sought out danger and physical challenge."

"That's just it, you see. I was at odds with myself, and that was something I had to examine when my life underwent a review in Shangri-la. In the novel, Hilton wrote something that imprinted on my psyche, though I didn't understand it at the time I read it. The high lama in the story told the hero that one of the first steps toward clarifying the mind is to obtain a 360-degree panoramic view of one's own past. Self-examination is difficult to do because of our bias to protect ourselves, but it is made much easier in our respective sanctuaries. Hilton wrote that when the hero had been in Shangri-la long enough, he would find his 'old life slipping gradually into focus as through a telescope when the lens is adjusted. Everything would stand out still and clear, duly proportioned and with its correct significance.' Works the same way here in the in-between."

Anson couldn't imagine anything more tedious, whiling away an eternity thinking about his earthly past. "Are you saying this is my Judgment Day?" He felt more than a little anxious. "I haven't exactly been a saint or an angel the last thirty-odd years."

Magee laughed. "Sainthood isn't accomplished overnight, and people on earth aren't supposed to be angels. Angels aren't angels either, at least not the way they're perceived earth-side, anyway. You're looking at human life through the construct of man-made, religious morality. No one is entirely good or entirely evil. Both tendencies exist simultaneously."

"But you didn't answer the question."

Magee shrugged. "Yes, you have been given the rare gift of a mid-life review from a higher perspective."

"What happens if I don't pass?"

"There won't be an exam at the end." The smile that wasn't a smile appeared again. "The rub is, we are faced with a paradox. Here in the in-between we can view our lives unemotionally, but we have no way of remedying the flaws or implementing what we've learned. Or, rather, we do, but it takes a very long time. On earth we can learn from our mistakes and make adjustments, but we don't have the information or detachment to change that easily. You have the best of both worlds and an opportunity to make a course correction like any good pilot."

"Whatever for? You just told me everything was going well … at least until it was abruptly stopped by gravity."

"Was your life truly going well?"

"You tell me what happened, then we'll both know."

"I wasn't living your life, Avroe."

That tears it! Anson grabbed a cue stick and slammed the table with it so hard that it broke in half. The part he wasn't holding ricocheted off Magee's chest, but the pilot-ghost didn't flinch. "I'm getting tired of these dribs and drabs of information," Anson shouted.

Magee placed his hands on his hips. "Anger serves you as a survival tactic, I see. You rely on it as a stimulant to motivate yourself and anyone around you who falls short of your standards. Is this not correct?"

Anson couldn't argue the point. "Chalk it up to a father in the military."

"Perhaps," Magee said. "I suspect your propensity toward anger sabotages your ambitions, your dreams, your relationships—virtually everything."

"You said you know nothing about me."

"If you haven't seen it already, we're alike, you and I. I'm here to help you to see that."

"What's the point?"

Magee exhaled and approached him. "There is a slim chance you might return to that lifeline, and if you do you need to be prepared."

"Prepared? For what?"

"We're both on need-to-know, Avroe."

He didn't like it, yet it seemed he had no choice but to go along with whatever this process was. "What do I have to do?"

"You've already begun. You need to go back for a longer look but this time with more deliberateness and control."

"How do I do that if I can't remember?"

"Fair enough. Let's start this way … do you have a prevailing question you want answered?"

"I suppose I'd like to know if I will be successful in my career as a pilot," he said.

"That's fortune telling. Doesn't fly in the in-between. Come on, I know there's something burning a hole in your skull or you wouldn't be here."

He considered a moment. "I would like to know what caused my accident. No … ." Anson raised a finger. "I'd like to know what the bloody hell happened to Vivianne."

"That is a good start. Amnesia is an illusion in the in-between, and, frankly, an excuse. You can't move on until you clear that up."

He let out a sigh of displeasure, fed up with the metaphysical mumbo jumbo, not to mention being held at the mercy of some invisible force and awaiting his fate. "Tell me what to do."

"Very well. Hold Vivianne's image in your mind's eye. Imagine yourself being with her as if your very life depends upon it. Pinpoint your attention on your single-most desire to see her."

As soon as Anson closed his eyes, a hurried montage of Vivianne images began tumbling in his mind—all the times he'd flown with her, made love with her, laughed with her, fought with her, watched her sleeping. The Vivianne memories balled up and overlapped one another. With effort, he managed to stretch the pictures into a row like a slideshow, but then the Viviannes moved past his mental viewfinder so rapidly that each dissolved into the next. He failed to freeze a single frame.

"You're trying too hard," Magee said. "Why don't you go back to your last memory of her? And when you succeed, just be the observer. The events have already taken place. You won't be able to change them even if you wanted to."

"Sounds Dickensian. Ghosts of girlfriends past, and all that."

"Where do you think he got the idea? By the way, you don't need to close your eyes unless it helps."

"It does help." Anson peered into the darkness again, and eventually the black screen elongated into a tunnel with a light at the end of it. He heard a cacophony of church bells ringing in the distance, and the sound pulled him through the tunnel. Vivianne slowly came into view, sitting in her usual place in the flickering glow of the fireplace at the Yardarm in Norwich, England. She was reading a London rag and sipping a cup of tea. The date on the newspaper read Wednesday, 25 February, 1981. For reasons Anson could not yet recall, it was a critical day in their relationship. This image of Vivianne instantly triggered a river of memories that began flowing through his mind with vivid clarity and in proper order.

21

The Gypsy's Prediction

IT WAS A crisp, sunny day in early October, 1980, when Anson hastened Vivianne from Heathrow Airport to Victoria Station via the Underground and up the stairs into the chaotic streets of London. He splurged for a taxi to King's Cross, where they would eat lunch and then board the train north to Norfolk. The taxi took them past the parks and statues of Buckingham Palace and through the shopping district of Oxford Street. Vivianne swiveled between windows in the back of the cab, verbally enthralled by the mix of modern and antique buildings, the throng of people on every corner, the miniature-ness of the old and the towering of the new. Tears came to his eyes as he watched her open the gift that was his country, for he'd been estranged from home far too long.

It was a triumphant homecoming for him, carrying a fattened pilot's logbook in his luggage and towing a budding American journalist in his wake. He was both apprehensive and optimistic about his future, worried that he wouldn't be able to find more pilot work yet encouraged that he was at least moving forward with his five-year plan. Apart from a lightly-packed, oversized suitcase, Vivianne traveled with her heavy camera bag and a zippered portfolio displaying her newspaper clippings from the *Daily Record*. He meant to show her off like a trophy, and his honor depended in part on the face she presented to his world.

After a pub lunch and a couple of pints, Anson yanked Vivianne away from neck-craning in London and whisked her to northern Norfolk via the King's Lynn train to meet his parents.

He recalled the tension he felt as they tried to absorb this curio their only son had brought home from America. Vivianne seemed to enjoy their hospitality, but he found them subtly reticent to give their stamp of approval, leery that this young foreign woman would distract him from paying debts now that his career had finally taken off. He was disappointed they didn't know him better than that.

Visiting his parents provoked his anxiousness to become airborne again. But it was autumn—the season when fields are tilled and put to bed and crop-spraying is forgotten until spring. He decided to make the most of this hiatus and show Vivianne a bit of East Anglia, and he was happy to do so. With luck they'd both be able to find some kind of work to support themselves, having arrived with just a few hundred dollars of Vivianne's insurance money. To that end Anson ushered Vivianne into the city of Norwich to avail himself upon the mercy of friends.

———

Vivianne exited the taxi and paused to peruse the Yardarm wedged between a derelict shoe factory and a row of blocky government buildings. It was a stark contrast to the castle and city center they'd driven past to arrive here. "Looks like a run-down gingerbread house for grown men," she said.

Anson couldn't tell if she was being sarcastic or enchanted, such was her dry humor. He gazed upon his pub. "Yes, I see it. Sort of a shoebox covered in ginger-biscuit masonry. A pitched roof layered with icing shingles and a gumdrop chimney on top. If it weren't for the beer barrels stacked around the perimeter, I'd say it was very nearly edible."

"Oh, you don't eat it," she said. "You drink it." Anson pulled the suitcases from the trunk of the cab and set them on the curb, while she reached for her camera bag. "I've got to get a picture."

"Time for that later. Now, before we go inside I must warn you not to be offended. The owner's a bit gruff." The bell on the door jingled as he opened it and led her into the pub. A round man with a mop of brown hair was pulling a pint of ale with one of the wooden handles on the bar. He placed the mug in front of a male patron and then eyed the newcomers. "We're closing soon."

"I've been away to America for three years, and this is all the man says to me," Anson said. "Vivianne, meet Mack McSorely. He owns the place. Better smile, Mack, or she'll think you're being serious."

His old friend showed his teeth. "Pleased to meet you, Vivvy dear. I'm just taking the piss out of the tosser." He fetched two glasses from the shelf. "What are you drinking?"

"She tends toward the darks. What do you recommend?"

"I have a lovely stout from Belgium unless the lady prefers a Guinness."

"I do," Vivianne said. She'd already acquired a taste for it.

"And perhaps a brown ale from Newcastle for the gentleman?"

Anson rubbed his hands together. "I'd like it in my mug." He winked at Vivianne to appease the look of confusion on her face, while Mack unhooked Anson's pewter stein from a long row of mugs lining the back of the bar. "Pour yourself a pint of whatever you like, Mack," he added.

"Oh, you're in money now," Mack said.

"Had a lucrative flying job in Oklahoma. Vivianne worked on the newspaper there as the energy and agriculture editor."

Mack looked impressed. "Is that so?"

"Soil and oil reporter, the paper called it," she said.

"She's being modest," Anson said. "Quite a photographer too. Show him your portfolio, sweetheart."

"Another time, perhaps," she said.

Anson scanned the pub's bare-wood floors, nicotine-stained walls, and smoke-black ceilings. The smooth, wooden bar, worn from decades of toweling beer spills, felt like a reunion with a long-lost lover. "Ah, everything looks just as I left it," he said. "Mack built this place from practically nothing, Vivianne."

"Oh?" She leaned forward to hear more.

Mack's eyes lit up, and he rested his elbows on the bar. "I managed a pub not too far from here, but I was fed up with making another man rich while I worked for wages. I scouted around and found this pub, only it didn't look like this. Built a hundred years ago, it had been closed for a couple of decades and the building condemned. I applied for a license to it, and my customers from the other pub helped me refurbish it to its present glory. The floor and bar are original. Everything else we installed."

"What does yardarm mean?" she asked.

Mack explained that, traditionally, ship captains didn't sanction alcohol consumption until the sun crossed the yard-arm—the upper horizontal spar from which hang the square sailcloths—around eleven a.m. in the Atlantic. "We're near the River Wensum, which connects Norwich to the North Sea via several tributaries. I believe the pub first catered to sailors and merchants."

"Now he serves lorry drivers and Bentley owners alike," Anson added. "All threads off the same sailcloth, independent thinkers and wunderkinds in our own way."

"That's rather poetically put," Mack said.

"I'm glad to be home." The brown ale from Newcastle was already making Anson feel warm and nostalgic.

"The sign on the building says the pub is a free-house," Vivianne said. "What does that mean?"

"Well, it means I'm not tied to nationally-franchised breweries and am free to sell ale made by independents," he replied. "The Yardarm offers the best and rarest 'real' ales made with traditional ingredients and methods. I'm building a brewery in the ground floor of the cottage next door."

That piqued Anson's interest, but the bell on the door interrupted his response. The three of them looked up to see a woman with bleached-blonde hair wearing a tight, pink sweater over a cornucopia of curves.

"Ah, Portia, my love!" Anson stood and crossed to her with open arms. "You're looking fit."

"Anson Roe, I can't believe it's you," Portia said. She hugged him and turned her face so that he could peck her cheek. She then noticed Vivianne and surveyed her from her thick, black hair to her scuffed boots. "Who's this?"

"Portia, I'd like you to meet my girlfriend from America, Vivianne." He squeezed Vivianne's shoulders and grinned.

She stood to shake Portia's hand. They exchanged pleasantries like two felines circling each other before an attack. Portia then spotted the luggage near the door. "You're not thinking of staying with us, are you, Anson?"

Anson feigned offense. "I was thinking no such thing."

"I'd keep an eye on him," she said to Vivianne.

Anson watched as question marks formed on Vivianne's face. "Oi, I'm a full-fledged aerial sprayer now. She's a reporter on sabbatical from her newspaper in Oklahoma. Both of us will be searching for comparable work until spraying jobs open in the spring. I'm afraid we may need to go to London until then, though I'd like to show Vivianne a bit of East Anglia. And I'm curious about this brewery of yours."

Anson knew that Portia didn't like other women underfoot, and she didn't like anyone taking advantage of her. Even so, she was business minded. He hoped she might see a way to work Anson and Vivianne to her advantage. She looked at her husband, who shrugged in turn. "We can use the help," Mack said. "You can take the room upstairs for ten pounds a week and work the pub for a pound an hour."

"As long as it's temporary." Portia scrutinized Vivianne again and finally gave her a tight smile.

"I suppose that's fair." The situation wasn't ideal, Anson thought, but they had few choices. Vivianne nodded approval despite looking dubious. He knew she would later comment on his making arrangements without warning her in advance. He would tell her that they were in his country now, and it was up to him to find accommodations for them both.

The McSorely family lived in a flat above the pub, which opened into the adjoining, gutted cottage used mainly for storage and spill-over from the pub. Their little room was tucked off a large hall where the folk singers and chess club met every week. The room had a window with a view of a tree-lined courtyard below, but it was unheated and barely larger than the square footage of a double-sized mattress on the floor. Their thin wooden door could not be locked except by a hook from the inside, which Vivianne later fussed did little to block noise or intruders. They were given access to a bathroom to be shared with the McSorely children and space in the pub kitchen to cook and store food items. It all suited Anson, and Vivianne seemed eager to embrace the adventure.

———

Anson didn't recognize the young woman who approached him at the tea stall in the Norwich Provisions Market until she collapsed her black brollie and grinned at him. He bent to greet Vivianne with a kiss. "Your nose is cold," he said. "Just like an

English girl's. Is that new?" He looked over the gray, knee-length coat with brass buttons down the front.

"Sort of. Paid two pounds for it. Do you like it?"

"Hmm. Looks a bit frumpy."

She'd followed his advice to buy anything she needed upon arrival with some of the money she'd brought from Oklahoma. "What do you expect me to do? The U.S. dollar is useless when converted into British pound sterling and even further diminished by Britain's inflated cost of living. I'm worried I won't be ready for the cold, damp weather, and you told me not to buy anything too trendy."

"I suppose it will do," he said. "Oh, I've brought you a prezzie." He reached into the pocket of his tweed coat and pulled out a brown paper bag.

She looked inside. "An eggplant?"

"We call it an aubergine. It's in honor of your Thanksgiving. Couldn't find a pumpkin."

"Oh! How sweet of you." She smiled and placed the dark purple vegetable into her macramé bag, looking perplexed.

"Cuppa cha, my love?"

"Dying for one."

They'd been in Norwich for more than a month, and he felt satisfied with the way she'd adapted. He was driving a taxi now, and they'd only seen each other in passing the past few days. They'd planned this late-afternoon rendezvous, but he had only thirty minutes or so before he had to make himself available to evening commuters.

The tea stall operator poured a steady stream of milky-brown liquid from a large pail across rows of teacups placed over a grate. He then shoveled out sugar in much the same wholesale fashion. Anson realized how funny that must look to her. "Bowl of mushy peas to go with it?" he asked.

She wrinkled her nose. "Mint jelly or no, I don't think I will ever get used to that stuff. I'll just settle for a scone. Buy yourself a bowl, though."

They enjoyed their tea while standing at the counter of the mushy pea stall and watched pedestrians trying unsuccessfully to avoid getting drenched in the downpour. "How old do you suppose this market is?"

He looked down the long aisle of canopy-covered booths, knowing there were about 200 such stalls on the square. "I believe the market has been on this site continuously for at least 900 years. The city became a major wool-trading hub for East Anglia about a thousand years ago, but its history dates back at least 2,000 years."

She shook her head and laughed. "For the past week I've been roaming through museums, churches, and the castle, and everyone says: 'This building is older than your constitution, dearie.'"

"Stating the obvious."

"It's the emphasis on 'constitution' that catches my ear, as if there's some resentment left over from the Revolution."

"Nah, they're making sure you're not feeling too arrogant. What will you explore next?"

"I'm conducting a study on whether it's true, that Norwich has a pub for every day of the year and a church for every Sunday."

"Ho, that sounds like a worthwhile project."

"I love it here. This morning I went downstairs early when no one else was awake. As I was building a fire, I noticed a truck pull up and deposit two glass bottles of milk at the front door. We haven't had our milk delivered that way since the sixties, and ours is homogenized. I scooped off the cream at the top and poured it over a bowl of Mandarin orange wedges."

"One of our many culinary pleasures," Anson said. English food was a point of pride for him.

"I wouldn't go that far. After breakfast Portia handed me a long grocery list for her pub lunch menu. Had to go to five different specialty shops for it all. I helped her make sandwiches and then ate a buttered sausage roll with some crisps. You can keep the pâté and mackerel." She made a face at the thought. "Worked the lunch session and practiced my accent."

He had advised her to study the accent, suspecting her shortened vowels and softened consonants rankled his mother's ears. "Careful not to go too broad."

"I'm not sure what that means."

"Don't pick up too much of the local dialect," Anson said. "What else did you do?"

"When the pub closed at two, I walked to town with my twine market bag and wandered through the winding streets, inhaling the aromas from the chocolate factory and rummaging through antique and thrift stores. Got the coat and umbrella today."

"You've had your exercise, then."

"Glad we got the little electric heater for the room. I'm freezing."

"You'll have to grow a layer of fat to stave off the cold."

"Beer and scones will probably help," she said, scrunching a corner of her mouth in self-admonition. "But Portia is worried I'm losing weight."

"She would. How are you getting along with them?'

"Well, Mack is full of stories of Viking-like aggression. He never changes his clothes, and if the ale-induced gas builds up inside him, he naturally lets it go without consideration for anyone around him. He has the same control over his mouth—the more vulgar, the better."

"He's an acquired taste, I know. One of my closest friends. That's why I brought you to him."

"So, did you hear what happened last night?"

Anson wrinkled a brow as he frowned. "Hear about what?"

"This guy made a rather crude pass at me."

"Bound to happen in a nearly all-male pub." He finished off the peas and wiped his mouth with a serviette. "I assume you took care of yourself."

"Didn't give it much thought until I heard that Mack met him outside with a blow to the nose."

"Ho, did he?" He smiled and his eyes brightened in approval. "See? I told you the man is a gem."

"Maybe just a coincidence."

"I don't think so. You've underestimated him. I'm sure Portia didn't like that he had to defend your honor."

"She hasn't said anything, though I'm surprised. Portia feels it her duty to straighten out her husband and everyone else within her purview. One of the bartenders told me that she ridicules people she doesn't like until they stop coming back, particularly women."

"She'll grow to love you once she sees you're not a threat." Anson knew Vivianne was intimidated by Portia, knowing her stay at the pub was probational as a favor to him. To her credit, Vivianne worked hard to get into Portia's favor by making herself useful, settling quickly into a daily routine as bar maid plus errand runner and au pair to the McSorely children.

"Are you covering the evening shift tonight?"

"Thankfully, they don't need me. I think I'll read some in the room and listen to the concert of the city's church bells."

"Good, I don't want anyone else chatting you up while I'm at work," he said, half jokingly.

"If I'm lured downstairs by the noise, I'll be rude and not talk to anyone."

"There's a good girl," he said. "This Saturday we should buy a car at auction so that you're not always on foot."

"Good idea. You think I can learn to drive on the left?"

"Pah! Of course, you can. I have full confidence in you. Got to go. The rain's good for business." He gave her a hug and a kiss on the forehead. "I'll get a curry take-away tonight after my shift," he said, already a few steps down the walkway.

Anson purchased an old Triumph Herald for £150 with Vivianne's insurance money from her burned-out VW Bus. The Herald had only a few months left on its Ministry of Transport tag, which meant that the owner sold it for next to nothing to avoid paying for the required—and expensive—repairs that would make it roadworthy for another year. It wasn't half bad for a Triumph, he'd thought, never mind that it didn't have a reverse gear. Vivianne would have to drive it forward wherever she went until he found someone to fix it. Legally she could drive on her U.S. license for two years, which made her popular among newfound friends who hadn't yet passed the stiff examination required of citizens.

Much to her annoyance, he inaugurated the car with a beer-drenched hunting spree of pheasant in an outlying Norwich neighborhood. He aimed a shotgun out one back window and then the other, while Vivianne drove and shouted her alarm. After that, they followed tamer pursuits on their days off, moseying along the winding hedgerow-lined lanes of Norfolk, visiting his friends and touring the sights. All said, she imbibed in England in large gulps, and he found that gratifying.

––––––

On New Year's Eve Vivianne stormed into the bar section of the Yardarm where Anson was washing a number of pint-sized beer glasses. Her fists were clenched by her side and her face was pinched, but she kept her tone even-keeled. "I've just received a person-to-person call from my father."

Smiling to himself, he reached for a bar towel and wiped his wet hands. "Oh, what did he have to say?"

"Don't play coy with me, English. Apparently you awakened him in the middle of the night to ask his permission to marry me."

"Oh, come now. It was four in the morning there ... hardly the middle of the night. But is that a crime? I should think you'd be pleased. Flattered at the very least."

"I think you're testing me."

He tossed the towel aside and began placing the clean glasses on the shelves. The Yardarm would open in an hour, and he didn't want to row with her right now. Even so, he was thankful Mack and Portia were out for the afternoon and that they had the pub to themselves in case there was shouting.

Vivianne stood her ground. "I deserve an answer."

"So do I."

"I'm not ready to marry you, especially not after you've tried to manipulate me by going through my father. What did he say to you?"

"That it was your decision to accept my proposal."

"That's right. And not only that, you haven't actually proposed." She pulled her hands to her hips. "I want to know why you're forcing this when we're so unsettled."

"Very well." She was correct—he didn't trust that she was in England to explore their relationship for a lifetime commitment, and he was growing more frustrated by the day. "Frankly, you're becoming a worry, dear."

Shock crossed Vivanne's face. "What? I've been working hard for Mack and Portia. We came here on my money."

"Yes, but that's gone now ,and you earn barely a pittance."

"You help spend the money, mostly on beer for your friends."

He didn't want to defend his social style right now with more important matters at hand. "My parents are increasingly concerned with the enormous debt I still owe for flight school, and they're worried about what will become of you when I begin working on the opposite side of the country or the world. They're pressuring me to encourage you to get some kind of real job or, barring that, to go home to America. I don't agree with them, but I don't want to be distracted when I resume flying."

"I'm not a citizen, and I don't have a national insurance number that makes me legal to work. You know that."

"We've been in England for three months now, and you haven't even tried to figure out something. It's as if you've lost your aspirations." He'd been catching whispers from people—most loudly from Portia—that writing stories about bugs in Oklahoma did not a real journalist make. He'd defended her by saying she had to start somewhere, but now he was beginning to wonder.

Vivianne started to say something when the door's bell announced Mack's entrance. "Ah, Vivvy. Just the woman I was hoping to see." He rested the box he was carrying on the bar and began unloading supplies for the evening's party.

"This isn't the time, Mack," Anson said. He knew what his friend was going to say, and he was beginning to have second thoughts about a scheme they'd cooked up together.

"Only take a minute. Anson tells me you're willing to give me your return ticket to America in exchange for a job here to help promote the brewery.

"What?" If she'd been shocked before, she was horrified now. "Anson, how could you? That's my ticket home. I don't even know if it's possible to transfer it to another person."

"Oh." Mack's face dropped. "That's all I needed to hear." He glared at Anson. "The deal is off." He disappeared into the kitchen.

"You should have gone along with the story," Anson scolded. "You could have had room, board, and a wage here while I'm gone, but now he will never trust either one of us."

"Who pays for a job, anyway?" With tears streaming down her face, Vivianne fled from the pub for their room upstairs.

"It was just meant to be a token of your loyalty to him," he yelled after her with no response. He'd leave her alone to lick her wounds, and he'd make up for it that night. Maybe it wasn't the best idea to offer Mack the ticket now that he thought about it, but he'd felt there was no other way to help her stay in England.

Vivianne got his message anyway. New Year's Day sparked fresh resolutions and ideas for her. All she could do, she told him, was what was right in front of her. One idea included freelancing an article on Mack's piecemeal brewery he was building, which would put them back in his good graces.

She pulled together an outfit of odds and ends and called on editorial staff at local print media. The city editor of the largest newspaper in Norfolk was more interested in her personal story than in hiring her or buying freelance articles. With Norwich itself being surrounded by agriculture, the newspaper ran a small feature on her reporting job in Oklahoma, complete with a three-column photo of her. Another publication agreed to a speculative story on Mack's brewery and, much to her chagrin, ran the article she wrote under a staff reporter's by-line without paying or crediting her. Surrendering, she settled for a job as a waitress for low, unreported wages and tips in an American-style steak house where, she told him in amazement, the customers ate burgers with knives and forks. It wasn't what he'd hoped for, but at least she would earn more in tips than what the MacSorelys paid her.

By February Anson was finally landing short-term flying jobs around the country, first in Kent and then near Brighton. He was beginning to receive inquiries about aerial spraying work in

Kenya, Libya, and the Sudan. Although nothing was confirmed, it made more urgent the decision of what she would do with herself while he was away for weeks and months at a time. When she had a couple of days off in a row, she drove down to Southern England in her Triumph Herald to visit him. Then, just like that, he was back in Norfolk spraying crops around Norwich.

Despite a happy reunion, Anson's growing frustration with her created more tension between them. As long as she stalled her decision, he felt unresolved and incomplete. Portia and Mack had allowed Vivianne to remain in their little room while he was away, but Portia let him know that her patience was running thin. Now that he was back, it was clear that their relationship was not returning to normal.

————

One evening in late February, Anson and Vivianne attended a large house party together where there was free-flowing alcohol. A young woman from Anson's past cornered him while Vivianne involved herself in conversation in another room. He could not recall this woman being so attentive, and he found her quite enticing in her short, tightly-fitting red dress. They sat together on the carpet and shared a party-sized can of beer. Before long she snuggled under his arm, and he didn't dissuade her. That's when Vivianne spotted them together. She came at him like a lioness and splattered his face with wine. After wiping his eyes on his shirtsleeve, he looked around to find everyone staring at him. Mack laughed in amusement, while Portia frowned with displeasure. The girl in the red dress bolted. Vivianne vanished.

When he crept downstairs the following morning, he found her reading the newspaper in front of the fireplace. He made himself a cup of tea and sat with her at the table. She held up the broadsheet in front of her to avoid looking at him. The dateline on the paper was the twenty-fifth of February, 1981.

The headline touted the engagement announcement of Prince Charles to Lady Diana the previous day. The royal courtship had been playing out in the tabloids for months, but Anson barely gave it a thought. He suspected Vivianne was tracking on the developing romance and perhaps contrasting it to her own relationship with him. On the page that faced him was an article about an American husband and wife team becoming the first hot air balloonists to sail over the geographic North Pole. While Vivianne may have yearned for the princess fairy tale, he craved the more mutually esteemed partnership of the balloonists. He thought Vivianne was just such a partner, but now he wasn't so sure.

He decided to break the silence first. "Portia would like us to move out as soon as … ."

"I assumed she wasn't amused by last night's disastrous performance at the party."

"Where did you sleep?"

"At your friend Robert's house."

"Ah, Lord of the Manor." Anson pictured the tall, stuffy looking man and felt a tinge of jealousy.

Vivianne's eyes widened as she described the fifteenth-century hall on its pastoral estate. Robert had inherited the house and rented rooms to students. "When I escaped the party through the front door, I soon discovered I was locked out of the house. Robert came out and gave me a talking to about English relationships. He said I shouldn't be bothered by what happened."

"Don't know whether I should punch the tosser in the eye or shake his hand. Did you sleep with him?"

"None of your business, though he advised me to keep you guessing. He was quite decent."

"Peerage and money aside, I'm told women aren't attracted to him," he said with confidence.

"Humph!" She hated being predictable. "I did consider it."

"The wine stung my eyes for quite some time, but I'm not going to ask for an apology." He felt entitled to sympathy, especially since her behavior also bruised his ego.

"You want me to apologize? I should think you owe one to me."

"For what, having a drink with a bit-of-stuff?"

She creased her forehead and shook her head. "Maybe you'd be kinder if I became the woman you want me to be. Let it be known that I'm tired of trying to learn the accent and balancing peas on the back of a fork in my left hand. You just want me to be the female version of you."

"I want you to be the woman I know you are." Anson started to say something else but he held his tongue.

Vivianne rested her face in her hand and stared into the distance, perhaps to plan her next line of attack. "You remember that chess master who comes to the pub for tournaments?"

"Nigel, I think his name is. Follows a guru called Ram Somebody. Dark cloud over his head."

"That's him. He asked if England seemed drab to me."

"What did you say?"

"I had no response, but it was like asking a newlywed if the honeymoon is over, and it's not over until someone asks."

"Interesting analogy." Anson could see she had some things to get off her chest.

"I was so happy when we first came here last October. The landscape, the architecture, the history, the language, the 'cheers-lovely-thank you-ta' manners."

"East Anglia isn't even the posh part of the country, but I was pleased to see you enjoy yourself."

"And the rain ... being a creature of high country desert, I can't tell you how exuberant I felt in all the moisture and greenery.

Now the soles of my boots have worn thin, and my feet get wet from the icy rains blowing in from the North Sea every time I cross the river."

"Buy some Wellies."

"It isn't just that. There's a certain pall that hangs over this country, all the people out of work and 'on the dole,' all the factories being imploded. Everyone grieving the death of John Lennon."

"He was gunned down in New York, not here. Look, you're suffering from the winter blues. Wait until you see our English summer."

Vivianne glared at him, for they both knew she wouldn't be there that long. Her six-month visa was due to expire in a matter of weeks. "Now that I've been here a few months, I can see a complacency in this ancient, ready-made world you people are born into. There's no ambition, no spark."

"I beg your pardon," he said in mock offense.

"Okay, you're the exception to the rule. But recently I realized the churches and great halls smell of mold. Those ballads the folk singers wail in the light of dozens of votive candles are beginning to sound like funeral dirges. If it weren't for the punkers with their orange or purple hair livening up the place, I think I'd lose my mind."

"Now, you're just being silly."

"There's more to it than that. Last week I had my palm read by a gypsy woman who blew through the front door of the pub during that snowstorm."

"Surprised Portia didn't sweep her right back out."

"Portia and Mack were out and I was curious, so I invited her to join me at the corner table. I have to say she was the most rancid woman I've ever smelled. The hair under her lacy scarf was gray and dirty. Her skin was as wrinkled as the layers of cotton dresses she wore, and the rings on all her fingers gave her the appearance of being linked to the other world. First thing, she asked me to cross her palm with paper. Not silver, mind you."

"That's inflation for you," he said.

"When I laid a one-pound note in her hand, she said, 'broader.' I gave her another pound and told her that was all I had. She accepted it, reluctantly, and began studying my palm with the practiced eye of a professional. She put on quite a show."

Anson laughed. "Come on … what did she say?"

"Are you sure you want to know?"

"Of course, I do. Unless it's about me." He hated it when she felt a need to choose her words carefully.

She drew in a deep breath, then belted out the gypsy's prediction. "She said that the man I was with was making a fool out of me."

Anson's grin of delight turned into a frown.

"She said that I would be lucky in my career, that I was going to gain a little weight, that I was going to have a son, but that I was unlucky in love."

"Should have paid for the five-pound fortune." He was making a joke, but he stopped when he saw the pain coming through those coppery eyes of hers. Suddenly he realized that something had shifted in her. She wasn't looking at him as adoringly as she had when they'd met the previous summer in Oklahoma. Upon closer scrutiny he saw that she'd changed in the month he'd been away flying. She'd lived and worked without his help, and she'd even cut her hair. *Maybe I've been too hard on her.*

"Why did you come to England?"

"You invited me."

"But why did you want to come?"

"Wanderlust," she answered without a moment's consideration, but he already knew she loved traveling. It was one of her redeeming qualities, and it was how he had enticed her to follow him. Now he couldn't help but feel used.

"Don't get me wrong," she continued. "I wouldn't have come here with just anybody. Even so, I wanted to get out and see the world, explore exotic places to live. If that included love then so much the better. But as you have so clearly stated, living here requires more wherewithal than I have. I was hoping for a miracle job to fall into place, but that takes time and you don't have the patience to wait."

"All I want is for us to be equals and for you to take advantage of your time in England. Make hay while the sun's shining, that sort of thing. I hate waste."

Vivianne nodded. "I've been trying. I've applied to a dozen or more publications all over East Anglia, but no takers, mainly because of the recent demise of two London dailies. I thought I had a chance when one clueless editor asked if I was a member of the National Union of Journalists. I told him I'm an American. He said, 'Oh, you did it that way, did you?' As if I'd chosen to be born there."

"Wouldn't put it past you," he said.

Vivianne shook her head, not enjoying the teasing. "I contacted a photography studio for freelance work and even offered to do an apprenticeship if they didn't want to pay me. The owner said I was 'a bit long in the tooth' for that and also that I should stop rolling my own cigarettes because I look like I've been in 'nic.'"

"Sound advice."

"Get this. Portia suggested I try selling an exposé to a London tabloid. People in this country mistake that for journalism."

"I can see her point."

"Anyway, last week I picked up a magazine of aerial photos of England," she continued. "It reminded me of how I'd fallen in love with aviation when we first met."

"I thought you were just attracted to me."

She scowled, so immune had she become to his charm. "A few days ago when you were spraying the fields nearby, I drove out to watch."

"I didn't see you."

The sad look on her face said to him: "When did you ever really see me?" She shrugged. "It was such a beautiful day, no rain, no wind, and I saw once again the ballet you perform with your plane in the sky. That's when I realized I was envious of your flying. So I headed for the Norwich airport and hired a plane and a pilot for an hour to shoot aerials of the city and countryside."

Her actions amazed Anson. "Y'all gal! How was it?"

Her face brightened. "We flew over the cathedral and the castle and followed the Yare out to the Broads. The green patchwork of farms bordered by clumps of forests and meandering lanes and waterways—beautiful!"

"It is, isn't it?"

"While I was up there, I had an epiphany." She fought back her tears as she spoke. "I am not a member of your special corner of the top one percent. I'm an average girl who thought that if I lived on the edge with you, I would transform into someone who leads a more exciting life than the one I had back home."

"You do lead such a life."

"Yes, but gathering the necessary skills and money takes more than risk. It takes plenty of time to practice and learn from your mistakes. I've decided that while you're at loose ends, I don't have the luxury of doing that here. I have to go home and regroup. Maybe I'll take flying lessons."

Anson's face dropped again. He didn't know whether to be sad or relieved, but he did know that he wasn't ready for her to go. "Tell you what, let's have a nice meal at Lamb's and talk it over." Vivianne agreed and all was forgiven—or so he'd thought. He spent the evening basking in his newfound respect for her. As coincidence would have it, he would be completing his local aerial job the next day. They planned for her to quit her job at the steak and burger restaurant, and they'd take off in the Herald on a tour of France. They'd spend some time together before she left for America and he moved to some exotic location to fly. They retired to their little room early and packed.

When he returned to the Yardarm after spraying his last field the following day, Vivianne's things were gone. She had packed her enormous suitcase and left.

22

ZAGAZIG

"**WHERE DID SHE** go?" John Magee asked Anson when he returned his attention to the Oklahoma lounge setting.

"Back to the States, I discovered later." His excursion into his memories had been disconcerting. He'd experienced the conflicting sensation of being the disengaged observer while lacking the free will to correct his own actions or words. Meanwhile, the sensations that had attended his experiences the first time intensified as he suffered them again.

"Were you able to speak with her about her disappearance?"

"Eventually, yeah. She said she'd outstayed her welcome and didn't want to burden my flying career any longer. Said she needed to face her life rather than run away from it. I had no argument."

"So that was that?"

"We spoke on the phone a few times, exchanged some letters, acted as if we were still in a relationship, albeit a distant one. She said she was trying to devise a way to return to England and live independently. I encouraged her, but I had my doubts."

Anson stood and crossed to the pool table. Until now he had kept his emotions at bay. *What is done is done*, he told himself, only half believing it.

Without notice, all the emotions he'd suppressed in the weeks leading up to the accident came flooding over him now. He doubled over the table in agony.

"The worst has already happened," Magee said. "You might as well let the pain in."

"It's strange. If, as you say, I am not in my physical body, then why does loss feel so much more profound to me now? I'm afraid to say I feel quite overwhelmed."

"Human beings have invented all sorts of measures for warding off emotional pain, including creating a culture that suppresses it. Because you are still associated with your Anson Roe life, you are suffering from your recent traumatic events. What's more, you don't have flesh and bone to act as a buffer and protect you from your emotional reactions."

Anson accepted the explanation, which allowed him to regain his composure somewhat. "Only goes to show how complete the illusion is, I suppose."

Magee grinned. "There's that. So, what happened next?"

Anson turned and faced Magee as his mind began to unwrap more memories. "I soon acquired a flying assignment in Egypt, and about a week before I was to report to Cairo for work, Vivianne rang with a bit of news." He steadied his voice and expression. "Pregnant."

"That's good news, isn't it?"

"Perfectly natural, but it threw a spanner in the works."

"I have no doubt," Magee said dryly.

"I was … am prepared to do the right thing, mind you. I told her that once I settled into my job in Egypt, she should meet me in Cairo, and we would marry. I felt it best that she then move in with my parents in England, at least until the baby arrived."

"And what was her response?"

"She wasn't sure what she was going to do."

"Marriage was out of the question, then?"

"She maintained that we weren't compatible. She didn't think anything would change between us just because we were married co-parents."

"That would never have been accepted in my day, but she makes a sound argument."

"Social mores have relaxed quite a bit in the last forty years. She doesn't strike me as someone who would terminate the pregnancy or resort to adoption, but I disagree with the idea of a baby being raised by a single parent and told her so. She felt that love should be the requisite ingredient for a marriage to work. I argued that it didn't matter, that love would come later."

"You're a traditionalist, are you?

"In matters of marriage, yes."

"Did she accept your answer, that love would come later?"

"You know women—what do you think?"

Magee remained silent and neutral.

"That was the last time we spoke before I left for Cairo." He again wobbled and his knees weakened just thinking about Egypt. Magee and the lounge began to dissolve into a hospital-like scene. Excruciating pain seared through the wounds in his head and face as he fought to avoid this physical reality. An instant later, he was back in the lounge with Magee.

"Steady on, Avroe. If you want to go back into the body then do so. You can't fly at half-mast—your consciousness can't be in both places at once."

"The pain ... I can't describe it."

"I know. The best way to stop transporting yourself all over the cosmos is to keep talking. Focus on the here and now."

Anson exhaled slowly, trying to relax. "Have I lost everything?"

"We can't be certain at this point. It's all in flux. Tell me what you remember about Egypt."

The memory perked up Anson's mood. "Both disgusting and thrilling, hot, dusty, crowded, dirty. I checked into the El Nile Hotel and notified the Greek aerial company that had hired me that I was in country. I had my head and beard shaved by a razor in an underground barber shop to cope with the heat. Within a day or so I relocated to an apartment suite in Zagazig that was maintained by the company. Not long after that, I began flying."

"Do you remember the work you did?"

Anson scratched his head. "Ferrying equipment and spraying crops ... cotton, mostly. Over the first fortnight I'd sprayed about 2,000 *feddans*—a feddan is a 'yoke of oxen' roughly equal to an acre. Roundworms are ubiquitous in the Nile Delta and rather destructive. The job was fairly straightforward until I encountered a problem with one of the fields. Electrical pylons ran right through the center of it, which necessitated that I fly over the lines. That meant that a substantial area nearest the lines would not be covered by chemical."

Another memory pulled him up short, and he was suddenly gripped with apprehension. He glanced at Magee who nodded to encourage him. "I remember arguing with Egyptian agricultural officials in their tent," he continued. "They wanted me to fly below the lines, and I contended that there wasn't enough room. I was so fed up with the heat, the dust, the bloody bureaucratic chiefs, Vivianne's pregnancy, that I may have actually tried flying through the wires."

"*Through* the wires?"

Anson shrugged. "I learned in aviation school that if you approach the wires at an angle, the prop will cut right through them. But I have a terrible feeling the wires may have stretched out in the heat so that when I hit them, the plane became entangled and was slingshotted to the ground." He rubbed the back of his neck as he struggled to recall the details.

"I see. One would assume that hitting the wires would have been problematic for the aerial company. All that lost time awaiting expensive repairs in a disorganized country."

"To be fair, Egypt is becoming quite industrious. Only about four percent of the country is arable and suitable for farming, but the Aswan Dam project enabled Egypt to irrigate nearly two million more acres. Apart from that, it receives boatloads of money from the U.S. every year to keep the Suez Canal open to Israel."

"Israel?"

Anson realized that Magee had died a few years before the end of the British Mandate for Palestine and the establishment of the State of Israel in 1948. "Suffice it to say that tensions in the Arab world have been volatile ever since. Only this past January, Iran released dozens of U.S. diplomatic hostages after they'd spent more than a year in captivity." He paused for a moment as he reviewed history. "You do know we won World War II, don't you? There have been more than a few atrocities since then, and good things too. Mankind has been to the moon, in fact."

Magee shrugged. "If I concentrated on it, I could make myself generally aware of events on earth, but you have to understand that wars and the like are of little consequence in Eternity."

"If it makes so little difference, then why are we even discussing it?"

"Context, my friend. Context." He slapped Anson on the back. "In your case, politics may have played a role in your accident."

Magee's comment triggered another loathsome recollection. "Some of the Egyptian locals were throwing rocks and metal parts at our aircraft. We didn't know if they were protesting the chemicals on their land, or if they were angry with their own government. A farmer is limited to leasing only fifty feddans, for instance."

"Something went wrong, obviously."

"Even if I could remember the accident, I'm not sure I could accept it. Did you remember your own accident?"

"Not at first," Magee said. "I was too shocked. I mean, I had expected to die in the war—I'd prepared for it. I didn't know how it would happen, of course."

"Were you aware of the details of your demise?"

"Yes."

Anson found Magee's candidness and acceptance of his own death perplexing. He spoke the words, stated the facts, yet nothing about his spirit said 'death.' He seemed all the more vibrantly alive. "Is it important that I learn the truth about my, what, near-death?"

"Technically, no, but if nothing else it could give you some peace of mind. Would you be interested in seeing for yourself?"

"I certainly don't want to relive it!"

"No, no. We can watch it from the sidelines."

"We can do that?"

"It's one of my special powers." Magee flashed his signature smile.

"I have to admit, I do have a morbid curiosity, and I can do with some of that peace-of-mind stuff."

"That's the spirit."

Magee touched Anson's elbow, and an instant later they stood chest deep in a vast field of cotton shrubbery. The notorious power lines in question dissected the field, and Anson frowned at the sight of them. He heard a familiar engine roar and snapped his head sideways to see a Cessna Agtruck pull up steeply at the end of the field. The plane banked and looped sharply to align with the next swath.

He turned and looked at Magee in astonishment. "Is that me?"

"Yes, that is you."

Knowing that he himself was piloting the aircraft was nothing less than mind blowing. The familiar anxiety returned as he watched the Agtruck swoop over the plants and release the spray from the nozzles under each wing. The liquid swirled beneath the plane in parallel patterns.

Magee extended an arm across Anson's shoulders. "Well done, Avroe!"

"Not bad a'tall, if I do say so myself." Anson was pleased with his skill, and he was proud to show off a bit to the former fighter pilot. He also remembered being so nervous he'd prang the aircraft that he was never able to relax.

"How fast does she go?"

"Tops out at 120. Stalls at half that speed."

"The nose is, what, nearly ten feet long?"

"Uh huh," Anson answered without taking his eyes off the plane. "That's where the hopper is. Probably carrying a thousand liters of liquid chemical in there."

"I see you're not wearing your helmet."

Anson realized with dread that he had dispensed with the bulky head gear because of the heat.

"Watch what happens next," Magee said.

The Cessna slipped into slow motion as it approached them. The landing gear skimmed the very tips of the plants. He could see the expression of concentration on his own face through the windshield as the plane flew past them and headed directly for the power lines. "Looks like I'm going to try flying beneath them," he shouted to Magee.

About ten feet away from the lines, a handful of black-haired teenage boys popped up between the plants. Instantly, the Cessna lifted to miss the boys. Heavy with a ton of liquid in its hopper, the plane lacked the power and speed to stay horizontal, let alone to climb. The Cessna's stall alarm sounded, and the plane pitched dramatically downward, plowing nose first into the earth in a violent storm of plants, dirt, metal, and fluids. The engine separated from the mainframe and landed dozens of feet away as the propeller, nose, and wing struts crumpled and rose up to be shoved into the front of the cockpit. The sound of scrunching metal was deafening.

Sheer horror consumed Anson as he watched the terrible scene play out before him. "Get me out of here!" he shouted at Magee.

The pilot wrapped an arm across Anson's shoulders, turned him in the opposite direction, and steered him through the cotton plants away from the accident.

23

The Forces of Flight

ANSON STAGGERED FORLORNLY behind Magee like a man convicted by a high court and now sentenced to roam forever in this no-man's land of the in-between. He fought the urge to look back at the devastation. Not that he wasn't curious, but he sensed it best to avoid watching his limp body being dragged from the smoking wreckage. Still, no amount of effort allowed him to control his thoughts. His mind replayed the accident like a short film with alternate endings, each time presenting various ways he might have revised the outcome.

As the two pilots strolled farther away from the crash site, the lush vegetation and citrus trees transitioned into the more familiar cornstalks of Oklahoma, all bowing and swaying in the late-afternoon breezes. "Hard to believe anyone surviving a crash like that," Anson said when he was finally able to speak. "Let alone me." He stopped and bent to support his hands on his knees. "Bloody hell!"

Magee squeezed Anson's shoulder as if to console him. "You sacrificed your own safety to save theirs. That counts for something."

"Wasn't it their intention to kill me? I don't think they cared whether they died in the process or not."

"Imagine the international incident you've averted."

Anson nodded but the sentiment was no consolation. "Can't believe it happened to me. I'm ruined."

"Stop being so dramatic and put it behind you."

"That's a bit stiff-lipped," he said, offended by the man's evident lack of sympathy. "Thought you wanted me to look at what happened in Egypt."

"Examine it for clues into the puzzle that is you, but don't tumble it incessantly in your mind until you go mad. If you decide to rejoin that lifeline, you won't remember the details anyway, so it does no good to dwell on it now."

"If *I* decide? I thought you said the situation was fluid."

Magee shifted his weight. "As I've said, we've been on need-to-know all along. Now, apparently, it's down to you to consider whether you want to return to your life or to move onward. Here's the prickly part—it won't be easy."

"What do you mean?"

"Think about it. You took the full force of the impact in your face. You'll likely have multiple operations, which will irrevocably modify your appearance, and you can also expect to suffer some brain damage. You will live with the injuries for the rest of your Anson Roe lifetime."

This news shocked Anson. "That sounds neither appealing nor fair."

"Fairness doesn't come into it."

"And the alternative?"

"You will be given a completely different corporeal existence."

Anson flinched at the prospect. "A new life? How does that work?"

"You'll have a fresh body, with its own set of talents and drawbacks based on what you've earned and the genetics you're born into. The essential 'you' will remain roughly the same."

"If I believed in reincarnation, which I don't, that doesn't sound half bad."

"I must warn you, however, there is no guarantee that you wouldn't play out a similar scenario in your next incarnation."

"For the sake of argument, I'll accept your premise of being reborn into a new identity, but how do you know what will happen?"

"I've told you before, I can't predict your future, but I do know you. If you choose to move on to another life, you will likely retain most of the tendencies and attitudes you have now, and there is a high probability that you, yourself, will recreate the circumstances by which you will have another devastating, life-altering collision with something very dense."

"By what assessment?"

Magee paused and then continued as if newly inspired. "I presume you are familiar with the theory of flight."

"What? Yes, of course, but … why?"

"Because the basic forces that keep a plane airborne also govern the cosmos," Magee explained in a matter-of-fact manner.

Anson shook his head and glared at Magee in shock. "Either you're mad or this nightmare is actually a drug trip."

"Go on. What are these forces?"

"Lift and gravity, and thrust and drag. Elementary physics." He winced as he thought about it. "Unfortunately, the forces failed to unite properly enough to keep me in flight," he scoffed.

"Ah, your humor has returned at last. And the play of these dual sets of forces is based on what?"

Feeling foolish, Anson raised his palms and opposed them to each other in mock tension. "Sir Isaac Newton's third law of motion … to every action there is an equal and opposite reaction. Where is this leading?"

"It doesn't matter which force is the action and which is the reaction," Magee continued. "They always work in tandem. If a skater pushes a partner, they both move in opposite directions with equal speed. Likewise, you can't have lift without gravity nor thrust without drag. "

"Reminds me of relationships. No wonder Newton died a virgin."

"That's a good place to start. I'm willing to bet that if you asked yourself why Vivianne left, you would immediately present a whole host of rationalizations."

"I don't see what that has to do with Newton, but I can tell you she was unhappy in England, probably because of cultural shock or her stunted career. It could've all been alleviated had she married me. And before you ask why she wouldn't, you'd have to ask her."

"She was working. You pressured her to do more."

"Is that so wrong?"

"We're talking action and reaction here, not right and wrong. Would you deny that you had anything to do with her leaving?"

"Did I drive her away? How would I know? I may have played a role. I do know I put a lot of effort and energy into her, and *she* left *me*."

Magee nodded. "Remember, relationships are mutually inclusive. She put energy into you as well."

"What about her? Wasn't everything that happened to Vivianne her lookout?"

"Absolutely. Vivianne has her own complex of tendencies, and you have yours. Sounds like she condensed a lot of living into a short period of time. It will take her years to realize it, but all the hard prangs she received—which, by the way, she created herself—will motivate her into seeking out her own true nature. Our concern here is you. What if I were to tell you that her leaving was inevitable?"

Anson shrugged. "I'd probably have to agree with you, but it's disheartening, isn't it, the thought of being defeated before getting started simply given our incompatibility." He arched an eyebrow toward his visitor turned mentor. "What are you driving at, exactly? Out with it, man."

"All right. Everything that happens to you has to do with your very own impressions, tendencies, attitudes, and choices, and if not seen for what they are, they rule your life. It comes down to action and reaction." Magee travelled a few steps around Anson as he spoke. "The principle that there can never be an action—or cause—without an equal and opposite reaction—or effect—is the basis for all life on every plane of existence. Not only in the realm of physics, where Newton's third law applies, but also in all human endeavor, all thought, and all emotion."

Anson shook his head. "Are you saying that my thoughts are dictated by a law of physics?"

"I am saying that the cause-and-effect principle is a universal law. Whatever action you take, whatever word you express, whatever thought you create or feeling you emote produces an outcome of equal consequence."

"I understand that a grievous crime could send me to jail. Even yelling fire in a crowded theater can cause havoc. But what you're proposing sounds ludicrous. Thoughts and feelings can be so fleeting and irrelevant."

Magee rubbed his chin like a scientist. "This is the way it works ... whenever something happens to you, you create an impression and store it away. Certain attitudes build up around the impression, which dictate your judgment, which in turn can be a catalyst for specific actions and their corresponding responses. Enough attention devoted to a single theme, backed by enough intense emotion, can elevate a person to power and bring down a nation if not the world. Witness Hitler or the Japanese invasion of China."

"Those are rather extreme examples, wouldn't you say?"

"What is true for one is true for all."

"Give me a relevant example," he growled.

"All right. Wasn't your constant frustration at play in your relationship?"

"All I wanted was to fly—not to worry about a bloody woman."

"Wouldn't you say that part of your frustration stemmed from overstaying your visa in America and losing a year fighting to get your passport back?"

"Yes and yes! I gambled and won, eventually." The pitch of his voice raised an octave.

"Wouldn't you say that you carried your anxieties with you to Egypt?"

Anson blew air in exasperation. "Of course. I was being put through enormous stress and aggravation *caused* by the Egyptians' concern over the amount of chemicals I was or was not spraying on the field. I was worried about the damn power lines and all the other reasons we've discussed. You make it sound like my frustration led to the crash, but you saw for yourself how the locals put themselves in the middle of the flight path. There were larger political forces at work. It … was … not … my … fault!"

"I beg to differ." Magee's gentleness turned stern. "Let's start with not wearing your helmet. How about that shot of Dutch courage you knocked back before you started your day? Or the binge you and your colleagues went on the previous evening? Wouldn't it be fair to say these causes initiated by you had some effect on your reflexes during flight?"

"Might have done, but now you're blaming the victim." His defenses went on red alert again. "Do you want me to feel guilty about something that was beyond my control?"

Magee didn't let up. "Then there's the devil-may-care attitude you have toward machinery in general, the breakneck speeds at which you race a car or fly a plane without any concern for others or any forethought as to what might lie ahead."

"I've always had full confidence in my abilities to control any mode of transport I command." As soon as he said it, he realized he'd been proven wrong in Egypt. He felt sick to his stomach.

"It's all part of the larger picture. These attitudes catch up with us. You've heard the adage, 'you die the way you live.' Cause and effect, full stop."

"You were exactly the same way, 'beating up' unsuspecting farms and villages from the airspace over Canada and Great Britain." He was fuming now.

Magee nodded. "And you know the effect of that cause."

"What about the poor bloke you slammed into with your Spitfire?"

"It's tragic but I can't speak for him. Perhaps he'd led his entire life in a fog, completely oblivious to his surroundings. On the other hand, I can't blame him for being in the wrong place at the wrong time."

"You were both victims of poor timing, as was I."

"That is one way of looking at it. My point is that seemingly random events will organize themselves to fulfill our tendencies, choices, and attitudes, even if the cause isn't obvious."

Anson stopped his line of argument, suddenly understanding Magee's point. "Are you saying that my plane accident is the result of karma?" He rolled his eyes. "My generation is familiar with the overused saying: 'What goes around comes around.'"

"Don't dismiss it just because it's cliché. Karma is the traditional word for cause and effect. Eastern religions describe several kinds of karma based on the causes a person creates every day or has stored up over lifetimes. The Christian principle of 'reaping what you sow' is a simplified version of cause and effect. The biblical concept of 'an eye for an eye' is a metaphor for cause and effect, which became the basis for equitable crime and punish-ment laws and degenerated into a misguided creed for retaliation. The Greeks debated endlessly over modes of causality, complete with complex mathematical equations. Humanity didn't invent the concept. It merely tried to explain a universal principle."

Anson's head began to spin over Magee's take-no-prisoners interrogation and moral lecturing. He held up his hands in sur-render. "I've never abided by such religious concepts," he said.

"We're talking science, not religion. But you're right, it does no good to get entangled in the weeds. All said, earth-made labels perpetuate preconceived notions that are not necessarily accurate or applicable, not to mention that they muddy the waters with dogma. What's important is seeing the principle at work in your own life."

"So, what about the teenagers I nearly hit in the field? Do they have to pay retribution in this cause-effect system of yours?"

"The principle is not about paying retribution—it's simply about an initial cause and its resulting effect. Be that as it may, if the locals don't charge them with a crime, I'm sure they will be held responsible at some point in their lives with an event of equal weight, and if not during this life, then another. Who knows? They may have been mere actors in your karmic play. I'm not asking that we take their side on this, only that you see your part."

"Am I being punished by a sort of cosmic judicial system? If so, I'd like to speak to the judge."

"Again, it's not a matter of sin and punishment, nor good deed and reward for that matter. Karma seems random, but that is because it is impersonal and has its own ledger of checks and balances. The pendulum appears to swing between good and bad, but it is simply reacting to the hand that pushes it. As Goethe wrote: 'So divinely is the world organized that every one of us, in our place and time, is in balance with everything else.' The scheme is exact."

Anson stroked his beard. "I've made some mistakes, but I don't see how I deserved what has happened to me."

"You're quite certain of that? We don't always know when or where the original cause takes place. It all comes down to attitude and choice in the end."

"Sounds like a lot of malarkey to me."

Magee took in a deep breath and continued to explain. "I'm talking about the attitudes you develop after something happens to you. Feeling like a victim is an attitude. Feeling as though you are blameless in any situation is an attitude. As long as you see yourself as the brunt of some random cause, you remain a victim of the resulting effects. As long as you feel you are owed something, you will remain shortchanged and devoid of any power to alter your situation. You've learned nothing from your experience at that point."

Anson raised an index finger and opened his mouth to defend himself but found he had nothing to add. He closed his mouth and lowered his flag. "That's me told." He sank to his knees feeling defeated and bereft. He covered his face with both hands and bent to the ground in sudden pain as reality crashed down on him. *What have I done?*

"Now we're getting somewhere," Magee said enthusiastically. "Don't take it so hard, Avroe."

Anson looked up and raised an eyebrow. "What? I thought you wanted remorse from me."

"Seeing your own cause is important, but repenting achieves little in the in-between. Follow me." He turned and began pushing through a forest of stalks laden with ripened ears of corn. Anson exhaled audibly, stood, and followed on the pilot's heels. Magee shoved aside one last stalk to reveal a slowly-rotating wheel suspended in air and constructed from a material that was at once industrial-strength, translucent, and luminous. The wheel was so tall, its top was shrouded by an upper atmospheric haze. The countless chairs around its perimeter appeared to be empty.

"What have we here?"

"A Ferris wheel—or a soul wheel, as it were."

"What I mean is, why is it here?" he asked.

Magee continued in his professorial persona. "The wheel is the composite you. Each carriage represents an aspect of your psyche, which is fixed in position by rigid spokes to the center. Once secured in one of those chairs and in flight, you can't change to a different chair. You succumb to the illusion that you're traveling, but in fact you're spinning in circles and you're either on your way up or on your way down. When a soul is granted another lifetime … and believe me, it's a privilege, not a right … the wheel goes along with it."

"Oh, please. Spare me the metaphoric object lessons," Anson said.

Magee's face cracked into a smile. "Realize that all life is a metaphor. And I do so love a Ferris wheel."

"Go on, then," he surrendered. "Explain it to me."

"As I was saying, this entire wheel represents you. Each chair represents all of the various identities assigned to you, such as being a British male born to a father in the military, an impeccably English mother, and siblings with personalities as strong and as bright as yours. There is a seat for your religious and academic training, another for your sailing and car racing, another for your flying, others for your separate relationships with the opposite sex. Now that you've planted that concept firmly in your mind, multiply the chairs by the infinite number of lifetimes you've had—they're all on the wheel. Moreover, there are seats for each of the impressions, tendencies, and attitudes you've created throughout all of your lives."

"Example?"

Magee shrugged. "How about the time your father threw you into the Singapore Straight? Do you remember how you felt about that?"

"Rejected and dejected."

Suddenly the wheel stopped with a chair at ground level, open and ready to accept a passenger. Magee pointed to the chair. "That represents the impression you created and the attitude you developed about your father in that moment. If you were to sit in that chair, you would have to ride it clear around the circle until it came to a landing again."

Anson tried to calculate how long it would take to travel the wheel's entire circumference.

"I'll save you the trouble. You would sit in that pathetic attitude for an eternity, transferring it into multiple lifetimes until you can rebirth a new attitude. There's a chair on the wheel that represents the behavior you presented to your father that caused him to toss you into the drink in the first place. That chair was a carry-over from a previous life."

"It's interminable, isn't it? I think I'm getting the picture," Anson said. "Confused, though. Do you sit in only one chair at a time?"

"No, you sit in all of them simultaneously. Mind you, some come into play more than others during a given life depending upon what is being emphasized."

"Cor blimey, all of them?" Although a simple concept, the idea of spending an eternity in each and every attitude was too much for him to fathom.

"You eventually earn the right to pick and choose which ones you want to work on. For your information, Avroe, you're on the cusp of that stage."

Anson didn't hear him, for he started to sink into the depths of self-loathing. "Do I have any redeeming qualities?"

"Oh, certainly," Magee said, nodding with enthusiasm. "You have a tremendous capacity for optimism. You are vitally curious about people and places—the more bizarre or remote, the more transfixed you become. People are fascinated by you in return. You're fearless when it comes to physicality, be it flying or racing or sailing. You're generous to a fault, and you're amazed to find that others are not always as giving. You have a strong work ethic. Loads of self-confidence. There are carriages for every one of these traits on your wheel as well."

"Sounds brilliant." Anson beamed. "What's the problem, then?"

"Well, again, it's like flying: lift, gravity, thrust, drag. What gives you elevation also bottoms you out. What propels you forward in your life also holds you back."

"I need more details."

Magee held up the thumb on his right hand. "You are charming, ideal, ambitious, fearless … lift." He extended his index finger. "You have the drive, discipline, and willingness to work hard for anything you set your mind on … thrust." He unfolded the thumb and index finger on his left hand. "But you over-think, and over-thinking causes paralysis, and you tend to over-react to circumstances or cause friction with others, especially when you judge that they're not carrying their load … drag. Finally, you are easily dissuaded by any negativity around you, and you plummet to the depths of apathy and despair steeped in alcohol … gravity."

Anson sighed and nodded. "Sounds about right. What about you? What's on your wheel?"

"Okay, let's talk about my John Magee life. You put your finger on it earlier. You suggested that my craving for adventure and challenge killed me."

"We call that an adrenalin addiction."

"Quite right." Magee's eyes widened in acknowledgment. "I wanted to exercise my intellect and settle down with Elinor, my primrose, but I sabotaged myself."

"How did you do that? You were blind-sided by cloud cover when you collided with the other plane."

"Yes, but my tendencies still caused the accident. Let's put it this way ... the attitudes I had, and the choices I made, accumulated and eventually attracted circumstances that resulted in the accident that caused my own death."

"How so?"

"I was a prodigy, both academically and as a pilot. Everyone acknowledged it. I exercised my genius freely and without caution. I didn't need an aeroplane to do that."

"Apparently, ego follows one into the afterlife."

"As goes the mind so goes the ego—the two are incontrovertibly woven. I was Icarus, whose hubris caused me to fly too close to the sun. My wings melted. I wasn't focused, and I didn't have a healthy respect for the fragility of life, mine or anyone else's. I flew with reckless abandon to escape the feeling of separation from England and my beloved. I was irreverent and immature, and I thought that I could bend the rules because I was above them and invincible."

"I can relate," Anson said, sighing.

"Just when Elinor was beginning to see me with new eyes, I flew even more haphazardly. I died before I could have the love I wanted."

"You were reprimanded for your wrongdoings."

"No! I was chained to my own tendency by the law of cause and effect. An accident of this order was inevitable. The cause-and-effect principle is a universal law that must be obeyed."

"How can you be so complacent about it?"

"Who said I was complacent? Despite my sojourn in the in-between, I was frustrated and angry. And I'm afraid I've carried that anger into my next lifetime."

"You were born again?" Anson was bowled over.

"Yes, of course, I have been born again. I can tell you I went into my new life already disillusioned, miserable, unhappy, and full of underpinning rage."

"I don't believe you. You seem so full of light. Not a care in the world."

"That is because I am not on the temporal plane at this moment and neither are you. You are experiencing my ethereal being as I am experiencing yours. But I've yet to escape the wheel despite appearances."

Anson found his explanation difficult to comprehend.

"As John Magee, I was on the right track. I was beginning to grasp the higher truths of life, but I was interrupted by my very own causes, which I am addressing in my next go-round. So now, in my new life, I have an entirely different genetic and circumstantial disposition than what John Magee had, although I've hung on to a few core attributes. I've kept my physicality and my spirit and my fearless sense of adventure. Even so, I've put a damper on my creativity as a poet, as well as my capacity to love and be loved, because I don't want to feel pain. Consequently, I've retained my addiction to high risks and speeds and chase it all with alcohol."

Anson reflected on Magee's new corporeality, and it reminded him of his own, yet it also didn't make sense. How could the pilot-spirit be so full of wisdom now, while also being the wretched being he described? "You've sussed out this cause-and-effect thing, and yet you say you fail on the next go-round."

"Wisdom is easy in the in-between where we have the advantage of hindsight and perspective. Here we have no true attachments to our earthbound identities and states of consciousness. Here we are the whole of ourselves as soul although we've yet to realize the depth of what that means. And yet, we are only the sum total of what we've experienced. The only way we can learn more is by participating in the wheel through human life."

Anson sighed at the overwhelming prospect of it all. "Is it so impossible to change chairs on the wheel?"

"Ah, that is the question, isn't it? Admitting that you play a role in the outcome of all your endeavors goes a long way toward diffusing the power it has over you. Thus, you begin to see that the power of all your causes lies within you."

"Is it possible to make the wheel stop completely?"

Magee proceeded in a sympathetic tone. "The wheel is self-perpetuating because every day we create new causes with the simple act of walking the earth. We are accursed to live out the effect of even our good deeds. Moreover, we are limited by our capacity to cope with no more than two or three major issues per lifetime. You're not going to believe me when I say this, but we are all held captive by the wheel, or rather, by the forces that put the wheel into motion. In a sense, you are not at fault for anything you do."

This declaration surprised Anson. "You've come full circle from where we started. Was this all for naught?" He was referring more to the purpose of life than to the review of his own life.

"That is a riddle for us all to work out. Now, before you become disheartened, there is another way to loosen the wheel's grip on you."

"And what is that?"

"By focusing on the center."

"I don't understand."

"You may have noticed that all spokes connect to the center, but there is no movement at the center itself. That's where the power lies, and it's within you. You have to understand that your attention represents your soul power, and wherever you place your attention is where your power goes. Your soul is locked into each one of those chairs on the wheel until you catch on to the game. If you can find a way to focus on the middle, between the extremes, you might learn to discriminate more clearly or at the very least to see your role in your own fate."

"How do I do that?"

"With practice. Plato wrote: 'The soul reasons best when nothing disturbs it—neither hearing, nor sight, nor pain, nor pleasure of any kind. It retires as much as possible within itself, taking leave of the body, and thus it discovers that which is.' Contemplation on the center of the wheel loosens the slavery of your attention."

"Sounds rather lofty. What is the point in having a physical body if it weighs down the soul?"

"That is a good question." Magee looked upward at the wheel and then returned his gaze toward Anson. "All things happen to you because you are a spiritual being, and everything is designed to bring you into resonance with the power at the center. But it goes deeper than that. Perhaps our soul is meant to evolve through the cultivation of our imagination. Icarus's father constructed wings of feathers and wax through his imagination. Icarus took a leap of faith and learned to fly though his imagination. He slipped the surly bonds of earth, the labyrinth of the mind. Realize that your hubris may have made you crash, Avroe, but your creativity gives you the impetus to free your spirit. These are the parallel lessons of the Icarus myth."

"Lift and gravity."

"Indeed. We must acknowledge the mortal boundaries of our physical bodies while also searching for the boundless, immortal soul."

Anson became abstract as he mused over the expansiveness of the wheel. "If there is a soul, then wouldn't it follow that there is also a superbeing in command—a man behind the curtain?"

"The wheel of cause and effect that keeps in balance the tandem forces binding all life is virtually self-ruling and automatic. The system is worshiped as God, but it is not God. Now, a superpower indeed emanates from a region far above the mechanism of cause and effect. I am told that this superpower, which created everything on earth and here in the in-between and beyond, cannot exist within the space-time continuum nor the worlds of matter and energy, and so it sends a singular force, an omni-current to sustain it."

"Do you know this power?"

Tears pooled in his eyes. "In my John Magee life, I'd discovered a power all around me when I flew my Spitfire to 30,000 feet. I didn't understand that the power that gave me my imagination was inside me and had been with me even when I was on the ground."

"How can I believe in what I do not know exists?"

"I can only tell you what I've experienced, but that wouldn't persuade you. You need to experience it for yourself."

"If this is heaven, then why do I not feel the power now?"

"Heaven is not a location. Heaven is a level of consciousness. That power is actually ringing you like Big Ben right now, but your soul has too many encumbrances to perceive it. Perhaps the disturbances will be calmed for you soon." He paused and placed a hand on each of Anson's shoulders while looking at him squarely in the eye. "First, my friend, you must decide what you are going to do. Do you want to move on to your next incarnation, or do you want to return to your current life?"

"Might I tarry here in the in-between?" The thought of staying in No Man's Land for a while without facing his troubles felt comforting.

"You can stay here for an eternity, but your Anson Roe body doesn't have that kind of time. Besides, what's the purpose in staying? Nothing will change. You can't remain in the same place in consciousness … you're either moving forward or you're moving backward. Why put off the inevitable?"

Anson felt defeated. *This is indeed a rum day*, he thought. It was all too overwhelming—his returning memories, the twice-experienced accident in Egypt, the cosmological meeting with the fighter pilot-poet. The decision before him seemed a losing proposition no matter what he chose and none of it too pleasant. He'd have to take what the Magee spirit told him on faith, for he had no proof. If he were to catch the next flight to a new life, he could become damaged again, but returning to his old life to pick up the pieces sounded like a condemnation to hell.

"You're looking at it all wrong, Avroe," Magee said. "You're forgetting the dual forces at work in everything. What comes down must also go up. There is good within the bad and vice versa."

"The proverbial silver lining."

"Don't discount it. Inherent in every experience is a consolation prize, sometimes in the form of personal insight."

"What's the point?"

"The system is carefully designed for you to see more clearly the perfection of the soul."

"I doubt I will be able to change."

"You're not expected to. Becoming more aware is all that's asked."

"Is there an upside to going back to Anson Roe?"

"Yes, if you go back, you will begin to diminish some of your destructive tendencies. Your injuries will ground you, and although you may continue to live recklessly and will refuse to allow anyone to tell you what to do, at least you will not have run away from your effects. You will have lived them out, and that's something to be proud of. You will probably be rewarded with a new and improved situation next go-round."

Anson had much to consider. If he had an eternity to decide, then he had no desire to rush. He required some of Plato's divine reasoning of his own to guide his decision. He stretched out on his back in the grass and gazed upon the immense wheel rotating leisurely above him. He found that if he tried to follow an individual chair as it moved vertically in its circuitous route, he felt dizzy and nauseous. But if he concentrated on the center of the wheel, which was indeed static, all sensory perceptions began to fade. The effect was mesmerizing, and it began to reveal a sense of hyper-knowingness within himself. He liked the feeling. From this heightened awareness he could view the entire 360-degree scope of his life with a bit less attachment, a bit less fear.

Anson was tempted to start afresh with a new identity, but if Magee's assessment of his behavior was correct, then choosing that option would be risky. The alternative felt no less daunting. If what Magee had said was true, not only would he be required to live with the physical injuries of the plane accident, but he'd also have to play out the same injurious effects in all his relationships.

He thought about Vivianne, about how he had misjudged her. He had confused her quiet, mild personality with weakness and indecisiveness. That misjudgment had given him a swift kick in the hind end, and now he was certain he had lost her. Then again, if they were to get back together, the odds were they would start their dance of causality all over again. He certainly didn't want to carry that into his next lifetime.

With lightning bolt clarity, Anson realized a single compelling reason to return to his current life—the child Vivianne carried. Even if she refused to return to England and marry him, he'd know the child existed in the world and that someday they would meet. Now he was desperate to know her plans. There was only one way to discover her decision.

Then, quite suddenly, he felt ... It! The floodlight he'd perceived just before he emerged at the Oklahoma airfield that morning illuminated his cranium once again. The Power reverberated through him like the hum of a finely-tuned engine. That hum felt like love, an overwhelming, transporting, all-consuming love. It knew him and had known him for an eternity. He sensed with absolute clarity that nothing surprised or disappointed It. He sensed that as soul he was one with It and as such he, too, existed everywhere. The sensations were over in an instant, but they left a glow in the pit of his being.

Feeling redeemed, Anson emerged from his contemplation of the wheel clearer now than he'd ever known himself to be. He noticed the lateness of the day—only the crown of the sun still shined above the western horizon, setting choral fire to the clouds. He could feel his stint here coming to a close. He hopped to his feet and faced Magee.

"I will go back and not for the reasons you've noted. I've decided that I won't let anyone or any*thing* take my life—or rather, that life—away from me. At least not before I'm done with it."

"Now, that's the Anson Roe I know and love, and that's being the cause rather than the effect. Congratulations, Avroe! Good decision. I admire your bravery."

"You know, I might consider coming back as a doctor next go-around. Help other people for a change."

"That can be arranged ... if you've earned it."

"There is one thing I want from you."

"From me?" Magee pointed a thumb toward his chest.

"Yes, I implore you to tell me who—or what—you really are?"

"Why do you want to know?"

"Maybe it's because I've spent all day in Eternity with you, but I have a sneaking suspicion we've met before."

"It isn't essential that you know who I am. It is only important to take advantage of your second coming. All you have is in the moment."

He sighed and cocked his head. "Next time we play pool, I break first."

The John Magee spirit smiled his non-smile. "That's a deal."

Anson grinned in return, feeling genuinely pleased with himself and his decision. "When do I go back?"

"Now."

24

On Laughter-Silvered Wings

MAGEE SPREAD BOTH arms skyward. Before Anson could react, a Supermarine Spitfire materialized at the ready on the grassy knoll next to the soul wheel, drenched in what he could only describe as a vibrant, divine substance that radiated infinitely in all directions. It was the most beautiful sight he'd ever beheld. "Your ride, Avroe." Magee gripped his shoulder.

Anson put a hand on his chest. "There's only one seat."

"You don't need me. You already know how to fly it. Go on. It's nearly time."

Anson shook his head. For once he was overtaken by apprehension, unsure of how to proceed—and he didn't mean the flying. No, he was anxious about returning to his life, frightened of how he would cope with the challenges he was sure to face.

"In truth, soul is powerful. Don't squander your precious energies on trying to change your effects … rather, change your causes and all effects will follow. Understand, you will always have a choice in how you respond to whatever happens to you. Strive for the middle distance. Don't let the sun melt the wax in your wings nor the sea dampen your feathers."

"You make it sound easy."

"It isn't easy, but recall the RCAF motto?"

"Through adversity to the stars."

"That's right. Life on earth is the dream. This is the reality. Heal the dream."

"I can't make any promises."

"You have to imagine a new ideal of yourself."

"What should that ideal be?"

John Magee grinned. "Icarus renatus, Avroe! Icarus reborn!"

Anson thought, *I can live with that.* "Will I see you again?"

"I am always with you."

Feeling emotional, Anson embraced the spirit being. When he faced the Spitfire, its canopy opened magically. He floated up the ladder and stepped onto the wing. He looked for Magee on the ground to ask about a helmet and parachute, but the spirit was gone.

The Spitfire's engine was already purring when Anson seated himself inside it. He didn't need to handle the yoke or rudders. He needed only to think *lift*, and the aircraft ascended vertically like a Harrier Jump Jet.

Anson maneuvered the Spitfire in a series of aerobatic stunts with his thoughts, and the buoyancy thrilled him. As the sun sank below the horizon, the sky turned shades of light to dark blue, revealing legions of stars alive with song. He positioned the Spitfire for optimal view of his soul wheel.

A tiny flame flared within the wheel's center, rapidly spread outward along the spokes, and ignited the individual chairs in a burst of fire. The wheel looked like a flower with countless spinning, humming petals burning brightly. The sight filled him with an all-consuming yearning to know the power that resided within it. Anson aimed toward the center of the wheel, and the Spitfire thrust forward to pierce the heart of Love.

25

HEALING THE DREAM

A HUSHED CONVERSATION blended with the mechanical white noise encapsulating Anson's body. He lingered in a twilight reverie, soaring through unknown worlds with nothing but his arms for wings and his feet for rudders. Waking reality persisted until he eventually opened his eyes, and the dream images scattered into oblivion.

Peering at his surroundings through the swelling and bandaging proved difficult. His eyes could not focus well now that there appeared to be two of everything. He lay prone in a bed—his head and shoulders felt bolted in place and couldn't be budged. Tubes led from his body to nearby beeping and whooshing devices. He wasn't alarmed—he'd been intermittently cognizant enough to know that he'd had some sort of an accident and that he'd learn more in due course. Surprisingly, and mercifully, he didn't feel as much pain as one would expect given the shape he was in. *Probably the opiates*, he imagined. *If only I could smoke a cigarette.*

A male voice continued to drone on in the hallway, a doctor perhaps, speaking of a "Mr. Roe." Certain disquieting words summarized all he needed to know about his medical status— every bone in his face fractured, a broken clavicle and forearm, edema of the brain, and cerebral fluid leaking from his nose. Apparently, he was stable enough for the first of several surgeries.

"What will the operations entail?" another voice asked. The voice belonged to Anson's father, and knowing he was present gave him solace. He pictured his father in his mind, remembering him to be a large, formidable man in command of his domain. Now he sounded humbled and worried.

The doctor detailed the task of wiring together the bones in his face to prevent it from collapsing. He would also screw a halo frame into his skull to keep it rigid. The very thought shook Anson, and he began to escape back into unconsciousness. *No, no, stay*, he commanded himself.

"He's awake!" a female voice exclaimed moments later, which Anson recognized as his mother. He was happy to know she was present. The petite and normally stoic woman rushed to his side to hold his free arm, the other being in a plaster splint. Even through the gauze he could see the shock that colored her face. He tried to form questions but found he didn't have much control over his vocal cords.

"Don't try to talk," his father said gently. He pulled up a chair next to the bed and seated himself. "You had a very bad aeroplane accident in Egypt three days ago. You were given a tracheotomy in the field and then driven directly to Zagazig University Hospital within the hour, where they stabilized you with a transfusion and intravenous drug therapy. You were flown to London in a cargo plane this morning with a doctor and nurse. You're being well cared for here at a hospital near Heathrow."

"Staff will come in soon to prep you for surgery," his mother said. Anson thought he detected a hint of tearfulness in her voice. "You've been disoriented every time you've awakened, but doctors are pleased with your responses and confident you will recover reasonably well. You're lucky they got you to hospital in Zagazig when they did."

"We've spoken to Vivianne," his father continued after a brief pause. "She won't be able to come here any time soon but sends her love. Says she's taking flying lessons." He paused. "Did you know she's pregnant?"

At first Anson didn't think he'd heard his father correctly, and then he needed another moment to absorb the full meaning of the older man's words. *Vivianne is going to have a baby.* The significance of the statement registered slowly in his mind. Vivianne was planning to carry the baby full term and raise it herself if she had to. That was the real message she'd hoped his father would convey to him, or else she would not have informed his family of her incredible decision.

He felt broken and stripped of all he knew to be true yet he was ecstatic to be alive. To whom or what he owed the privilege of his life, he didn't know. He'd had some crazy dreams about flying and a sort of heroic teacher who, though shadowy, felt closer to him than his very breath. The future was uncertain to him, the past a vague memory. All he had was now, and within this now-moment he had a child and the prospect of winning back Vivianne's affection.

As he mulled over the new direction his life had taken, he felt a quickening inside his chest. He attributed the sensation to his wounds or to an undiscovered cracked rib or a mild heart attack. Then he experienced the sensation again—it radiated warmth like sunrays throughout his body, softly pulsing *I love* deep within in the recesses of his being.

"Did you hear me?" his father asked. "Vivianne is going to have a baby."

It occurred to Anson that his damaged face failed to communicate his feelings. There were so many things he wanted to say to his father, but he couldn't quite form the words. Then he realized that nothing was wrong with his vocal cords, only that he hadn't used them in days. He decided to try to speak, if only to cheer his father. After several attempts he managed to whisper a single word.

"Good."

THE INDIVIDUAL STORIES of Anson Vincent Roe and John Gillespie Magee, Jr., are true. Their interaction in the "in-between" is, of course, a product of the author's extrapolation and imagination. The names of Anson Roe and Vivianne Keene were invented, and some details of their relationship were changed to fit the scope of the novel. They never married, but Vivianne did have a son and continued a career as a writer/photographer. Anson became a truck driver and died in 2013 at age 64, having spent exactly half a lifetime dealing with his physical and mental deterioration created by his plane accident near Zagazig, Egypt, in 1981. His father told me that despite his complaints, he was optimistic at heart to the end.

John Magee tells his own story in *A Day in Eternity*, gleaned from nearly two dozen poems and more than a hundred letters he sent to his family over the final four years of his life. These materials are archived in the John G. Magee Family Papers, Record Group No. 242, Special Collections, Yale Divinity School Library (used with permission). Much appreciation is due to Special Collections Librarian Martha Smalley and Senior Archives Assistant Joan Duffy at the Yale Divinity School Library for their help in accessing the files.

John Magee's sonnet, "High Flight," was first published shortly after his death (December 11, 1941) in his father's church bulletin in Washington, D.C., and rapidly spread through print media. The poem is traditionally read at eulogies for pilots, and President Ronald Reagan paraphrased it in his tribute to the astronauts who died aboard the Space Shuttle Challenger in 1986.

As stated in chapter 15, "High Flight" was heavily influenced by the book, *Icarus: An Anthology of the Poetry of Flight* (Macmillan, London, 1938), which contained the poem, "The Blind Man Flies," by Cuthbert Hicks. The anthology was compiled by R de la Bere and "three flight cadets of the Royal Air Force College, Cranwell." Magee also borrowed lines from G.W.N. Dunn's poem, "New World," and C.A.F.B.'s poem, "Dominion over Air," both published in the *Icarus* anthology.

Elinor Lyon became the author of more than twenty children's books, most notably her series on the adventures of Ian and Sovra in Scotland. She married Peter Wright, an RAF pilot and Rugby School English teacher, and they had four children. She died in 2008 at age 86. Her unpublished poetry and notes, used with permission from her son Roger Wright, are archived at the Seven Stories, National Centre for Children's Books in New Castle, U.K. Special thanks to Archivist Kristopher McKie for his help in accessing her materials.

I'd like to thank my dear friends Deborah Malone and Irene Swain for their generosity of time and patience as sounding boards over the years. The same can be said for Robin Tawney and Stan Byron, who between them edited several drafts of the novel. I always learn so much about the English language from Robin, who is himself a poet. Stan, as a physicist, was helpful in comparing Newton's third law of motion to the metaphysical principle of cause and effect. Credit for the Ferris wheel metaphor ultimately goes to my spiritual teacher, Sri Gary Olsen. An extra special thank you to Linda DeVine for her final deep cleaning and polishing of the novel. Further gratitude is due Jane and Dr. John Taylor and to Margaret and Terry Jeffrey for their hospitality during our trip to England in 2013. Much love to my husband David Loving, U.S. Air Force veteran and WWII film buff, for helping me keep the aircraft and history of that era straight and for his boundless enthusiasm and humor.

FURTHER READING

THE FOLLOWING BOOKS provided additional biographical information on John G. Magee, Jr., and Elinor Lyon:

Sunward I've Climbed, by Hermann Hagedorn, The MacMillan Company, 1942.

The Complete Works of John Magee, The Pilot Poet, compiled by Stephen Garnett, This England Books, 1989.

The Spitfire Smiths: A Unique Story of Brothers in Arms, by Squadron Leader R.I.A. Smith DFC & Bar with Christopher Shores, Grub Street, 2008.

High Flight, by Roger Cole, Fighting High Ltd., 2013.

Touching the Face of God," by Ray Haas, High Flight Productions, 2014.

Other fiction by Kathryn Gabriel Loving:

The Logos of Soul, A Novel on the Light and Sound, SoulJourn Books, 2011.

Non-fiction books by Kathryn Gabriel (Loving):

Marietta Wetherill: Life with the Navajos in Chaco Canyon, University of New Mexico Press, 1997.

Roads to Center Place: A Cultural Atlas to Chaco Canyon and the Anasazi, Johnson Books, 1991.

Gambler Way: Indian Gaming in Mythology, History, and Archaeology in North America, Johnson Books, 1996.

Country Towns of New Mexico, Country Roads Press, 1997.

Please visit souljournbooks.com for articles and news by the author.

Cessna AGtruck over Oklahoma Panhandle fields, 1980 (photo by the author).